SEAL & SHELTER | BOOK ONE

Baby Consealed

Leah Miles

Black Rose Writing | Texas

The author grants the final approval for this literary material.

First printing

This is a work of fiction. Names, characters, businesses, places, events, and incidents are either the products of the author's imagination or used in a fictitious manner. Any resemblance to actual persons, living or dead, or actual events is purely coincidental.

ISBN: 978-1-68513-733-5
LIBRARY OF CONGRESS CONTROL NUMBER: 2025947315
PUBLISHED BY BLACK ROSE WRITING
www.blackrosewriting.com

Printed in the United States of America
Suggested Retail Price (SRP) $19.95

Baby ConSEALed is printed in Garamond Premier Pro

*As a planet-friendly publisher, Black Rose Writing does its best to eliminate unnecessary waste to reduce paper usage and energy costs, while never compromising the reading experience. As a result, the final word count vs. page count may not meet common expectations.

Cover by Lia Davis with Glowing Moon Creative.

For Mom.

We started this journey together, and you've read every single version with fresh eyes and endless enthusiasm. Your love and support mean everything to me, and I'm thankful for you.

Praise for
Baby ConSEALed

Baby ConSEALed won the 2024 Georgia Romance Writers' "Maggie Award"

"A tightly plotted, fast-paced whirlwind of a ride fraught with secrets, danger, and an emotional love story that focuses on family—the kind you choose."
–Lena Diaz, Publishers Weekly best-selling author

"I couldn't put this book down, even when I had to go to work!"
–Jillian David, best-selling romantic suspense author and physician, who was late to start hospital rounds because of Leah Miles' book

"What a fantastic new voice in the military romance genre!"
–J.M.Madden, *NY Times* and *USA Today* bestselling author

"A heart-racing, gripping thriller that only pauses to deliver scenes of smoldering romance."
–Christopher Amato, author of *Peace River Village*

Baby Consealed

CHAPTER 1

Almost three years ago.
San Diego, California, (Cicadas Bar)

Cicadas bar was packed, the air thick with laughter, spilled beer, and the occasional whiff of too-strong cologne. Marissa Parker adjusted her glasses and glanced around, nerves fluttering in her stomach. The upbeat music of the live band filled the space, drowning out conversations. Her best friend, Liesel, stood beside her, arms raised, singing along with the rowdy birthday crowd.

"Happy birthday to you, happy birthday to you, happy birthday ..."

After the song ended, a server weaved through the throng, handing out plastic tubes filled with a neon-green liquid.

Rissa shook her head. "I'm good, thanks."

Liesel nudged her shoulder. "It's your twenty-first birthday. Scratch that—our birthday. Live a little!" She waggled a tube under Rissa's nose.

"What's in it?" Rissa eyed the drink as if it might bite. The idea of letting loose sounded great in theory, but she'd never been that kind of girl.

Liesel rolled her eyes. "Does it matter? It's free, and we're celebrating."

Half of their weekend together had already slipped away, and tomorrow, she'd be flying home. Rissa sighed, her resistance crumbling under Liesel's infectious energy. She grabbed the shot and knocked it back. The alcohol hit her tongue like gasoline and burned all the way down.

Throwing her arms in the air, Liesel whooped. "That's my girl! It's our birthday, and we can do what we want to!"

"What we want to!" Rissa croaked, her throat on fire, but she still joined in on the last line.

Liesel giggled and fell back against the man she'd been dancing with. "This is the best night!"

"Come on, babe. I love this song," her dance partner murmured, tugging her toward the floor.

Liesel shot her a look, a clear invitation to join. But Rissa wasn't about to be the third wheel. "You go ahead," she called over the music.

As the birthday crowd thinned, Rissa found herself standing alone—except for one guy lingering nearby. He looked even shyer than she felt, nursing a beer and glancing at her before quickly averting his gaze. Should she strike up a conversation?

Nerves took over, and she veered toward the bar instead, claiming the only empty stool. There went her big plan of putting herself out there tonight. Meeting someone would be fun, but what was the point anyway, since she flew home tomorrow.

The bartender paused in front of her. "What'll you have?" His wavy brown hair tumbled down his forehead, and he wore a fitted tank with the bar name "Cicadas" emblazoned on it, showcasing his incredibly muscular arms. Someone shouted for his attention farther down the bar, but he ignored them and waited for her reply.

"Uh ..." She had already finished one drink, not counting the radioactive shot ... but it *was* a celebration. "A Cosmopolitan, please."

After this, she'd call it a night. Get a cab back to Liesel's place. Maybe read a few chapters of a book. *Wild and crazy. That's me.*

She took a sip of the drink he delivered, letting the tart cranberry linger on her tongue as she watched the television mounted above the bar. A bowling tournament played, of all things, the announcer droning on about a perfect strike. A man slid between her stool and the next one, close enough that the heat of his body radiated toward her.

"Sorry to crowd you." His voice was deep, smooth, and impossibly calm despite the chaos of the crowd around them.

She turned—and nearly forgot how to breathe.

He was tall and built like he actually used his gym membership. His dark skin contrasted against the crisp blue of his button-down, and when he tilted his head, the light caught his short black curls. But it was his eyes that stole her attention, a golden shade, piercing yet unreadable.

For a moment, she thought he might be about to hit on her, but he only raised a hand, signaling to the bartender. Of course, he wasn't interested in her. She needed to finish her drink and go back to the apartment. Rissa gulped down a large swallow and barely managed not to cough.

"Patrick. Beer for me and one of those for the lady."

She blinked. "You're buying me a drink?"

Amusement flickered in those striking eyes. "Only if you want it." He wedged himself farther into the space, turning sideways to fit, with one elbow propped on the bar and his free hand tucked in his pocket.

She absently swirled a finger through the condensation on her mostly empty glass. One more drink might be too much. "I think I want a soda," she said.

He gave a slight nod of approval and called out the order to the bartender. While he did, she took the chance to study him more closely. The sharp angles of his face, the short-cropped hair, and the faintest hint of a scar cutting through his left eyebrow.

"The golden color of your eyes reminds me of a stray cat I sometimes feed near my apartment. I mean, they're nice," she added quickly, when she realized that may have sounded a little weird. "Not that I'm calling you a cat."

He chuckled, a low, rich sound. "I've been called worse."

She glanced down at her glass, unsure what to say next.

"You here alone?" he asked.

"No. My friend is over there." She motioned toward Liesel, who was dancing with a guy who looked like he belonged on a recruitment poster.

His gaze followed hers, and something flickered in his expression. "The guy she's dancing with is from my SEAL team."

Rissa's stomach dropped at his words. "You're a Navy SEAL?" He was so far out of her league.

"Nine years." His eyes locked on her, and he seemed to be waiting for her to comment.

She didn't know much about military ranks, but the way he carried himself suggested he wasn't just some guy on weekend leave. "I've seen that TV show, *Navy SEAL*, but I don't know anyone in the military."

His eyes crinkled at the corners. "You do now."

The bartender set down their drinks. "Good to see you, Burn."

"You too, Patrick. Your bar is doing well, and I see Dominick is back with the band. You two doing okay?"

"We're fine. He loves all the attention," Patrick chuckled. "And I can't complain. The Forget Me Nots are getting some traction in San Diego and starting to really draw in a crowd. Having them as our house band is good for the bottom line. Hey, I'd love to chat, but I'm down a bartender and server tonight. Yell out if you need anything or climb back here and get it yourself."

"Later," Burn said, tipping his chin in response.

"Your name is Burn?"

He exhaled through his nose, like the nickname both amused and annoyed him. "It's actually Bernie, short for Bernard. My teammates call me Burn."

"My name's Marissa, but everyone calls me Rissa."

"Rissa," he repeated, rolling the 'r' slightly. "Nice to meet you." He tapped his beer against her soda in a quiet toast, his golden eyes locked on her.

Warmth unfurled in her belly. She wasn't sure if it was from the alcohol or the way he watched her. Like she was the most interesting thing in the room.

"Tell me something about yourself, Rissa," he said, taking a swig from his beer.

"Um." What could she say? *I live alone. I work all the time and don't have time to make friends.* "I'm celebrating my birthday today, although it was technically yesterday. My friend Liesel and I were born on the same day, and we came out tonight to celebrate."

"Nice. I heard the singing. Happy Birthday."

"Thanks," she said, taking a drink from the soda. She was glad she'd opted against more alcohol. It was better to have a clear head.

"Dance with me?" he asked.

Her first inclination was to decline, but something about the hopefulness in his voice made her reconsider. She slid off the stool. "Yes, I'd like that. One dance would be fun."

"Maybe more than one." His lips curved, and he took her hand, leading her through the crowd to the dance floor. The band had slowed things down, and Rissa's pulse jumped as his hands settled on her waist; firm but not intrusive, giving her space to move. "This okay?"

She nodded, winding her arms loosely around his neck.

They swayed in easy rhythm, the crowd around them blurring. He smelled like soap and something faintly sweet.

"Why do I smell chocolate?"

He chuckled, and his lips brushed against her ear. "I have a thing for Rolos. Do you want one?"

"Maybe later," she giggled, then her breath hitched as his fingers flexed against her hip. The music changed, but neither of them moved to leave.

After a few more songs, he murmured, "Want to get some air?"

Her heart raced. She wasn't the type to leave with a guy she'd just met, but Burn wasn't just any guy. "Yes."

He laced his fingers through hers and led her toward the exit. The night air cooled her flushed skin. She took a steadying breath as he turned her toward him, his eyes flicking over her face as if he were memorizing every detail.

For once, she didn't want to overthink it.

"I like this," he said quietly.

"This?" she echoed.

This was supposed to be one night. A story she could tell herself later about the time she danced with a ridiculously gorgeous Navy SEAL on her twenty-first birthday. But as he pulled her closer, as her hands slid up his chest, the unsettling realization hit her—this was the beginning of something she wouldn't be able to forget.

CHAPTER 2

**Present Day — Wednesday in San Antonio, Texas
(The home of Amelia Iglesias)**

The wail of the house alarm jolted Rissa from a light sleep. She jerked upright, her heart hammering with disorientation. The cushioned chair creaked under her sudden movement as she fumbled for her glasses, shoved them onto her face, and checked the digital clock—just after one. The muted glow of the television flickered against the walls, casting eerie shadows across the ornate bedroom.

Mrs. Iglesias was already awake.

Her elderly employer pressed the remote with steady fingers, and the bed motor whirred as her torso rose. She folded her hands over the comforter, calm as someone settling in for tea rather than a potential break-in. Her lined face was unreadable, yet her sharp brown eyes cut through the dim light, focused.

The alarm abruptly stopped, plunging them into a chilling silence. They were the only two people in the house until six, so who had turned off the alarm? Rissa got up from the chair to stare at the closed bedroom door. The security company would call after an alarm was triggered—she knew that because she had set it off a few days ago by mistake. If someone had broken inside the house, help would come.

She held her breath, counted to three, and was relieved when the phone by the bed rang. Before she could answer it, someone else did. Her breath hitched, and she swiveled her gaze toward Mrs. Iglesias, because burglars don't answer calls from security people. Moving closer, she whispered, "We need to call the police."

"No, *chica*," Mrs. Iglesias' fingers tightened on the remote, but her voice stayed level. "I want you to hide in the coat closet behind the bedroom door."

Rissa's pulse thundered. "The closet? What about you? You should hide, too."

"I'll be fine. Do as I say," she said, punctuating the order with jabs of her arthritic fingers toward the closet.

"I can't leave you. There's someone in the house," Rissa whispered, glancing at the door and back at her boss. "The police—"

"I don't need them." Mrs. Iglesias cut her off. The old woman's voice didn't waver, but for the first time in the weeks Rissa had been there, she saw something different in Mrs. Iglesias's expression.

Fear. And resignation. Almost imperceptible, but there.

Mrs. Iglesias plucked a gun from her nightstand and stuffed it under the edge of the comforter. A gun? She was eighty-eight.

Rissa's hands went numb. The room tilted, and she gripped the bedframe to steady herself. "This is crazy—"

"Hush and listen. I know who is in my house, and I don't want him to see you." She clamped her fingers on Rissa's arm. "If something happens, press on the center panel of the left closet wall. It will open to a hidden room."

"You have a safe room?"

"Listen to me," Mrs. Iglesias said. "When you're on the other side, look for a small leather bag. You'll need what's in it, so take it with you."

Her throat closed. She forced herself to swallow. "Take it where?"

"This is important." Mrs. Iglesias said, digging her long, manicured nails into Rissa's arm. "When you're on the other side of the panel, don't come out, no matter what you hear."

"I can't leave ..." Rissa's voice faded when the heavy thud of a door closing echoed from the hall.

"*Chica,* are you listening? Trust no one."

Rissa nodded. That wouldn't be a problem. "Trust no one" was pretty much her entire existence. Her parents made sure of that when, after her high school graduation, she came home to find her suitcase on the porch. Three years of scraping by, job to job, and now this. If she died tonight, what would happen to Shelby?

Were those voices? Rissa spun toward the door, expecting someone to burst through any second.

Mrs. Iglesias's voice shook when she said, "Look at me."

"What do we do?" Rissa said, her air coming in short, useless gasps.

"If something happens and you have to leave—"

"Leave?" Rissa squeaked.

"Shut up and listen. After you go through the panel, you'll find another door which opens into the utility room by the garage."

"I can't leave you here," Rissa said, her heart clambering into her throat.

"You can and you will." Mrs. Iglesias released Rissa to smooth the covers over her lap. Over the gun. "The spare key to my Mercedes hangs on the wall inside the utility room. Take the car if things go wrong and you need to leave. Now, hurry. There's no more time." Mrs. Iglesias made a shooing motion.

Two male voices drifted from the hallway, growing louder with each word. She didn't want to go, but Mrs. Iglesias's fierce stare left no room for argument. Rissa rushed to the small closet, slipped inside, and wriggled among the winter coats just as the bedroom door slammed open.

She had a good view of Mrs. Iglesias on the bed through the closet's slats, but not much else. Then, a shadow blocked the light as a man stepped into view.

"*You.*" Mrs. Iglesias's face flushed a deep red, and her lips twisted to show a bit of teeth.

Memories of gossip from the day shift nurse flashed through her mind. She had warned Rissa to be wary of Mrs. Iglesias' temper.

"Hello, Amelia. I was in San Antonio this evening and thought I'd drop in for a visit." The man's deep, raspy voice was a predator's purr that sent shivers down Rissa's spine. His perfectly tailored suit and black Stetson hat likely cost more than she made in a month.

Mrs. Iglesias scowled up at him. "It's the middle of the night. You have no business arriving at this hour."

He grunted in response and brushed a speck of lint from his sleeve. Then, as if he sensed her presence, his pale green eyes fixed on the closet door. Rissa had to bite down on her knuckle to remain calm.

Mrs. Iglesias broke the silence. "Go home, Terrance."

His gaze shifted back to the old woman. "But I'm here about your letter. You said there was some urgency."

Rissa's heart hammered so loud she almost missed their words.

"I wanted to speak to you," Mrs. Iglesias said, her tone clipped, sharp. "Not him. You aren't supposed to bring him to my home."

Terrance swiveled his gaze to the other side of the room. "Rick, I don't think Amelia likes you being here."

"Seems that way, boss," a second man said as he stepped into Rissa's line of sight. Rick wore a uniform, and his black utility belt glinted, with the unmistakable bulk of a police-issued service weapon resting on his hip.

Mrs. Iglesias's voice vibrated with fury, and her frail fingers clenched the blanket. "I have nothing to say in front of your father's filth."

"Now, now." Terrance tsked. "That's no way to talk to my half-brother."

"This is how you repay me for all I've done for you?"

"You think you were doing me a favor, old woman?" He threw out his arms, momentarily blocking Rissa's view before he dropped them.

Mrs. Iglesias inhaled deeply through her nose and exhaled from her mouth. Then she picked up the cup on her nightstand and took a sip of water, making him wait for her answer. "Calm down, *mijo*. Your father was penniless when I married him, so yes, I did you both a favor. As for my invitation to come here, I didn't ask you to come in the middle of the night."

Rissa struggled to keep her breathing quiet. *Mijo?*

"Too bad. I'm here now." Terrance stalked around the expansive bedroom, which allowed Rissa occasional glimpses of his hand-tooled Lucchese boots, the kind with the silver threading. Something she could never afford, although she had window-shopped plenty.

Mrs. Iglesias tucked her hands beneath the comforter. "We can't have a conversation with you acting this way. Besides, I'm old and need my rest. Leave now and come back *mañana*."

"No." Terrance halted his sporadic pacing to draw closer to the bed. "We deal with this now. I'm sick of your bullshit. *Come here. Come there. I need this. Get me that.* This time, if you intended to piss me off," he slow-clapped a few times, "then bravo, you fucking succeeded."

The man he'd called Rick moved in front of the closet, standing so close that his back brushed against the wood. Rissa clamped her hand tightly over her mouth as an involuntary shudder rippled through her.

"You disrespectful ingrate." Mrs. Iglesias's querulous voice morphed into the steely tone of a queen. "I'm your mother, Terrance. You'd be *nada,* nothing, if not for me."

Rick's hand moved to his belt, resting on his gun. Then he shifted a few feet away, allowing Rissa a better view. Mrs. Iglesias's face may have been white as chalk, but her lips were set in a firm line.

"Stepmother," Terrance growled before spitting on the white Berber carpet. "I was ten when my father took pity on a pathetic old woman and married you. You're not my mother."

She bared her teeth. "Well, you're forty-eight now. Old enough to know when you're not welcome. *Lárgate de mi vista.* Get out of my sight."

"Old woman, the days are past when I follow your orders—"

"How about this order?" Mrs. Iglesias pointed the gun at his chest. "Leave my home and never return."

Terrance spread his arms wide. "Put down the gun. We both know you won't use that on me."

Her voice shook, but her arm didn't waver. "You wouldn't treat me this way if your *papi* were alive."

"Now ... Amelia," Terrance said, dropping his arms and shifting closer to the bed.

"Stay back. I thought about sharing interesting information I learned, but I've changed my mind. You don't deserve to know." The motor on the bed whirred as Mrs. Iglesias raised it further. "Leave now, Terrance. I'm finished with you, for good this time."

He groaned dramatically and pressed both hands to his temples. "You're giving me a headache."

"I mean it." She wagged the barrel of the gun toward the door. "Get out, or I will use this. I swear on your father's grave."

Terrance took another step closer. "Don't be stupid. You need me to care for you and bring the family business into this century. *Papi* is dead, and I'm in charge. Besides, he had no vision for the future."

Mrs. Iglesias' shoulders bunched as she adjusted her position, bringing up her other hand to help support the weapon. "Don't be disrespectful of your father."

Terrance blew out a breath. "Respect has to be earned, and he never earned mine." Fists clenched, he hovered closer. "You saw the way he beat me. Why didn't you ever stop him? Did you enjoy watching me bleed?"

"Terrance, that's very far in the past." Mrs. Iglesias shifted her focus off him. "Besides, it was his right as your father."

His head reared back. "Something else we disagree on, but it doesn't matter. You are right about one thing. That was in the past. Things are different now."

"Different?"

"Yes. Now, I'm in charge. But since you disapprove of change, I can arrange for you to join *Papi*."

"Not likely." Mrs. Iglesias's lips curled, and a gunshot shattered the air.

Terrance staggered and clutched his side. "You bitch," he shouted, leaping forward to slam her wrist against the nightstand. A second later, the weapon dropped to the carpet with a dull thud.

"No—" Mrs. Iglesias exclaimed right before Terrance fastened a hand around her throat.

He held her in place while punching her over and over, fist against flesh in sickening thuds.

A whimper escaped Rissa, and unable to watch without doing anything, she reached for the door handle, only stopping when Mrs. Iglesias's hands fell limply to the bedcovers. Was she dead? Her field of vision contracted to a pinprick. *Breathe, dammit. Don't pass out. You'll die if you pass out.* She kept the mantra going and buried her face against the soft lapel of a Kashmir coat.

Terrance had killed his mother, and if he murdered her also, Shelby would be alone. Why had she run from her baby's daddy like a naïve virgin? Who was she kidding? She was a naïve virgin. Or had been. Back then, she'd had no one to help her. It wasn't like her pregnancy had made a difference to her parents. They'd kicked her out at eighteen, and a newborn granddaughter three years later meant nothing to them.

No. Should've, would've, could've spun out the window as soon as she slipped from Burn's bed. If she got out of this mess, she'd try harder to find her baby's father. She'd attempted to call him on the base and even searched for him on social media, but she needed to do better. If something happened to her, even a stranger was preferable to foster care for her little girl.

"She get you, boss?" Rick asked.

"I'll live." Terrance hissed, pressing a hand to his side. "Hit the light switch by the door. I can't see a damn thing."

Rissa stifled a gasp when the closet light flicked on with the overhead in the bedroom. She blinked, adjusting to the new illumination, and watched as Terrance stripped off his jacket to reveal a blossoming red stain on a stark white shirt. When he shrugged off the shirt, Rissa cringed. Ragged scars crisscrossed his thick, muscular back.

"You check the house?" Terrance's gaze swept the room and stopped on the chair where Rissa had been sitting.

"It's empty," Rick said.

"Then who does this belong to?" Terrance held up her pink phone with blood-smeared fingers.

"If that isn't Amelia's, then the owner must've left it," Rick said. "Only car in the garage is her Mercedes, and the groundskeeper's cottage behind the house is vacant."

"My stepmother had round-the-clock sitters. Someone is here. Find her before she slips away."

"If she's here, I'll get her. What do you want done with her?"

"Kill her," he said, pressing his wadded-up shirt to his side.

Rissa locked her knees and concentrated on breathing as quietly as possible.

"And Rick?" He turned around.

"Yeah, boss?"

"Get me the first aid kit from the top shelf of the pantry. I need to stop this bleeding before we leave."

A roadmap of long white stripes with painful-looking ridges covered his chest. Beneath the black Stetson, his pale green eyes fixed on her hiding place, ramping her pulse to a stampede as she waited for him to cross over and open the door.

"I have the kit," Rick said, returning to the room. "Do you want the doctor here?"

"No." Terrance ground out the words in his deep voice. "Neighbors might notice the traffic. Bring him to my house in a few hours. And call the cleaners."

"On it." Rick jogged away.

Terrance placed his Stetson on the nightstand and unzipped the red bag Rick had given him. Rissa willed herself to remain calm, watching as he ripped open a pouch and pressed a gauze square against his side. He had trouble reaching the wound, and after dropping several pads on the floor, he cursed, scooped up the bag, and moved out of sight. Seconds later, she heard water running in the bathroom.

Now was her chance to find the panel. She scooted left and ran her fingers along the edge of the closet wall. No. Mrs. Iglesias had said to press in the middle. She did, and nothing happened.

Had she meant left, facing the closet?

Rissa's hands shook so much that she knocked against the hangers as she moved toward the other side. The tinkling racket, like trumpets, broadcasted her location. Breath snagged in her throat as she waited to be discovered.

But the door didn't burst open, and water still ran in the bathroom. With a steadying breath, she moved more carefully, reaching out to push both palms against the opposite sidewall—and barely caught herself when it swung inward.

A way out.

She edged forward, careful not to disturb more of the hangers. As she was about to let the secret panel shut, her cell rang. Rissa stuck her fingers in the gap to keep the panel open a sliver. The water stopped, and a few seconds later, the phone shut off mid-ring.

"Hello … hello? Marissa, is that you?" Mrs. Griffin's familiar voice floated toward her. "Shelby's been throwing up, and I need you to come get her. We're leaving early tomorrow to celebrate Labor Day weekend with my daughter, and we need our rest."

"Who's this?" Terrance rasped.

"I'm sorry. Did I call the wrong number? I'm trying to reach Marissa Parker."

"You have the right number, but she's unavailable now."

"Well, who are you?" Mrs. Griffin demanded.

"I'm a friend of Marissa. Give me your address, and I'll come get … Shelby."

"I don't think so. Have her call me." Then, a dial tone.

"Stupid woman," he snarled. A loud thunk followed.

Rissa jerked back, and her foot struck something on the floor, surprising her into releasing the panel. Incredibly, the thing had a hydraulic hinge and closed without a sound just as he burst into the closet. Frozen in pitch darkness, Rissa shrank away from the muffled cursing and rattling hangers on the other side.

If he knew about the panel, she was dead.

CHAPTER 3

Unknown place in Afghanistan
(Same time as the San Antonio murder, halfway around the world.)

Ding, ding, ding.

Warrant Officer Bernard Cruz swung his focus from the interview to locate the sound. A woman in a voluminous blue burqa stood a few paces away, holding a metal tray filled with tiny cups of *kahwah*. Instead of placing their tea on the table, she remained in place, shaking hard enough for the cups to clink against each other.

"Three o'clock. Possible tango," Burn murmured, alerting his team through their comms.

His number two, Palmer Watson, nicknamed Scoot for his proclivity to dance, sat on the other side of the informant. Scoot was a little too American for this part of the sandbox, with his reddish-brown hair and freckled skin, but his translation skills surpassed Burn's. Especially his Pashto.

Burn tipped his chin at Scoot. "Ask Hakim about the woman holding the tea."

Scoot murmured something in Pashto. After the man replied, Scoot said, "The woman is the daughter of his cousin. Hakim took her in last year after her family was killed."

Warning bells clanged in Burn's head, and he had to wonder if Americans were involved in the death of her family.

Hakim jerked to standing, both arms outstretched. "*Salaam.* Our tea." He said something else in Pashto and waved the woman forward.

Instead of moving, she lifted trembling fingers holding a cylinder device with a cord looping up her sleeve. In the standard dialect, she said, "American demons must die," or something like that. The words too quick for Burn to get an exact translation, but his rear brain kicked in.

"*Bomb!*" Diving sideways, he yanked Scoot to the ground with him in the same moment as she detonated the device.

He lost his grip on Scoot when they hit the stone floor, and a roof section collapsed. Acrid smoke engulfed the shop, turning the air thick and sour with the bomb's accelerant and burning flesh. Burn struggled to pull in a breath as it seemed the weight of the building pressed him into the broken tile floor. His ears buzzed, and darkness dragged at him. Where was his team?

"Chief? Where are you? Chief!"

Pan called his name. The last time he'd seen Pete Serrano, a.k.a. Pan, he'd been scaling the building next door like a human spider. Why the hell wasn't he in place on overwatch? Burn flattened his hands on the rough floor, but the debris on his back kept him from bending his knees. "Here. I'm here," he croaked.

Most of the buildings in this area were built with homemade mud bricks. Good thing, too. Better to end up under those than solid concrete.

Pan whooped. "Chief!"

Hands dragged Burn free from the rubble. As soon as he was clear, he rolled to a sitting position, blinking his bleary, dirt-encrusted eyes. "Where's Scoot?" He coughed with the effort to speak.

Pan crouched beside him and pushed a canteen into his hand. "Blast threw him clear, but he took a lick to the head."

"Anyone else?"

"Drink. Some debris from the wall outside landed on Mack, but he's on his feet and watching the front. Only casualties were the informant and the woman." Pan's gaze swept around them as he spoke.

Burn sloshed water on his face to clear his vision. Movement in his peripheral revealed Scoot struggling to rise. *Thank God.* He shoved the canteen back at Pan and heaved himself upright. Then, together, they helped Scoot to his feet.

"Ah ..." Scoot muttered and lolled sideways, his face a wash of blood and grit.

Burn slung Scoot's arm over his shoulder and supported him around the waist. He jerked his chin at Pan. "Head out."

Rifle up and ready, Pan led as they exited the demolished building. Outside, Mack leaned against the remains of a wall, his med kit open on the ground and his leg wrapped in an inflated splint.

Relief punched Burn in the gut. "You good?"

Mack spoke through clenched teeth. "Negative, Chief. My leg is shit."

"Hang tight. We'll get you out of here," Burn said.

This shouldn't have happened. The meet with the informant had been pure clockwork. An easy five-man mission. Styles on the perimeter, Mack out front, and Pan on overwatch. He and Scoot had been the only ones inside to parlay with a man purported to know the American they'd spent the last several weeks hunting. The slippery bastard was selling truckloads of American weapons to insurgents.

His team had been tasked with finding the American and erasing him from the planet. This fuck-up was on Burn. He'd been so certain they'd get him this time he'd rushed the intel.

"Time to leave, Chief," Pan blurted, his head still on a swivel. "We stay here any longer, and the neighbors will get the party invitation."

Burn dipped his chin in agreement, regretting his decision to split the eight-man SEAL team. He'd like to have his other three guys here right now, but they were in the helo, waiting to rendezvous at the evac point. If the neighbors dropped in before his team vamoosed, they were toast. "Where's Styles with our ride?"

"Thirty seconds."

"I've got Scoot. See if Mack needs anything."

The ancient cargo van screeched to a halt in front of them, and Styles yelled out the open window. "Need a ride, Chief?"

"Fuck yeah," Burn snarled, half-lifting Scoot onto the middle bench seat before helping Pan settle Mack on the back row. Then Burn slid into the front passenger side while agile, five-foot-nine Pan scrambled over the back seat to cover their rear.

Styles hit the gas, spinning the tires as they shot down the narrow street. Burn glanced over his shoulder, and despite their injuries, Scoot and Mack were weapons ready, eyes peeled for pursuers at the side windows. He was damn proud of his team.

"That suicide bomber came out of nowhere." Styles glanced at him. "No way to plan for that."

Burn's team trained for every contingency, but sometimes things went to shit. "Save your breath. Debrief can wait till we're on the helo. Let's get out of here first."

They rode in silence the rest of the way to the rendezvous point. After topping the last hill, they watched as the sleek, black bird dipped to land.

Styles let out a jubilant cheer and hit the gas a little harder. "Hot damn, that's our taxi!"

Burn took a deep breath, relieved that something was going as planned. Then, out of the east, a ground-to-air missile blew away the helicopter's tail, sending it into a spin and slamming it hard against the rocky hillside.

"Fuck!" Styles yelled, dropping speed as they drew closer to the wreck.

"Get the van as close as you can. We'll grab the guys and detonate the bird. Coal will have his gear." Assuming everyone in the aircraft was alive and mobile. "The distraction of the blast will give us time to reach the second evac point. Scoot, get on the radio, but stay frosty. Mack, you too. Both of you cover us while we get our team." Burn gripped his door handle, ready to leap out as soon as they stopped.

The van rocked to a halt a dozen feet from the helicopter. No visible flames, but black smoke poured from the tail section. Kama, the team medic, and Butter, his newest team member, climbed down the side of the bird carrying multiple duffels. But where were Coal and the Marine pilot?

"Styles, help load in the gear. Pan and I will find him." No need to explain. They knew he meant Coal. No teammate is ever left behind. Not on his watch. Burn called out to Kama and Butter. "Is Coal still in there? Injured?"

"No injuries, Chief. But that last little spin took our breath away. Maggie would kill me if I let anything happen to her husband." Butter hopped down the last few feet. "Coal and the pilot are setting charges. We thought it'd be a nice welcome gift when they come looking for us," he said, his perpetual five o'clock shadow made darker by the soot streaking his face.

Lightheaded with relief, Burn scanned the smoking heap. "I'm glad that pretty face of yours survived the crash. Otherwise, we'd have to come up with a new nickname for you."

"Nah, the ladies would still love me with a few scars." Butter grinned, his teeth flashing white against his olive skin and his smoky gray eyes lighting up with humor.

Finally, Coal poked his head out from the sideways cockpit, followed by a second man. Both slid down the nose of the craft and hurried toward them.

"Charges are set." Coal used an elbow to mop the soot from his eyes. "But the heat might set 'em off before we're ready."

Burn thumped him on the back. "Let's get out of here, then. Whiskey Team, time to go."

"Easy day," Coal said as they jogged back to the waiting van.

Blowing the aircraft gave them a few minutes head start on the tangos, but it wasn't long before the telltale rising dust appeared in the distance.

"Got a visual," Pan called from the van's cargo area.

Coal sat behind Styles, checking the map and arranging coordinates for a new extraction point. The original spot had been east of their location— the direction from which the missile had originated. They could go to ground and call for air support, but Mack needed medical attention soon.

"Chief. We have an issue." Styles thumped the steering wheel.

Of course, they did. "Report."

Style's lips thinned, but he didn't slow the van as they raced over the winding two-lane road. "Gas is low."

"How's that possible? We filled up last night. Should've been good for three hundred-plus miles."

"Gauge is flashing. Something must've nicked the tank."

Burn slammed a fist against the dash. "Options?"

"Keep driving and see what happens or ditch the van. If we ditch, we could go straight into the tree line and climb to higher ground to rendezvous with the evac helo."

Burn twisted to focus on his navigator. "Coal, where do we stand on the alternative exfil?"

Coal tipped his head but didn't glance up from the maps and devices he was using to plan their retreat. "Working on logistics, Chief, but higher ground would be good. Wilson, hold up that paper map you had on the bird so I can see it."

The addition of Coal to the Whiskey Team might be what pulled them out of this crack. Not only was he physically strong, but his genius-level intellect and photographic memory also allowed him to remember every map he had ever seen. He'd gone into Basic Underwater Demolition training, or BUD/S SEAL training, right out of college and fast-tracked through all the training before the Whiskey Team snapped him up.

His real name was Rockford Murphy and not only did he win the lottery in brains and looks, he had a gorgeous wife who was completely in love with him. With Lucky Coal on board, there was no way they were dying in this sandbox today.

Burn studied the faces of his team. "Okay, boys. We gotta get to higher ground for the pick up, so we have two choices. Drive till the van gives out and hope our location is defendable, or climb to higher ground and meet the helicopter."

"Chief," the Marine pilot spoke. "I'd rather be in the trees than the open." His patch read: WILSON.

They'd borrowed the helicopter and this pilot as a backup for today's meeting, so Burn didn't know Wilson all that well, but he'd done a helluva job setting down that damaged bird.

Burn nodded. "How about the rest of you?"

"Let's hike," Styles said.

"Agreed—yeah—good plan." Multiple affirmative replies came from the team.

Burn pointed at Coal. "Genius, find us a route." Then he spun a finger toward Styles. "Take off."

Styles sent the van bumping overland, climbing higher. The engine whined and strained as they raced toward the trees. Miraculously, they reached the first stand of trees and shrubs about the time the van choked out.

"Let's move," Burn ordered, popping open his door. The team exited the van on both sides, spreading out, the lean form of Wilson joining Pan to chop camouflage foliage to hide the van while Coal planned the route and Styles assembled the gear.

"I've got Scoot, but we got a problem with Mack," Kama said.

Haikili Kama was the team medic, and he'd been with Burn since the beginning. Though born and raised in San Diego, his grandfather had tagged him with the name of the god of thunder, Haikili. He refused to answer to it, and Doc didn't seem to fit the six-foot-four bald, dark-skinned Hawaiian, so they used his last name.

Mack was out cold. Butter helped shift him into the open door of the van. The smelling salts roused him, but no way he could run.

"We'll take turns carrying him," Burn said, tipping Mack over his shoulder in a firefighter's carry.

Butter jerked his head in agreement. "I'll stay close, and you can hand him off to me."

"Head out and stay alert," Burn ordered as they took the hill at a fast trot, a cross-country sprint for their lives in this sandpit. He fell behind the group under the weight of Mack's two-hundred-plus-pound frame. He, Mack, and Kama were the only three original team members. Mack was a sharpshooter and had been the best translator on the team until Scoot joined them three years ago.

Butter flanked him and watched for any hazards on the rugged trail. The team had plenty of juice left, except for Scoot, who resembled a horror movie extra with all the blood on his head. Kama had him tucked against his side, keeping him on his feet as they ran.

They climbed for fifteen minutes before he handed Mack off to Butter. Another fifteen, and they swapped again. With no time for anything else, they'd dosed Mack on morphine and antibiotics. The guy hadn't complained once. Tough bastard.

Burn thumped Mack's good leg. "Hang in there, sailor. Your pretty wife is expecting to see you home soon. Preferably before your daughter makes her appearance."

"Roger … that."

Burn's gut hollowed out at the reedy sound of his teammate's voice. "Hey, you hear me, Mack Dempsy? When we're outta here, there's a diet in your future."

Mack wheezed. "Don't hurt my feelings, Chief."

"Always the comedian," Burn chuffed. "Coal," he called to the SEAL up ahead, who was bird-dogging for them.

Coal held up a thumb. "We're closing in. Less than a mile," he shouted, never glancing back as he set the pace, following an internal compass in his giant photographic brain.

Wilson jogged close to Burn's other side. He couldn't be much over twenty-five, but the dirt-streaked lines of his face were fierce and battle-hardened. "Chief, we've got plumes kicking up below us. Appears to be four separate vehicles. I suggest digging in for the fight."

Marines loved a good fight, but Burn outranked him. "I'd rather shoot them from the cabin. You can bring up the rear and lay down fire if necessary. The only calm day was yesterday. We all leave together. Hooyah!"

Most of his team called back a rejoinder, and Wilson saluted him with a loud "Oorah!" before dropping back out of sight.

"Chopper!" shouted Coal.

The rumble grew louder. An NH90. Thank you, Marines. This bigger ship could handle their group and get them out of there fast. Sweet Jesus, they were going to make it. "On me, boys. Push!" Burn ordered. His muscles burned from carrying Mac's weight even as he cranked his speed up a notch.

Knobby outcroppings and knee-high shrubs threatened to trip him as he ran across the open area, Butter close at his side, supporting him when he might've stumbled. The gunship fired over their heads, and bullets from the insurgents pinged around them, spraying dirt and sand on all sides.

Styles yelled, "Hooyah!"

The team zigged and zagged toward the open bay of their ride.

A sharp pain sliced through Burn's upper arm, but he kept a firm grip on Mack's legs.

Pan and Coal hurled themselves into the bay, followed by Kama and Scoot.

Finally, they made it, and hands reached down to pull Mack inside. Then, he and Butter planted themselves by the skid to lay cover.

Wilson flew past.

Where was Styles? Burn spotted the crazy bastard twenty long feet away, still firing. "Harry, get your ass inside!"

Burn boosted himself on the edge, snapped a strap to his belt, and opened fire in a wide arc to give the idiot time to board. Which he did, an instant before the bird spun up and away, pullets pinging off the metal as they rose. They hit cruising speed in under twenty seconds. The best way to avoid more missiles was to get the hell out.

"Ha ha!" Styles was jubilant, no doubt adrenaline burning out his last few brain cells. "We kicked ass."

Burn's team took up positions at both doors of the helicopter. He watched as Kama dosed Mack with more morphine. "How's he doing?"

The big Hawaiian grunted. "We need to get him on a flight to Germany the minute we land. He's gonna need a surgeon."

Coal wound a fat roll of clean gauze around Scoot's head on the opposite side of the cabin. "Palmer's good. In and out, but he's talking and told me he loves me."

"Asshole," growled Scoot, covering his eyes with his hand.

Palmer "Scoot" Watson was far from good, but a German hospital with MRI machines was his best option. Now, they needed to convince the commanding officer it was a priority for them to leave with the wounded so he could keep his team together.

Their ride, the big NH90, was a powered boomerang with a top cruising speed of over one hundred fifty miles per hour. It didn't take long for them to make it back to the safe zone.

If anywhere could be called safe in this godforsaken place.

CHAPTER 4

Shelby's little arms had a python-like hold around Rissa's neck, and the relief of holding her child was indescribable. "Sorry it took me so long to get here, Mrs. G." A hysterical giggle built inside Rissa's throat. The trip back to the apartment had taken longer than she'd wanted. She'd taken time to ditch Mrs. Iglesias' car in a hotel parking lot across town, in case it had LoJack installed, and catch a cab the rest of the way.

"What delayed you?" The woman's hawk eyes studied her.

Rissa faltered, thinking of the last few hours. Should she tell her about the hidden door and the stolen car she used to escape from a murderer? "Lots of things. I'll tell you about it sometime." Not really, but Mrs. G. was nosy, and Rissa needed to offer something.

"Home, Mommy," whispered Shelby, her breath tinged with the unpleasant scent of soured milk.

"In a second, sweetie." Rissa tucked her closer without breaking eye contact with Mrs. G. "Do you—"

"Who answered your phone?" she interrupted.

Rissa dropped her gaze. She hated to lie, but if there was ever a time, it was now. "I ... I lost it."

"That's irresponsible, Rissa," scolded Mrs. G. "And why are you so pale? Are you sick?"

"I don't think so, but I'm ... off work for a few days. I'll keep Shelby home with me," Rissa promised. She handed Mrs. G. two one-hundred-dollar bills. "Here's the money I owe for tonight and the last three nights."

With a smug purse of her lips, the older woman tucked the cash into the pocket of her housecoat. She crossed her arms and studied Rissa over her half-glasses. "You rarely pay me before Friday."

"I got paid early this time." From a leather bag full of money in a secret closet. Money she'd already used to pay for a cab and now her babysitter.

"It's good you can be home for a day or two. We'll only be gone one night, so if you need me after that, let me know. Goodnight, then."

"Wait." Rissa stuck out a hand to prevent the door from shutting. "Do you have the extra key I gave you to my place?"

Mrs. G. gave a disapproving grunt. "You lost that too?"

Not lost. "Yes." Her keys and bus pass lay on the kitchen counter at Mrs. Iglesias' house, next to the coffeemaker. Thankfully, she still had her driver's license in her apartment. Even though she didn't have a car, she needed it for identification.

"Of all the stupid things." Mrs. G. grabbed a key from a hook Rissa knew was behind the door. "Make a copy of this tomorrow."

"Thanks. I'll do that. Goodnight." After Mrs. G. shut her door, Rissa rushed across the hall to her apartment, securing the lock behind them. She placed her daughter on the couch, where she groaned and stretched, but her eyes remained closed. Hopefully, Shelby would stay asleep and give her time to pack their things.

Rissa dashed into the bedroom and grabbed her suitcase from the closet. She tossed in clothes for both of them, along with shoes, personal documents from her nightstand, toiletries, and hair accessories. What else? She returned to the living room to get Shelby's backpack and added more clean clothes, socks, and an empty sippy cup.

Almost done. She sank onto the bed beside the open case and pressed a hand to her chest, trying to slow her frantic heartbeat. Her meager savings, spare glasses, license, and a few papers she didn't want to pack in the suitcase were laid out next to Mrs. Iglesias' oblong leather bag.

Should she even be using it? There was a second backpack in her closet, but this crossover style fit securely at her hip and would be easier to manage since she also had Shelby's bag. Mrs. Iglesias wouldn't miss it, and if someone else came for it, she'd probably already be dead.

Rissa poked at the money inside. The paper bands around the bills were printed with various dollar amounts. Not all the stacks were hundreds, but this was more money than she'd ever seen in her life. She would use it to keep them safe and worry about the consequences later—if they had a later.

Decision made, Rissa pulled out a stack and placed five of the hundreds in the front pouch of the leather bag. That should cover the cost of train tickets and any other expenses they might need for now. She stuffed the rest of the money back inside and tossed her other things on top.

Then she paused for one last check before scooping up her daughter and entering the hall. This place wasn't much or even very nice, but it'd been hers for the last three years, and she would probably never see it again.

Acid pushed up her throat, and she hauled in a steadying breath. She had no time to be sick because getting her daughter out of danger was the only thing that mattered. The city bus came every thirty minutes. If she hurried, they could still catch the four o'clock.

Outside, she rolled the suitcase to the nearby stop. From the bus station, she'd get them on a train to Austin, and then to San Diego. She needed to figure out her Plan B—rather, Plan Burn.

Time to find her Navy SEAL.

•　　•　　•

Terrance closed his eyes and tipped his head against the cherry wood of the high-backed chair in his dining room. Road construction had turned his two-hour drive home to Austin into three, then he'd had to wait for Rick to bring the doctor.

He clenched his jaw as Dr. George examined his wound. George was in his late forties and barely competent, but he was discreet. Besides, who else could Terrance get to come to his house in the middle of the night?

"I can't detect any fragments," George said, snapping off thin blue gloves and rocking back on his heels. He smoothed one hand over his thinning blond hair and licked his lips nervously. "The bullet may have done damage I can't see, even though I irrigated the area thoroughly. IV antibiotics might be a good precaution—"

"No." Terrance reached for his tumbler of gin. A shitty drink, but about right, given the day he'd had. He perused the ragged flesh on his side. Amelia had gotten the last word after all. "Sew it or fucking tape it," he growled.

Rick shuffled his feet, drawing Terrance's attention to the other side of the table.

"Did you find—" Terrance bit off his words. He'd almost asked about news at the station, but one witness a night was enough.

Dr. George smeared cream over the wound before applying a bandage. "That's it. I'll leave you antibiotic pills, but if ..." He stammered, the words trailing away.

He was wearing on Terrance's nerves. "Spit it out."

Beads of sweat dotted the doctor's face. He dropped a handful of gauze and scrambled to collect it again. "If the ... area turns red or becomes more tender—more than now—have Rick call me."

"Fine. Now get out of my sight." Terrance turned up his drink and jiggled the ice.

Dr. George held his bag against his chest. "Before I go, could I—"

Terrance motioned for him to stop talking. "Rick. Give George enough heroin for three days. No more."

Separating from the shadows, Rick said, "Come with me."

"Yes, sir, absolutely," George sniveled, holding his medical bag like a lifeline.

Terrance smirked as the man took a step toward Rick. As if *he* was the safer bet. *Idiot.* "Rick. Bring me another drink when you come back."

Rick grasped the doctor's upper arm and pushed him forward. When George stumbled, Rick whispered something that made him whimper and try to back away.

Terrance chuckled. Although his half-brother might appear weak, at only five feet, five inches, Rick was wholly unburdened by a conscience. As Terrance's enforcer, he doled out consequences as needed. Their blood relationship had never been acknowledged, but they'd been raised together on the family's mausoleum of a ranch. Two motherless boys. Rick's mother disappeared after one of his father's infamous parties, and Terrance's mother didn't live to see his first birthday.

Papi had been like Dr. George. His alcohol addiction left him unable to manage his finances. Whenever his business faced a decline, he vented his frustrations on his sons. Their lives improved somewhat when he married Amelia Iglesias, a wealthy widow twenty-eight years his senior. She introduced *Papi* to cartel connections and a profitable Middle Eastern group—men who dealt in weapons and heroin.

Rick returned, a bottle of bourbon and thick glass tumblers in hands. "George is waiting in the kitchen until we're done," he said, pausing beside the table.

Terrance kicked an adjacent chair in a silent invitation. "Did you go by your precinct?"

Rick took a seat. Though he hadn't slept, he was freshly showered, wearing jeans and an Austin Spurs t-shirt. "I checked the log. Nothing of interest. No reports on a murder in your mother's vicinity."

Terrance winced as he reached for the bourbon. The pain injection the doctor had given him was already wearing off. The fool probably hadn't done it right. "No news is good news, I suppose." He tipped the bottle over both tumblers, filling them with a generous amount of amber liquid. "But I wonder why the sitter hasn't called the cops yet."

Rick nudged the cell phone in the thick pink case resting on the table. "It pissed me off when that motor revved up the driveway. No time to catch it."

"If the old cow had turned on the cameras I installed, we'd have a picture."

"She watched too much television and thought the FBI spied on everyone. The upside is there's no record of our visit." Rick drained his glass.

"True." Terrance shifted to cross his leg, and a sharp pain jabbed his side. *Fuck.* "My being caught with a gunshot wound on the premises would've raised questions."

Rick tapped his empty tumbler against the smooth wood. "It's been hours. She's not going to report it."

"Why so confident?"

"It's been too long." Rick refilled his glass. "I assume she saw my uniform or was hiding in the garage. She probably heard the gunshot."

"Regardless, we need to find her."

Rick gave a perfunctory nod. "It's only a matter of time. I'll get the GPS location on the Mercedes. Do you want me to green light the cleaners? We only have another hour until daybreak."

"Yes. Have them move fast. The woman might reconsider or tell someone else."

Rick sent a text and downed the rest of his bourbon.

"You're guzzling that like cheap beer. It's Blanton's Silver, for fuck's sake."

Rick shrugged. "One's the same as another."

Terrance swirled his drink, the aroma of the amber liquid a perfect antidote for the overpowering antiseptic the doctor had used. "What would you have done if she'd killed me?"

Rick filled his glass a third time and held it up for a toast. "Killed her right back, boss." When Terrance mirrored him, he added, "The past is dead and gone. Good riddance."

Terrance fingered the deepest scar on his chest, visible above the white bandage. "Bitch loved watching him beat on us."

Rick leaned back on two chair legs. "I'm curious. She called you down there for a big secret. Did she take it to the grave?"

He blew out his cheeks and hoisted himself upright, careful not to crease his side. "I don't—" An idea struck him. "Text the cleaners back. Tell them to save every piece of paper or notebook they find. Box it all up and deliver it here. Afterward, they can torch the house with her in it. That way, I won't waste time pretending to be sad standing beside a casket."

Rick pulled out his phone. "Why the papers?"

The liquor and pain reliever scorched Terrance's gut. He sucked a slow breath through his nose. "Amelia kept journals and wrote notes on every damn thing that happened."

CHAPTER 5

Rissa pressed her cheek against the cold window, peering into the darkness beyond the reach of the station lights. She had scored two seats near the bathroom, and the aisle seat in their row remained empty.

Shelby slept across her lap. Her daughter had bawled her eyes out right after they boarded, begging for Mrs. G. and pleading to go home. Because, exhausted and ill, nothing satisfied her.

This was, without doubt, the longest night of Rissa's life. And not over yet. They were leaving San Antonio, but instead of relief, fear of what lay ahead dominated her thoughts.

"Do you need a blanket, honey?"

The woman's gentle question made her jump, and Rissa barely prevented Shelby from rolling off her lap.

"What?" she managed, her teeth chattering.

"I'm sorry. I didn't mean to startle you," the attendant apologized and offered up a folded blanket from her stack. "I thought your little one might need one of these."

"Thank you," Rissa whispered through dry lips as she draped the blanket over her daughter. Shelby had finally cried herself to sleep, and Rissa hoped she wouldn't wake until they arrived in Austin.

The bulky weight of Mrs. Iglesias' oblong leather bag pressed against her ribcage. Spending the money felt wrong, but she had no choice. Besides, the old woman didn't need it anymore, and she had told her to take it. There was no way to count it on the train, but Rissa hoped it contained enough cash to get them where they needed to go and keep them fed while she figured out what to do next. She'd figure things out when they were safe. Maybe even get a job.

Rissa pressed a hand to her eyes, trying to erase the image of Terrance lunging at Mrs. Iglesias. If she thought about that, she'd panic, and she needed to focus on getting them to San Diego. Once her daughter was safe, she'd allow herself to cry. She had no doubt Terrance would come after her, and that thought had bile trickling up her throat.

He knew her name thanks to Mrs. G.'s call, but perhaps other women were named Marissa Parker in San Antonio, like in *Terminator*, where the killer robot searches for Sarah Connor but ends up targeting women with the same name. Ugh, that sounded awful. She should've gone straight to the cops, but the second man, Rick, was a cop, and she'd been afraid.

Her stomach lurched, and she forced deep, rapid breaths through her mouth to quell the nausea. Running to the bathroom to be sick wasn't an option because she couldn't leave Shelby or carry her and all their stuff with them.

Desperation weighed on her as she considered her options. Who could she turn to? For sure, not her parents. The last time she spoke to her mother was shortly after her birthday trip to San Diego. She had hoped her mother would be happy about a grandchild, but Evonne Parker had kicked her out a second time.

The words still hurt.

Knots coiled in Rissa's belly as she pressed the doorbell, listening to the chime resonate through the heavy oak door. When no one answered, she took a deep breath and dared to use the key she still had to her parents' house. Tuesday was Evonne Parker's "me" day, so she should be home.

Entering uninvited might prove foolish, but Rissa had taken the morning off work, and she couldn't afford to lose any more time. Her rent had increased, and she hadn't caught up from the money she'd spent flying to San Diego for her birthday. Fear was a sour taste in her mouth as her mind raced with worries about her job, rent, and doctor bills.

"Hello? Mother? It's me, Rissa. Hello? Are you home?" She'd never been particularly close to her parents, and since she turned eighteen and they'd made her move out on her own, she only saw them once or twice a year.

"Marissa?" Evonne Montano Parker appeared at the top of the staircase. "What are you doing here? Aren't you supposed to be working?"

Rissa tucked trembling fingers in the pockets of her jeans. "I … uh … wanted to see you."

"Did you call in sick? You know jobs are difficult to come by, and if you're lazy or call out for no reason, you'll get fired. Don't expect any help from me if you lose your position."

Rissa licked her lips and told a lie. "They gave me the morning off."

Evonne squinted at her and retied the belt of her silk robe. "Then wait for me in the living room."

Okay, so her mother didn't want her roaming around. At least she hadn't immediately told her to leave. Rissa crossed the marble floor of the foyer to enter the formal living room, a space that had been off-limits in her childhood due to its array of valuable items. Now, as she pressed a hand to her flat stomach, she silently promised that her future son or daughter would never be shut out from any room in her home.

At one end of the expansive room, a grand piano stood proudly with a pair of pristine white couches facing it as if anticipating a concert. Though her father was a talented pianist, he'd never allowed her to touch his precious instrument.

The scent of sickly-sweet magnolia blooms wafted from the giant vase on the coffee table, making Rissa gag, so she moved close to the fireplace, as far away from the flowers as she could get. Along the mantle, between a pair of enormous crystal candlesticks, stood a row of photographs of her parents, grandparents, and a few of her father's nieces. Not a single one of her. It was like she'd never been part of this family.

In truth, the only person she'd been close to was Granny Montano, her maternal grandmother. Granny Monty had lived alone and kept Rissa when Evonne had to work, filling at least some of her childhood with warm memories *of baking cookies and petting her half-dozen cats—a stark contrast to her mother, who detested both cooking and house pets. She wished for the comfort of Granny Monty's arms, but she knew that was no longer an option as she passed when Rissa was eleven.*

She'd only met her dad's parents a couple of times. When she was small, he'd gone alone to his family events, or they'd left her with Granny Monty. It struck Rissa as odd to see a photo of her parents and his smiling together. Maybe they'd patched up whatever had pulled them apart.

"What are you looking at?"

Rissa spun to face the open doorway. Evonne Montano Parker wore a deep burgundy sweater dress with a cowl neck, black tights, and her customary black leather Jimmy Choo pumps.

"Hello, Mother. I was admiring the photos. That one surprised me." She pointed at one of her parents with Mr. and Mrs. Parker.

"Why?"

"Seeing you all together. I mean, it's a nice change."

"What are you talking about? We're together all the time." Her mother gestured dismissively and moved to adjust the arrangement of magnolia blooms. "Did you stop by to look at my photos?"

"No. I need to talk to you."

Evonne's head popped up, and she frowned. "Sit in that chair. I recently had the couches recovered."

"I have some news," Marissa said, settling into the black-striped high-back chair while her mother perched on the edge of the couch cushion.

Evonne didn't speak, only arched her manicured brows.

Rissa shrugged and decided just to spit out the reason for her visit. "Surprise. You're going to be a grandmother."

"What?" Evonne sprang to her feet to pace across the room. "You're pregnant? Who's the father?"

"I ... uh ..."

Evonne froze, her eyes wide and her mouth a round O. "You don't know?"

"No, I do." Rissa half-rose, but nausea forced her to sit again. "He's in San Diego. I met him when I visited Liesel for our birthday."

Evonne's gaze burned into Rissa as she sank slowly back onto the couch. "Let me get this straight. You finished your nursing associate so you could work in a care home, and now you're pregnant with no husband to help you? Have you contacted the father?"

Rissa felt like a little girl again, recalling how her mother used to call her stupid, saying her friend's little girls would always be smarter and prettier. "No, I only know his nickname, but he's a Navy SEAL. They call him Burn."

"Why don't you know his real name?"

"Well, I left quickly, because I didn't expect that I would see him again. I was hoping you'd loan me some money to fly out there so I can talk to him."

"You promiscuous little fool." Evonne snapped to her feet and crossed her arms. "Pregnant by a stranger whose name you can't recall."

Rissa jerked to her feet. "I thought you'd want to know you're about to become a grandmother. And I'd hoped—"

"Don't pretend you're here to tell me good news. You're here for my money. Well, you can't have any. This child is your responsibility. I did my best for you in spite of everything."

"What do you mean? In spite of what?"

"It doesn't matter. You need to leave my house. This time for good. Give me your key."

Rissa choked on a sob. The room spun, and she thought she might faint. "Mother—"

"No. Don't call me that anymore. I'm Mrs. Parker now, should you ever have a reason to contact me—which you won't."

A long time ago now, but the words still jabbed spears into her heart. If Liesel hadn't sent her money, she might have ended up back in the shelter, this time with a newborn.

Rissa gently brushed Shelby's hair back and caressed her soft cheek. She'd been promiscuous precisely one time, yet that one time turned out to be the best thing that ever happened to her. Would her baby's dad be willing to help them? Other than him, Liesel was the only person she knew wouldn't turn her away.

They had remained friends since their high school days. Back then, people had commented on their comically different appearance. Rissa, with her light green eyes, short stature, and brown skin and hair. Her eyes were her best feature, except she was mostly blind without her glasses. In contrast, Liesel stood six feet without shoes, had smooth, pale skin, blonde hair, and vision-perfect, baby-blue eyes. Liesel had rescued Rissa from the shelter after graduation, and they'd lived together for an entire year after high school before Liesel moved to California to pursue a modeling career.

Rissa shivered, lonelier than she'd ever been in her entire life. "I'm going to look for your daddy, but I hope it's not a mistake. We only had one night, and he doesn't know about you. Can you understand why I was too afraid to find him?" She brushed a tear away with the back of her hand. "I had no money, and I was scared he might want to take you away. It's been better with just us. Only now … now things have changed. We need his help."

She planned to stay in Austin for a few nights, but after disembarking at the station, Rissa discovered an express train to San Diego leaving in only fifteen minutes. Shelby still asleep in her arms, Rissa lugged the heavy suitcase to the ticket desk. They could spend the night here, but it was pitch dark outside, and she'd have to catch a cab and find a hotel with all this stuff. Easier to board another train and get to San Diego faster.

At the counter, she bought tickets and checked the bag before hurrying to the station's newsstand to buy a cheap phone.

"One more quick stop," she murmured to her sleeping daughter.

They had only a few minutes before the train left, but she needed a phone. Inside the small shop, a young man leaned on the counter, flirting with the giggling cashier, so caught up in each other that they didn't notice her arrival.

Rissa wrinkled her nose at the multitude of odors in the train station—coffee, pastries, and too much perfume on a woman standing in front of a souvenir rack. She hitched Shelby higher on her shoulder and coughed, but no response. A whistle blew in the distance, signaling an impending departure.

Time ticked by. Rissa unzipped her bag and pulled out two one-hundred-dollar bills, holding them up like a flag. "Excuse me," she said.

They didn't notice.

She needed to hurry. "Excuse me, miss? I need to make a purchase. My train leaves soon."

Their heads separated slowly, and the man twisted around to face her with his butt against the counter.

"Move back, Chris," the cashier said. "What'd you need?"

"I'd like to buy a phone."

Now, both of them appeared interested.

Rissa's petite size and ponytail made her appear younger than she was, so she pushed her shoulders back and placed both bills on the counter. "Here. I lost my phone and need to call my husband."

The cashier reached behind her and grabbed two boxes containing phones. "These are the only ones we have in stock. This one costs—"

"It doesn't matter," Rissa said, cutting her off. "Give me the best one. And do you have any bottled water?" Her mouth was dry and her throat tight as she struggled to keep her emotions under control.

"In the back, there's a long cooler with drinks." The cashier pointed.

Rissa slumped. "Never mind." No way was she walking that far.

"Here." The man, Chris, held out a bottle of water. "It's not open. I can grab another one."

"Thank you."

The cashier gazed dreamily at him. "Isn't he sweet?"

"Yes, he is." Rissa pushed the water toward the girl. "Can you ring us up?" She grabbed some packs of crackers by the register and added them to her purchases.

When the cashier gave a total, Rissa swung Shelby's backpack down to unzip one-handed and stuffed the crackers, water, and one bill inside. The box with the phone wouldn't fit, so she put the backpack on her shoulder and scooped up the box in her free hand.

The girl held out her change.

Rissa didn't want to put everything down again. "Keep it," she said, rushing to catch their train.

•   •   •

Rissa shifted uneasily on the worn upholstery of the bench seat. The train was cramped and stuffy, with narrow aisles and rows of seats packed with sleepy passengers. Shelby slept cuddled in her lap. The trip would take thirteen hours, and she'd programmed the cellphone right after boarding, but since Austin was two hours ahead of San Diego, she had to wait to call Liesel. Finally, it was six a.m. in San Diego, and she couldn't wait another minute. Hopefully, her friend would be home and willing to help them. The line rang seven times, and Rissa almost hung up when a groggy voice answered.

"Hello?"

"Liesel." Relief made her breathless. "It's me, Rissa. Sorry to call this early."

"It's alright. I usually wake up around this time, but I stayed out late last night. I almost didn't answer because I didn't recognize this number. Gosh, it's been a few months since we've spoken. What's going on?"

"It's a long story." The sound of Liesel's voice loosened something in her chest, and Rissa broke into sobs.

"Riss? What's wrong?"

"I ... I was afraid you wouldn't be home ... I miss you." Rissa hiccupped, trying to control her gasping breaths, aware of other passengers watching her curiously.

"I miss you too, honey. Guess what? I have exciting news. My agent booked me for that perfume shoot in LA, and he got me a sweet six-month contract in Japan. I leave in three weeks for Tokyo. I cannot wait. The amenities in the hotels are fantastic, and they really roll out the red carpet for the models."

"Japan?" Rissa struggled to keep her voice steady. "The last time I saw you was right before you went there."

"You're right. I flew out on the Monday after our twenty-first birthday celebration. I can't believe it's been nearly three years. That job really propelled my career. Best decision I could've made. Tell you what. I'll visit Texas when I return from Japan. Or you could come here. We have got to get together again. I'm dying to meet the little princess."

"I want you to meet her also. She's perfect." Rissa hadn't been able to visit Liesel or even look for Shelby's father because she had used all her money on food, rent, and childcare. A woman across the aisle handed her a little pack of tissues. She covered the phone and gave her a watery smile. "Thanks."

"Riss? Are you still there?"

"I'm here, sorry." Rissa mopped at her eyes with the tissues. "So, Japan. Will you be with the same modeling agency?"

"I'm not entirely sure, but probably. It's a great opportunity. Besides, the pay is too good to pass up, and I won't be young forever."

"But you're home in San Diego right now?"

"Yes." Liesel let out a long yawn. "Until I go for that perfume shoot in L.A. Oh, exciting news. I might be on the cover of a French magazine again, if it doesn't conflict with the Japan trip. I can get Shelby another bunny. Does she still like that?"

Rissa fiddled with the tissue pack. "She won't sleep without it."

"That's sweet." Liesel groaned like she was stretching. "You never call me this early. What's up?"

She hated involving her friend in this, but she had no one else. "Liesel, I've been missing you, but that isn't why I called. I'm in trouble."

"What?" Liesel's voice sounded distant now. "Hang on, I dropped my phone!" Rustling sounds could be heard before Liesel spoke again. "Okay, say that again? What kind of trouble?"

Rissa swallowed past the tightness in her throat. "I left San Antonio last night, and I'm on a train right now."

"Don't make me pry it out of you, Marissa Parker." Liesel sounded fully awake now. "Tell me right now where you are headed."

"I'm coming to you. Can you help us?"

"Gosh, yes. Get your butt here. But what's going on?" Liesel demanded.

Rissa glanced at the nearby passengers. A few were sleeping, and some watched her like she was on the morning show. She cupped a hand over the phone to whisper, "There are too many people around me to talk freely, and Shelby is asleep. Can I explain when we see you?"

"Yes, definitely. I have something for work this afternoon, but I'll ask my neighbor to meet you. What time does your train arrive?"

"We'll be in after eight your time, so don't worry about anyone meeting us. I can grab a cab from the station."

"You have enough money? I can Venmo you."

"I have money." Stacks of money in a leather purse.

"If you're sure."

"Thank you, Liesel. I'll see you this evening." Rissa said goodbye and disconnected the call. She rested her head against the seat and closed her eyes. Exhaustion pulled at her, and they had hours yet to reach San Diego. She thought of Burn, afraid to hope he might help her when no one other than Liesel ever had.

CHAPTER 6

Two years and nine months in the past.

Rissa shivered, not from the cool air swirling the curtains under the hotel windows but from the sensation of his hand tracing the contours of her back. He threaded his fingers through her hair, almost dislodging her glasses.

"Can I take these off?" he asked, even as he tipped them up and off her head.

A bolt of panic rushed through her. She could function without the glasses, but barely. "I need those to see," she said, grabbing them from him.

"How about we put them on the nightstand?" His lips quirked, and he extended his palm.

She wavered, feeling vulnerable without the thick lenses. "Okay."

Instead of moving her off his lap as she expected, he leaned them both straight back on the bed, reaching an arm out to lightly toss the glasses onto the nightstand with a tiny click.

"They're safe now. Where were we?" He sat them back up and captured her nape in one big hand, kissing her until her nerves dissolved and her blood sizzled.

He lifted her higher and pushed aside the silky barrier of her bra. Something heavy and needy spread through her veins, and she forgot to be self-conscious of her less-than-ample breasts. The drag of his mouth on her nipple had her moaning and pressing her face against his short curls. She sprawled across his lap on the end of the bed and wanted to be closer, to have more of him against her. Using his shoulder for leverage, she twisted and bunched her skirt to her waist so she could straddle him.

His hands positioned her over his thighs, but his legs were so thick her knees didn't quite touch the mattress. She pressed down against the ridge of his erection behind the zipper of his jeans.

Despite only having met a few hours before, she wanted this. Burn was smoking hot, and Rissa couldn't believe that they were going to have sex. The two-fold sensation of his warm mouth and the hard line of his erection had her squirming against him. She needed more.

"Can we move up on the bed?" she whispered.

His throat resonated with a low laugh, and he nuzzled her cheek. "Hold tight," he said, tucking her close and easily lifting her as he gained his feet.

She inhaled deeply, trying to memorize every little thing about him. An instant later, a cool pillow was behind her neck, and his warm breath tickled her lips.

"Can I take your clothes off?" His gaze tangled with hers, freezing her in place.

Rissa's heart fluttered with an emotion she couldn't identify. Burn gave her confidence and made her feel sexy—a new experience for her. She stretched her arms above her head. "I'm halfway there already."

"Halfway is no good." He eased back on his heels, and her nerves tingled in anticipation as he slid her skirt down her legs, taking her underwear with it.

She quivered with anticipation, waiting for him to say or do something. What was he waiting for?

"Oh, babe." He lay half over her, his jean-clad legs sliding across her bare ones as he pressed his weight against her side. "You're perfect." He cupped her jaw and held her in place for an all-consuming kiss.

She broke away enough to whisper, "Will you get undressed too?"

He contemplated her with an upward slant of his lips and slid off the bed to undress at lightning speed. "Your wish is mine."

Joy erupted inside her, reminding her of when she opened an unexpected gift or delicious treat. When she'd imagined having sex with someone, she'd never thought it would be this fun. Burn settled back over her, peppering her face with tiny kisses before slanting his mouth over hers. The heavy weight of his dick brushed against the inside of her thigh. She wanted to touch it and slipped a hand between them.

He snagged her fingers and brought her hands above their heads onto the pillow. "Uh uh." His lips tickled her ear. "Keep your hands right there for now. I want to make this good for you, and to do that, I need to be in control."

"Can I ..." Instead of finishing the sentence, she wiggled her legs out from under his and wrapped them around his hips. "Oh ..." The length of him pressing against her was exquisite.

"You're killing me here. Hit pause a second," he groaned and gently pushed one of her legs down before leaning over the edge of the bed to pull his jeans closer.

In another minute, she heard the crinkle of a wrapper. A condom. She should've thought of that. The room light was off, but streaks of moonlight spilled through the blinds. He settled on his heels to roll the condom into place. The semi-darkness gave her confidence, and she stroked the bottoms of her feet over his rock-hard thighs.

He stretched over her, supporting himself with one arm bent at the elbow by her head. "Wrap your legs around me."

She did as he asked, and he slid a hand between them to position himself.

"Are you ready for me?"

"Slow, okay?" A tingle of fear trickled down her spine. Should she tell him she hadn't done this before?

He paused when she tensed. "Rissa, I'm big, but we'll fit. Put your legs down, and I'll make it better for you."

Is he talking about going down on me? So not ready for that. "No. I mean ... yes, I'm good. Please don't make me wait. I'm soaked." She was as aroused as she'd ever been in her life.

His face hovered over hers, his eyes searching.

"Why are you waiting?" she asked.

White teeth flashed in the dark room. "No more waiting." He kissed her as he began a rhythmic, nudging motion with his cock, pushing himself slowly inside her body.

She spread her legs wider, easing the progress. So full. Not exactly painful, but more pressure than she'd imagined.

"You're tight. Are you okay?" he murmured.

"I need ..." She writhed, partially impaled. She needed something.

"Yes, baby, I know what you need." He licked his thumb and slid a hand between them, forcing her to remain still as he massaged her clit, slow, then fast, then—

Her eyes shut, and the world sheeted white. He plunged full hilt.

"Oh!" She gasped as her body clamped down on the intrusion.

He froze. "Sweet Jesus. Are you—? Please tell me you're twenty-one." He kept his voice low and kissed away the moisture from her cheeks. "Are you crying? Baby, I'm sorry."

She breathed through the pain and shook her head. "No, I promise I'm okay. And I'm twenty-one. You can check my ID, but not right now." She kissed his cheek, seeking his lips. The pain had subsided, and being impaled by him stirred a deep need inside her. She murmured, "Can we keep going?"

He pulled back to study her. "I don't want to hurt you."

"Please." She tried to wiggle her hips, but he held her in place. "I want this."

Whooshing out a breath, he brushed his mouth over hers. A gentle press, soothing her, then tangling his tongue with hers while he made incremental thrusts of his hips.

Tiny thrusts that had her digging her heels into his back. "Faster," she breathed, but he didn't alter his speed or his hold on her. Her torso clenched with an orgasm so intense, so deep inside her, she screamed his name when she exploded in ecstasy.

His thrusts faltered before speeding up, and he groaned, pumping out his release. He pressed his lips to hers before rolling them onto their sides, cuddling her close, their bodies still connected. He stroked his hand in long sweeping motions over her hair, down her back to her hip, and up again. Perfect ... except for one thing. She squirmed slightly as his semi-hard shaft remained inside of her, and it burned a little.

"You uncomfortable?" His deep voice rumbled near her ear.

"That was amazing. I ... do you mind if I take a shower?"

He stroked a hand over her hair one last time before sliding out of her body. When he did, a little gush of fluid trickled down the inside of her thigh.

"Stay where you are. I'll get ... oh shit." He rolled up onto the side of the bed.

"What's wrong?" she asked, sitting up, squinting in the dim light, and wishing she had her glasses.

"Babe, I'm sorry. The condom broke. *Shit.* Don't move. I'll be right back." He rushed to the bathroom.

"It's okay," she called tentatively.

"Not really." He returned with a warm, wet washcloth to gently wipe between her legs. "We should take a shower."

The night had been so great, and she hated that he was upset. "It's okay. I'm on the pill." However, she'd forgotten to bring the pack on this trip. But everyone forgets them sometimes.

He let out a relieved grunt and pulled her onto his lap. "That's good. I wish you had told me it was your first time. I would've been easier with you."

She rested her cheek against his chest, safe and cherished in his arms. "I liked it. After we shower, could we try again? If you don't mind?"

"Mind? Woman, you're a dream I hope to never wake from." He lifted her in his arms and carried her into the bathroom.

Hours later, she woke alone in bed. She could hear water running in the bathroom. They'd taken a shower together before making love again, but she'd been pretty sore. After that second time, they'd curled up and talked, and he'd made her feel like everything she said was important.

She untangled from the sheet and reached for her glasses. The digital clock read 5:48. Leaving before things got complicated would be the smart thing to do. Mind made up, she dressed but found nothing to write a note on. The shower shut off, and still no paper. Well, it was just for fun. He'd said that at the bar. They hadn't exchanged numbers or full names. If she left now, before any of the awkward stuff, this night would be a fantasy she would cherish forever.

CHAPTER 7

Burn settled into his seat as the big C130 rose off the tarmac. They were finally in the air for the six-hour flight to Germany. Kama Haikili, their corpsman, sat by Mack's stretcher, Scoot was between Coal and Pan, and the rest of them were spread out around the equipment-filled bay.

They'd all made it out. Not unscathed, but alive. Burn's upper arm smarted from the shallow bullet track he'd earned in the dash to the aircraft. He closed his eyes and leaned back, composing the mission report in his head.

"Chief." Styles dropped next to him.

He cracked open his eyelids to see Styles holding out a beer. Styles was the first one up for any mission and the first one to belly up at the bar. Unconventional, but someone you wanted at your back in a firefight.

Harrison Tucker was his real name, but he'd picked up the nickname "Harry Styles" in training when they'd had a karaoke night at a bar. The idiot could carry a tune and had the look of the popular singer with his brown hair and green eyes.

"Thanks." Burn accepted the beer. He wanted a nap, but it was easier to accept the beer than argue about it.

Styles relaxed in the seat beside him, took a swig from his can, and waggled his brows. "The first thing I'll do when we get back is find a certain co-ed. We hooked up before the team got spun up. I expect she's jonesing for round two."

Burn scrubbed a hand over his eyes. "You rely way too much on your pretty face. But honestly, I don't care. Although if I did, I'd point out that your co-ed won't be in Germany."

Unconcerned, Styles stretched his legs, set his now-empty can on the metal deck of the aircraft, and started shuffling a deck of cards. "I know, but we'll be home a few days after that. Do you want to play?"

"No." Burn closed his eyes again. This guy took living in the moment to a whole new level. "You think you're so good that co-ed will wait three months for an encore?" College girls were too young for him. At thirty-four, Burn was the team's oldest member, and the allure of a quick lay didn't hold the same appeal. Not since that night with Rissa.

"Absolutely." Styles bumped Burn's shoulder with his.

Ow. He didn't react to the tiny flash of pain, but it ground on his nerves.

Styles continued. "If you're not drinking that, I'll take it back."

Burn handed him the unopened beer.

"That co-ed had the biggest—"

"Harry. Do I seem interested in this conversation?" Burn twisted to glare at him.

"Just talking, Chief."

He crossed his arms to get his sore one farther from Styles. "If I tell you my plans, will you stop the chatter?"

"It's—"

"I'll spend time with my brother's family," Burn interrupted. "His wife had a new baby last month, whom I haven't met." And he couldn't wait to hold that little boy and remember why he did all the things he did for his country.

Styles' lips tilted. "Boy or girl?"

"Boy. They have two girls." Burn's mood improved as he thought of his five-year-old nieces. He didn't mind being wrapped around their tiny, identical fingers.

"You've got to be looking forward to seeing someone besides your family."

"Not really. Although there was a woman ... " After one night, he'd never found her again. His love-and-leave-'em dream girl. Rissa had been sweet, funny, and so very innocent. Images flooded his mind of their bodies soaking in the tub. After trying and failing to order room service, they satiated themselves on each other rather than food. "I'm sure she's moved on."

"SEAL bunny, huh?" Style scrunched his face in sympathy.

"Not really. She was special." Burn wondered why the image of the green-eyed beauty remained stamped in his memory. Incredible sex, but it had been so much more than that. They'd talked most of the night, and her determination impressed him. She'd recently completed her associate degree in nursing and done it on her own because her parents had kicked her out of the house at eighteen.

Stupidly, he hadn't even gotten the mystery woman's full name. During the early morning hours, he'd slipped into the bathroom to order them breakfast and grab a quick shower, but after he emerged, she had left. No note. Nothing.

Styles bumped his shoulder again. "You never know what a woman wants. Call them, don't call them—"

"Go bother someone else, and I'll buy you a six-pack when we get to Germany." He closed his eyes and listened as Styles moved away. He welcomed the familiar image of tumbling hair the color of pine bark and soft green eyes. Her face burned forever into his brain. And maybe his heart.

·   ·   ·

As Terrance had known they would, a pair of somber-looking Austin deputies arrived on his doorstep mid-morning with the news of a fire at his mother's house. It was fortunate he hadn't used a bullet, and that Rick had located the slug that had gone through him and into the wall. No forensics.

He feigned surprise and grief. Not too difficult, given his lack of sleep and the pain from both his hangover and his wound. Although perhaps a bit too convincing, as the officers insisted on coming inside to make sure he was okay.

The officer—Windham?—put a hand on his arm. "Can I call someone for you?"

He fantasized about snapping her fingers but managed a curt nod. "I'll call my brother. Did you know he's an officer with the East Substation?"

The pair made eye contact, then Windham pursed her lips. "The fire marshal from San Antonio only gave us your name. He indicated you were the only known relative."

Terrance shrugged, wondering if sitting would appear suspicious. "Rick is my ... foster brother. My father took him in as a boy. He had no relation to my stepmother."

The other officer spoke. "If there's nothing more we can do for you, we'll be on our way."

"Unless you need us to drive you to San Antonio?" Windham's brows arched.

What does she want?

Terrance wasn't worried about being a suspect, but if that changed, he had a rock-solid alibi. Yesterday, when he planned his trip to San Antonio, he made sure his housekeeper knew he would be home all night watching the boxing match on pay-per-view and drinking with Rick. What better character reference than a member of the Austin Police Force? They certainly downed the booze, but post-game, early morning.

"I'll be fine." He wanted them to leave so he could make coffee. "I need to call my brother," he said as he punched the numbers into his cell.

"This place is very secure," said Windham.

He glanced up, and her expression was blank. Too blank. "I don't have security personnel, but I have cameras around the entire property."

"I see."

He could tell she regarded him as a suspect, but it was inconsequential. Years earlier, he bought the adjacent house through a shell corporation and utilized it as a safe house and base for his business activities. Cameras monitored the exterior of his property, except for a hedge-lined path that led to a concealed gate between the two homes. A sedan and a truck registered to that same corporation were stored in the garage next door, enabling him to come and go unnoticed, while the cleaning service only interacted with a manager.

Last night, he and Rick drove the sedan to San Antonio for a business meeting with his Afghan associates. Rick's truck had been parked in front of his house, clearly visible on camera from around six p.m. until he left for the station that morning. They hadn't planned to stop by Amelia's house, but the timing worked out. So there was no proof that he and Rick hadn't spent the entire evening inside watching the game.

Terrance straightened his spine and squinted at the woman. "I'm not sure how that pertains to the fire. What was your name again?"

"Officer Windham," she said, never taking her eyes off him. Smart cop, checking his reactions. "And no, sir, it doesn't pertain to the fire. I was only making an observation."

"Well, if you're done with your observations, I'll see you both out." Terrance took a few steps toward the door. They didn't immediately follow, so he turned back and allowed his real fatigue to bleed into his expression. These two needed a push to leave, so he swung open the door and held up his cell. "I need to call my brother and see about my dear stepmother."

CHAPTER 8

The sun had set when the cab pulled up to a glass-fronted apartment building. Rissa sagged in relief at the sight of Liesel's condo. Fifteen hours of traveling with a toddler had taken a toll. The last six had been miserable with Shelby alternating between crying and wanting to run up and down the aisle of the train.

Shelby was sleeping now, and Rissa took a moment to stare up at the building she'd visited three years prior. A place filled with memories of that long-ago birthday trip. Only she wasn't on vacation this time. She had nowhere else to go, and there was no one she trusted more than Liesel. But coming here could put her friend in danger. Uncertainty pulled at Rissa, but she was too tired to come up with any other options, and it was too late for second guesses.

She leaned forward to hand the fare to her driver. "Thanks for the ride." Then she scooped up her sleeping daughter and slid out of the cab, exhaustion making her movements clumsy. Even worse, her glasses fogged over in the chilly evening air. She cuddled Shelby closer and tried to peer over the frames. If she could rest for a few hours, she'd figure out what to do. They were over a thousand miles from San Antonio. They were safe, right?

"Mommy? Home?" Shelby's green eyes blinked at her in the glow of the streetlights.

"Give me a minute, sweetie." Rissa kissed her forehead and turned to take her bag from the cab driver.

He shifted from foot to foot, seeming eager to get back on the road. "Are you alright to get it inside?"

She realized he was giving her an odd look. Had he noticed her distress? "Yes, we're fine." She had already tipped him, but then an incentive might help. "Wait a sec." Rissa shifted Shelby enough to unzip the leather bag and retrieve one of the hundred-dollar bills. "If anyone asks, please forget you saw us. My ex was … abusive, and we recently got away."

His eyes went wide. "Keep it. You might need it."

Rissa tried to smile, but her lips trembled too much to cooperate. "No, please take it. I have friends here, so we'll be okay." She held out the money until he reluctantly accepted it.

"Me want down," Shelby whined.

"Not yet, sweetie." Rissa gave the driver one last nod before rolling the bag toward the entrance.

Through the glass window, the lobby appeared unchanged. Pristine and cheerful, with an immaculate tile floor and several flowering plants in pots lining the walls. However, the doorman behind the reception desk was a different person from three years ago. This man had snow-white hair and wore a deep red jacket.

Rissa tugged at her rumpled shirt, which she'd put on yesterday before leaving to sit with Mrs. Iglesias. The past twenty-four hours had been one long, terrible nightmare.

"Home, Mommy?"

"No, we're at your Auntie Liesel's house."

Shelby's dark brows bunched, and she reached up to touch Rissa's cheek. "Auntie?"

"Yes, Auntie Liesel."

Thankfully, Shelby had recovered from her upset stomach. She had eaten most of a grilled cheese sandwich in the dining car a few hours earlier and taken another short nap before they arrived at the train station.

"Down?" Shelby wiggled again.

"Wait till we're inside, and I'll let you walk." Rissa pushed the glass door and propped it with her backside to drag the heavy suitcase over the threshold.

"May I help you?" A gnarled hand pushed the door wider.

"Yes, ah … I'm here to see my friend, Liesel Zolan."

"Santa," Shelby whispered.

The old man's entire countenance lit when he smiled. "That's a darlin' there."

The tension drained from Rissa's shoulders. He did resemble Santa Claus, but his nametag read Dean. "Thanks, Dean."

Now that they'd arrived, her body drooped as if buckets of sand were pouring into her bones. If she didn't sit soon, she might fall on her face.

"I'll buzz Ms. Zolan for you," Dean offered before stepping to the desk.

Shelby wiggled again, and Rissa let her down to explore. There wasn't anywhere for her to get lost in the lobby. Rissa propped against the counter while they waited. The lobby had a faint scent of citrus and cleaning products, but no heavy fragrance from the artificial flowering plants.

Seconds later, the elevator dinged. The doors slid open, revealing a man wearing a dark suit and a black Stetson with a silver band. *Terrance? He's here?*

Rissa's vision blurred. "Oh!" she got enough air to squeak, "Shelby!" *Where's my baby? Are we going to die right here?* A hand on her arm had Rissa scrambling backward.

"Is something wrong?" Dean's brown eyes filled with concern.

Where was her daughter? There! She was trying to pick a flower from the artificial plant on the far wall. "Shelby!"

The man in the suit stepped between them, and Rissa's vision tunneled, focusing only on the black fabric.

"Sugar, are you okay?" He cupped her elbow, holding her upright, his voice soft and accented. "What's wrong with her, Dean? Is she sick?" The cowboy's voice floated an octave above the killer's rough tone.

Relief had her knees buckling, but she got control of her breathing enough to whisper, "I'm fine." Terrance wasn't here. They were still safe. No one restrained her. Both men flanked her. They were helping her.

"My boyfriend's an EMT," the cowboy said as he put an arm around her back, supporting her weight. "He'll be here any minute to pick me up. Or I can call an ambulance?"

She staggered under a wave of nausea, but she managed to whisper, "No hospital." They would have records of her visit, making it easier for Terrance to find her. If he had someone on the police force helping him, they probably had some sort of search to find people. All that mattered was keeping Shelby safe.

"Breathe, Rissa. Can you hear me, honey? You need to chill, girl. You're scaring everyone."

Rissa leaned toward the sound. "Liesel?" She saw her then, blonde hair floating in voluminous waves around a pale face.

Liesel squeezed her in a warm hug. "Yes, honey, it's me," she said in her soothing, familiar drawl. "I got home thirty minutes ago and was about to call you to see how close you were, but you're here now." Liesel rattled on, talking about something that kept her at work late, and Rissa's lips twitched with humor.

"You know who she is?" the cowboy said in a bright tenor voice. "I see my boyfriend's truck pulling up now. I'll get him to park, and he can check her out."

Her friend was a full head taller than the nice cowboy, and Rissa had to clamp her lips together to prevent a hysterical giggle from escaping.

"I'm good. Please … I'm sorry. We had a long trip," Rissa said, taking in a shuddering breath. "Shelby? Come here, please."

Liesel pulled the cowboy into a side hug before taking his place beside Rissa. "I'll take care of her, Jack. You have a nice dinner with Andy. I'll get her upstairs and, if necessary, take her to the hospital later." She then scooped up Shelby with her free arm. "Are you the magnificent and famous Shelby?"

It amazed Rissa when her daughter didn't freak about a stranger holding her. Instead, she patted Liesel on one of her well-proportioned breasts.

"Big ones." Shelby chortled. "Auntie Liesel."

The cowboy laughed hard enough his fancy Stetson tumbled to the tile floor. Rissa wanted to bury her face in her hands and crawl under a rock.

"Big ones?" Liesel gave Rissa a wide-eyed stare.

Rissa's gut clenched in horror. "I had a picture of us at the beach on my refrigerator. Liesel, I'm sorry, I left it behind."

Still chuckling, Jack picked up his Stetson. "And Miss Zolan fills out her bikini very well."

Hiding a grin, Dean asked, "Do you need help getting upstairs?"

"No thanks, we're good. Come on," Liesel said, propelling her toward the elevator. She sent Dean and Jack air kisses and pressed the button for her floor.

"Wait! Don't forget this." Jack rolled the suitcase in beside them. "Call me if you need anything."

"I will, thank you." Liesel made a little squee sound and jiggled Shelby. "You came to visit me. I'm so excited I finally get to hold my princess."

Rissa wanted to thank the men again, but the doors were closing, and Jack stood several feet away in his wide-brimmed Stetson. She lost her voice as her mind flooded with memories of another man and another hat.

CHAPTER 9

Burn ended the connection with Mack's wife, Deena, and jammed his phone back into his pocket. Scoot's hospital room was brightly lit with white walls and tile floors reflecting against the fluorescent lights. He glanced around at his team. Kama and Coal had the only chairs, and Styles sat on the floor playing solitaire. Butter had left for more coffee and most likely to flirt with the nurses.

They had all been awake for the last thirty-six hours and weren't budging until Mack was out of surgery. A better group of guys didn't exist. They hadn't showered or eaten a meal not out of a machine since arriving, but not a single complaint.

Palmer Watson, a.k.a. Scoot, would make a full recovery. He had a hairline fracture in his skull, and because of that, the docs were requiring him to have at least one more scan before they cleared him to fly home. The German doctor had said three times that Scoot needed plenty of rest to recover. As if by repetition, he could convince a two-hundred-pound Navy SEAL to stand down.

"What'd Deena say when you told her about Mack?" Pan settled on the window ledge beside him.

Burn shook his head and scrubbed a hand over the rough stubble on his cheeks. Regret and fatigue weighed on him. "She thanked me."

Pan grunted. "For calling her?"

"Yeah. She was damn stoic." Burn pressed his fingers to his eyes. "Even though I couldn't tell her how he got injured."

Styles cleared his throat and shuffled his cards. "Deena's a military wife. She knows the drill."

The room was small, so small it was impossible to have a private conversation, so Burn wasn't surprised Styles was listening. "Deena said she'll get here as soon as possible, but she's five weeks from delivery, and her doctor has to sign off for her to fly."

Pan dipped his head. "Figured she'd come. That means their baby will be born in Germany."

Burn dipped his chin, and his team sat in silence for a few moments, digesting that fact. He could practically hear Pan making to-do lists in his head. He was a planner and excelled at logistics.

"Do you want me to contact the American base and arrange housing for when Mack gets out of the hospital?" Pan asked.

"Good thinking. No telling how long he'll be hospitalized. Deena will need somewhere to stay with the baby till they can fly back to the States. Check with the C.O. and find out who runs the spouses' group on base."

"I'm on it, Chief."

Burn watched as Pan slipped from the room on a mission to take care of his teammate. They'd all accepted the risk of being frontline warriors, but as their leader, the wounds of his team were Burn's responsibility. His intel had led them to that location. This team was his family, and he'd led them into danger.

The door to the room pushed open, and a bone-thin man of indeterminate age stepped inside. He wore a surgical cap and paper covers over his shoes. "Chief Cruz?" he asked in accented English.

Burn shot to his feet. "Yes, I'm here." His team all rose with him. Even Scoot sat up on the bed. It gratified him to have the team at his back.

"I'm Dr. Schmitz. Could we go somewhere to discuss—"

Burn interrupted. "Give it to us now. We all want to hear what you have to say."

Dr. Schmitz glanced at the five operators filling the small room, his jaw working silently. Then he focused on Burn. "Mr. Dempsey is out of surgery."

Burn wanted to shake the doctor to make him talk faster. "How's his leg?"

"We attempted to save it, as you requested." Dr. Schmitz heaved a sigh and squared his shoulders. "If the blood flow is not sufficient within twenty-four hours, we'll likely be forced to amputate."

"You did your best. That's all we ask," Burn said.

"When can we see him?" Styles asked, moving closer to Burn.

"Right now, he's in the recovery room. I'll have a nurse notify you when he's awake." Dr. Schmitz punctuated his words with a sharp nod before quickly exiting.

Burn scanned the faces of his team. They needed a mission, something to focus on besides Mack. He cleared his throat to be able to talk around the giant lump that seemed to have formed there. "Time to make plans for getting stateside."

Several of them spoke at once.

"Chief—"

"We—"

Burn folded his arms over his chest and waited for them to finish. Then he said, "Mack will be here for several weeks, and his wife is on her way. None of us wants to leave, but we head home as soon as he's stable."

He only hoped Scoot could leave with them.

•   •   •

Thursday morning at Liesel's apartment.

Rissa dumped a handful of colorful kids' cereal and a small amount of milk in a bowl before placing it on the coffee table. "Please don't spill this on Auntie Liesel's nice carpet."

"It's fine," Liesel said from her relaxed seat on the couch.

"You say that now, but this cream-colored carpet is pristine, and I want to keep it that way," Rissa said.

Shelby patted Rissa's leg and gave her a sweet smile. "Me watch Paw Patrol?"

Rissa double-checked the lid on the sippy cup. "Sweetie, we can try, but I don't know the channel."

"I've got it." Liesel leaned forward to scoop up the remote. "What about this one? It isn't what she asked for, but it's puppies."

"It works. She's already sucked in."

"Good. I need you in the kitchen," Liesel said. "I have questions for you, and we need to talk privately."

"Okay." Rissa trailed behind her and sat cross-legged on a chair at the retro blue Formica table in the brightly lit kitchen. Butterflies danced in her stomach. She had come to California seeking Liesel's help, but her whole body tensed at the thought of the danger she had brought with her.

"Do you want some coffee? I don't drink milk, so I only have caramel creamer. Do you want some of that?" Liesel asked. "Or there's tea. I'm sure I have some tea bags around here somewhere. Not sure if I have anything else."

Rissa's nerves eased into amusement. Liesel never said just one thing. "Coffee for me, please."

"Coming right up. I usually have flavored coffee, but I haven't been to the store recently," Liesel said as she pulled down another mug.

"Those are fancy pjs," Rissa said, eyeing Liesel's shimmering gold silk pajamas decorated with countless tiny yellow kittens in various poses.

Liesel snorted. "Everyone needs kitten pjs. I didn't buy these, though. Got them from a photo shoot. You'd be amazed at the stuff I get from photo shoots. I just have to wear them home, and nobody asks for it back."

"You wore the pajamas home?"

"Sure did." Liesel gave her a wide smile as she set down the mug. "Sometimes you gotta do what you gotta do."

"I don't even own pajamas." Rissa plucked at her oversized, plain t-shirt. "I'm underdressed in your kitchen."

"Yeah, right. You can have these as a gift, once I've washed them. For that matter, you're welcome to anything in my closet. My shoes won't fit you, though. You have small feet."

"I have average feet. You have big feet," Rissa teased, and Liesel tossed a napkin at her. "I'm only kidding, but I won't say no to the kittens. I wish you had them in Shelby's size. By the way, your apartment looks amazing. Is the couch new?"

"Yes, bought it last year when I redecorated. New paint and carpets too. One of the benefits of owning rather than renting. But, I think you're trying to distract me."

"Maybe. There's so much to tell you that I don't know where to start," Rissa said, grimacing when she sipped the black coffee.

"Hold on." Liesel jumped up to retrieve a container of sugar-free, fat-free, caramel-flavored creamer from the fridge. "Drink your coffee and take a few deep breaths to settle your thoughts. That's what I do when I'm trying to clear my mind for a job. While you're doing that, I'll fix us breakfast."

"You cook now?" Rissa grinned. Liesel had zero interest in domestic duties like cooking and cleaning, and no doubt had a cleaning service.

"Sure." Liesel's blue eyes sparkled with challenge as she plopped a box of chocolate protein cookies on the table. "Breakfast is ready. Now tell me what's happening. Last night, you were upset, and I only got part of it."

Rissa found the creamer's sweetness, mixed with the bitterness of the black coffee, much better tasting. She straightened in her seat and put her feet on the floor. Liesel had given them a place to stay, and she needed to be honest with her. "You know that I'm a nurse's aide, right?"

Liesel bobbed her head and fiddled with a clip in her hair. "You had finished your classes when you came out here last time."

"Yes. Well, even with a job, daycare is ridiculously expensive. I can't work during the day until Shelby is old enough for school. That's why I quit my job at the retirement home and signed with an agency that provides in-home skilled care to elders. Only working at night."

"Who looks after the munchkin?"

"My neighbor, Mrs. G., watches her for me. I pay her, but less than I'd have to pay someone during the day," Rissa said, pouring more cream into her coffee. "A few weeks ago, I got an offer for a position paying thirty-five dollars an hour, working six nights a week with an elderly lady."

Liesel's eyes widened. "Is that considered good? I mean, for sitting?"

Rissa rolled her eyes. Her friend had no idea how hard life had been living alone with a baby. "I usually get twenty-five an hour."

"Umm ..." Confusion clouded Liesel's expression.

"Yes, it's a great wage for an adult sitter."

"Sorry. Keep going."

"Anyway, Mrs. Iglesias was eighty-eight and in good health. I only had to be there in case she needed something during the night. Her mind was sharp, and she was kind, although she constantly tried to offer me food and random things. And she asked a lot of weird questions." Rissa cupped her fingers around her mug and thought about everything Mrs. Iglesias had said to her.

Liesel's eyes lit with interest. "Oh, the plot thickens. What kind of questions?"

Rissa shrugged. "A million and one things. Personal things about me and Shelby. That was the strange part. I had only been there a few weeks, and she kept asking me to bring Shelby to work with me."

"Too interested in your kid. That's a red flag for sure." Liesel waggled her fingers.

"I agree."

Liesel pushed a cookie toward her. "Get to the good stuff. I mean, you're here out of the blue. You're welcome here, but why did you jump on a train in the middle of the night with the munchkin?"

"I'm so sorry."

Liesel held up a hand. "Dang it, Rissa. Stop apologizing. I'm glad to see you. That isn't what I'm saying."

"Okay." Rissa exhaled deeply. "It's bad."

"I'm all ears. Don't keep me in suspense."

Rissa straightened her spine and pushed away her mug. "Last night, no, night before last, I watched Mrs. Iglesias get murdered."

Liesel recoiled in her seat. "What the fuck?" She slapped a hand over her mouth and swung her gaze to the living room.

"It's okay. She isn't listening," Rissa said.

"Are you for real? Actual murder? Tell me everything."

Rissa clenched her fingers in her lap. "Two men came into the house—"

"No way. They broke into the house when you were there?" Liesel's eyes doubled in size.

"Mrs. Iglesias was sleeping in her bed, and I was dozing in the chair beside her like I always did. The house alarm went off and woke us."

Rissa went on to tell her about the murder, the safe room, the bag of money, and escaping in Mrs. Iglesias' car before picking up Shelby and catching a bus to the train station.

"I think I need a drink." Liesel paced from one end of the kitchen to the other.

"It's eight-thirty in the morning."

Liesel flapped a hand. "Why didn't you call the police?"

"I should've, but all I thought about was getting to Shelby and escaping. Besides, the second man was a cop."

Liesel stopped pacing to scowl at her. "Honey, the police are the good guys. Running makes you look guilty." She whipped her head to the TV and back. "Have you checked the news?"

"No. I haven't had a chance and didn't think of it this morning."

"Let me grab my laptop," Liesel said, dashing into her bedroom. Moments later, she returned and opened her computer on the table. The soft clicks of the laptop keys were the only sound in the kitchen as Liesel scrolled through the news. "Okay, okay. Here it is."

Rissa moved to peer over her shoulder.

"I searched for San Antonio and Iglesias." Liesel tapped the screen. "The headline says, 'Heiress dies in her sleep ... Reports confirm an electrical fire completely consumed the house ... Her grieving stepson, Terrance Simmons, states his mother was a hoarder, and the place was stacked with newspapers and books.'"

Rissa shook her head. "Her place was as immaculate as a five-star hotel."

"The stepson claims the junk contributed to the fire."

"But Mrs. Iglesias had a cook *and* a housekeeper," Rissa stuttered. "They'll know the truth."

Liesel scrunched her shoulders. "I don't imagine they'll talk. Not after her demon spawn gets to them."

"He was her stepson," Rissa said.

"Whatever. It doesn't matter. The good news is that your name isn't in this story. Are you sure he knows who you are? I mean, he knows someone was there, but how can he know it was you?"

Rissa sank back in her chair. "Guess I left out that part of the story. Terrance didn't see me, but Mrs. G. called my phone because Shelby was sick."

"He heard it ring?"

"Even worse. He answered it on speaker, and she clearly said my full name."

Liesel smacked the table. "That *stupid* woman."

"Yeah."

"You need to report this to the police."

Rissa swallowed hard. "I promise to do that, but first, I want to find Shelby's father. Will you help me?"

Liesel's perfect brows rose. "An admirable goal, but it's been three years. What have you done to find him so far?"

"Umm ... not much," Rissa confessed.

The disappointment on Liesel's face had Rissa cringing with guilt. "I wanted to find him. I planned to, but money was tight, and I didn't know his full name. When I called the Navy base, they said I needed more information. I even sent a letter, but there was no response. Please. If something happens to me, Shelby needs a parent."

"Don't talk that way. You're going to be fine," Liesel said, shutting the laptop. "Here's what we'll do. Last week was Shelby's birthday. August twenty-third, right? Let's take her to the zoo today and have fun. Take your mind off things. We'll keep checking the computer, and you can call Mrs. G. to see if she's heard anything."

"But you'll help me find Shelby's father, won't you?"

Liesel nodded. "I'll always help. Have you thought about how to do it?"

Rissa put her mug in the sink and leaned against the counter. "I made a list in my head on the train of ways to look for him."

"Tell me."

"The first thing is to call the base again. Or maybe go there, but I doubt I could get past the guards. He liked to be called Burn, but his real name was

Bernie. If he told me his last name, I don't remember it, but he has one brother, and his parents live in San Diego."

Liesel laughed out loud. "We'll start there. Do you have any other ideas?"

"I don't. Unless you think we could return to that bar where we had our birthday party?"

"Cicadas? The odds are a million to one that he'll be there." Liesel began clearing away the uneaten protein cookies. "Riss, you know he could be married and living far away."

"True, but the bartender might be the same, and they were friends."

"Let's call the base first," Liesel insisted.

Rissa got her burner phone, and they found a number online and called the base. The switchboard operator thought it was a prank call and hung up on her. The third time she called, the lady threatened to call the cops for clogging up the phone system.

"I told you I tried this before."

Liesel tapped her chin. "What if we went to the base, took a note, and left it at the gate?"

"Maybe. I sent a letter once, asking him to call me and gave my number and address. I never heard anything. I addressed it to the Navy SEAL department/ Burn/Bernie. It probably went in the trash."

"Why don't you write another letter, and we'll go to that bar? It's a known base hangout, so there's bound to be a Navy SEAL there. Maybe we can ask the bartender if he knows anyone who would deliver a note."

"That's a fantastic idea. I can go alone if you want to stay here. Will you keep Shelby for me?"

Liesel shook her head. "No way am I letting you do this by yourself. We'll enlist Jack and Andy to watch the munchkin."

"Do you think they'll mind keeping her? She goes to bed at eight, but that's six o'clock here with the time change."

Liesel's lips quirked. "They need the practice, since they're discussing having a kid. They'll love Shelby. I'll call Jack right now."

Rissa tensed. "Please don't tell him."

"What?" Ever able to find humor in any situation, Liesel said, "Don't tell Jack you're on the hunt for your one-night-stand baby daddy? Or should I tell him you're a murder witness on the run?"

"It isn't funny. You might be in danger because of me."

"Sorry, bad joke. Don't you worry about me." Liesel wrapped her in a hug. "I haven't seen you in three years. What's the chance the murderer could find you here?" She paused. "Did you leave my address stuck on the fridge?"

"No, I tried to get everything. But last night when Shelby grabbed your chest?" Rissa stammered. "I remembered that photo of us on my fridge. It's still there."

CHAPTER 10

This changed everything.

Terrance rocked back in the chair he'd positioned between the boxes from his stepmother's house. His guestroom was now a chaotic mess, with papers strewn over the bed and the surrounding carpet. Most of the sandwich his housekeeper had prepared for his lunch sat uneaten nearby.

He'd located the sitter's name and address in Amelia's papers, but also something else: a manila envelope wrapped tightly in a thin pink ribbon that reeked of his stepmother's sweet, floral perfume. His name was scrawled in loopy letters across the front.

Terrance Simmons
My last gift for you.

Something frozen scurried through Terrance's belly as his fingers traced the smoothness of the thick envelope. The woman had hated him, so no doubt this gift was something he very much didn't want to receive. He shifted in his chair, pressing a hand to his side, then lifted the tiny metal wings of the tab to open the flap. Reaching inside, he slid out a handful of pages with a handwritten letter clipped to the front.

Terrance,

Your father pushed me out of the operations of my family business, and after his passing, you continued to disrespect me. All the Iglesias properties and accounts are deeded to me, and I'm leaving you nothing. Since I have no living blood kin that I care to recognize, my sole heir will be your daughter, Marissa Montano Parker.

This is probably a shock to you, and I would've enjoyed delivering this information in person. Twenty-five years ago, Evonne Montano showed up claiming you'd put a child in her belly. She was, of course, expecting a payoff. I countermanded my husband's kill order and provided her with an annual stipend on the condition that she raise the child and communicate only with me. Marissa graduated from high school with honors and supported herself through community college to get a nursing certificate. She has elevated herself above the sins of her father.

My death will trigger the estate's distribution, and, as this Will has already been probated, it is irrevocable. If something happens to Marissa, my entire fortune will be disbursed to a Catholic charity.

Burn in hell,

Amelia

Unbelievable.

The sitter who'd escaped was his *fucking* daughter.

Terrance seethed with fury, struggling not to crumple the letter. Instead, he shuffled the pages to examine the ten-page Will, which clearly designated Marissa Montano Parker as the sole heir of all Amelia's assets. The final page stated that if M. Parker were either deceased or unwilling to accept the inheritance, everything would be distributed to a Catholic charity. All the pages had been notarized and filed with the San Antonio Clerk of Court two years prior.

Terrance jerked to his feet only to be reminded of his gunshot wound as the rapid movement had pain knifing through his side. A burst of air spewed from his mouth, and he clutched his side over the bandage. Damn that old woman to hell. Amelia thought she'd sewn this thing up—but had she?

He eased back onto his chair and tipped his chin to stare at the ceiling, his mind whirling as he considered options. It was possible to contest the will in court, if he could prove Amelia wasn't of sound mind, but that wasn't a guaranteed outcome. Additionally, he didn't want any legal scrutiny that might reveal his frequent trips to the Middle East.

Terrance read the letter again and scrubbed a hand over his nose, trying to wipe away the floral perfume. The notion of having an adult child piqued his interest, although if no DNA test existed, it might not even be true. Was the girl aware of their relationship? And more importantly, could she be used to advance his plans, or did she pose a roadblock of epic proportions?

He rummaged through his memories. The name Evonne Montano didn't ring a bell. Twenty-five years ago, he would've been done with university, though he'd hit up plenty of frat parties after graduation.

It could be the pills he'd downed with coffee a few minutes ago, but he wasn't angry Amelia had well and truly outsmarted him. This new challenge was interesting, and if managed correctly, it might turn into gold. The girl hadn't reported the murder, so perhaps she had something to hide. Something he could exploit.

The first order of business was to locate his daughter's mother and discover who else was aware of the relationship. Terrance turned over the manila envelope, and a single crumpled sheet fluttered to the floor. Before he could pick it up, an alert beeped on his phone, indicating that the front door had opened. He checked the screen to verify what he already knew, because Rick was the only person he trusted with a key.

"In here," he called, scooping up the sheet.

"Boss?" Rick paused in the open doorway, his cap in his hands. "I'm on duty all weekend, but I got someone to cover me for an hour. I see the cleaners sent over the stuff. Did you find the sitter's address?"

"Yes. It's all here, but there's something else you need to see. Have a seat," Terrance said. Rick was his illegitimate brother, but they'd grown up together and he trusted him.

Rick set his cap on the dresser, kicked a few papers aside, and tugged an ottoman beside the wastebasket.

"I have a system," Terrance said, waving a hand at the bed. "Everything warranting a second look, I put over there. The rest I'm tossing. Most of it is useless crap, but this is a gift she left for me." He held out the sheaf of papers.

Rick gingerly held the edges while he read. A few minutes later, he gave a low whistle. "Did you know about this girl?"

"Not a clue. Amelia paid, probably well, to keep it quiet. *Papi* wouldn't have tolerated such a loose end." Terrance needed more coffee. The pain pills from earlier were giving him a coppery taste in his mouth.

After quickly flipping through the rest of it, Rick handed it back.

Terrance tossed the packet onto the bed and flattened the crumpled sheet against his thigh. "I'd shred it all, but the note claims the Will has been probated and the stamp from the Clerk of Court appears authentic."

"I wasn't aware you could do that before you died."

"I guess it's possible, but I'll need to confirm with my attorney. If Amelia's telling the truth ..."

"She had an ace in the hole." Rick crossed his arms. "But what about *Papi's* will? With her dead, shouldn't his estate revert to you?"

Terrance shook his head. "The ranch, her portfolio, the house in town, and the department store chain all belong to her. Her family owned all that before they married, and a copy of her prenup is attached. *Papi* also kept his investment accounts in her name to keep the money safe if he was ever investigated."

Rick shook his head slowly. "If all that's hers, what's left?"

"My personal real estate, these houses, and the cattle. But now I don't own the grass they're eating."

"You're going to fight it, aren't you?"

"Amelia never adopted me, so we have no legal relationship. Which means this girl is not related to her. Maybe that could help in court." Terrance read the sheet he'd flattened. "Shit," he said through clenched teeth before kicking a box across the floor.

"What is it?"

Terrance tossed him the page. "Another gift from Amelia."

"A police report." Rick scratched his head. "About a rape at a frat party."

"Yeah, now I know who Amelia's talking about." His lips thinned. "I'd forgotten her name, but I remember the cops were called."

"Says here, 'No suspect found.'"

"My friends got me out of there, and *Papi* got involved. Obviously, the girl was smart enough not to give my name to the police. Our family had a reputation."

Rick tilted his chin. "Why'd she have the kid? Don't hospitals give you pills for rape?"

"They're available, sure, but you don't have to take them. Maybe she's Catholic," Terrance said.

Rick snorted. "Or she rolled the dice, and her prize was a golden goose."

"She thought." Terrance's mind reeled with this information. "*Papi's* only been gone six years. I don't get how Amelia kept this a secret for more than twenty years."

"Doesn't matter. We'll kill her and make it look like an accident," Rick said, moving to the dresser to retrieve his cap.

"No, the letter mentions that. If she dies, a charity gets everything." Terrance wanted to punch something. He plucked his phone off the bed and searched the contacts for his attorney's firm. It was time for them to earn their money.

"I'm on shift the next few days, but I'll keep my nose to the ground and my ears open." He paused in the doorway, staring at Terrance.

"What?"

"Your daughter was in Amelia's house."

Terrance sawed out a humorless laugh. "I don't suppose her first impression of me was very good."

"We don't know what she did or didn't see. Do you have a plan to handle her?"

"I'll separate the girl from whatever herd she plans to hide in and bring her back here. Who knows? I might enjoy having a daughter. If she married you, we could keep it in the family."

Rick arched a brow. "Wouldn't I be her uncle? Half uncle?"

"Whatever. She has a child. After she signs the papers, we could kill her and keep her kid. In the meantime, I need to pay Evonne Montano a visit."

He reached over to a pile on the bed and held up an envelope. "Amelia saved old correspondence, and Evonne resided in San Antonio at least until five years ago. Can you check on this address?"

Rick took the envelope. "If she's still there, it'd be best if someone else handled that interview. After our relationship surfaces, there could be an inquiry."

Terrance shrugged. "Fine then. I'll text you my plans."

He wanted to pound on something. Perhaps he needed someone to beat, and who better than his own daughter?

Like father, like son.

CHAPTER 11

The sun hadn't risen when Terrance parked his Mercedes-Benz in front of the three-story low-income apartment building on Friday morning. What a dump, he thought as he took in the squat structure. The paint was weathered and dirty, and large chunks had stripped away entirely. All the windows were barred, as if whatever was inside might hold some value—not likely.

Rick pulled his cruiser in beside him, and Terrance stepped out of his vehicle. His brother's uniform would lend credibility to their breaking and entering if the girl wasn't home.

"I checked the place out last night. No cameras or security. Let's get in and out quick," Rick said.

Terrance gave a sharp nod, and they headed through the unlocked entrance. The linoleum inside was cracked in places, and the dingy gray walls hadn't seen a coat of paint in years. "This place is disgusting," Terrance murmured.

Rick shrugged. "No cameras and no doorman. Stairs or elevator?"

"Elevator," Terrance said because his wound throbbed from the long drive, and he'd run out of gauze this morning. They rode in silence to the third floor, every jolt of the creaky elevator making him wince as it rattled his injury.

The second door in the musty hallway was apartment J. There was no bell to ring, just layers of chipping paint. Rick stepped out of sight, and Terrance rapped on the wood.

No response.

"Open it," Terrance ordered.

Rick got to work with a lockpick. "Wait here," he murmured before moving farther into the apartment. He soon returned. "No one's home, boss."

Terrance pulled on gloves as he stepped inside. The kitchen opened to the living area, and a single door connected to another room. The shabby, secondhand furniture was barely adequate. A sour taste filled his mouth. His daughter was a pauper.

"You check that side," he said, motioning Rick toward the kitchen, before crossing to the single door. With gloved fingers, he twisted the knob to reveal an unmade bed, a nightstand, a dresser, and a crib against the wall. A bathroom lay beyond. At least it wouldn't take long to search.

He checked the dresser first, but all three drawers were empty. For now, she was one step ahead of them. Rick appeared in the doorway.

"I found this on the fridge," he said, holding out a Polaroid photo.

It was a picture of two smiling women: a striking, curvy blonde in a string bikini and a shorter, brown-skinned woman with dark hair, an average build, and bright green eyes.

"Marissa is the short one," Terrance said.

"How do you know?"

"The eyes. It's a shame she doesn't look more like her friend." Flipping the photo over, Terrance noticed faint pencil marks. "With L by the sea." He tucked the photo into his shirt pocket. "Nothing else useful so far. Let's finish up and get out of here."

Without another word, Rick left to continue searching around the apartment.

Terrance scanned the rest of the bedroom, his gaze locking onto the nightstand. Perhaps in her haste to leave, the girl left something for him to find. With a pained sigh, he perched on the edge of the mattress and opened the top drawer. It contained nothing but hair ties and a blank notebook.

The bottom drawer was empty, and no one had an empty nightstand drawer. He slammed it shut in frustration, but it caught on something, preventing it from closing all the way.

Terrance jerked out the drawer, dropping it to the carpet with a soft thud. When he leaned over to peer inside, pain had him jerking upright.

"Fucking Amelia," he muttered, knocking off the lamp as he picked up the flimsy nightstand and set it on the bed.

A single red envelope was pushed flat against the wood in the back. Nothing was in it, but it had a two-year-old postmark over a Christmas tree stamp. There was also a return address label. Liesel Zolan in San Diego, California.

Could this be L by the Sea?

Knock, knock.

Terrance stuffed the envelope in his pocket and met Rick in the living room. "Stay out of sight," he ordered, before swinging open the apartment door.

"Good morning," he smiled at the middle-aged woman.

Her gray-streaked brown hair was secured in a tight bun at her nape, and her eyes were sharp with suspicion. She held a phone in one hand and tapped it methodically against the other, narrowing a frown at him. "I thought I saw someone come in here. Who are you?"

He barely kept his smile in place. "Are you looking for my niece? She's out right now."

The woman's mouth pinched as she examined him. "I'm her neighbor, and she's never mentioned an uncle." Her gaze fixed on his gloved hand. "Why are you wearing leather gloves inside?"

A little too observant. She would need to stay.

"Please, come in," Terrance said, opening the door wide and glancing over the woman's head to see if any other doors had opened. They were all closed tight. "We'll have coffee and wait for Marissa together. I didn't catch your name?"

"I'm Mrs. Griffin. I don't want any coffee, but thank you," she mumbled, backing a step.

He pointed behind her. "There's Marissa now."

When Mrs. Griffin turned to look, he caught her by the neck with one hand and yanked her into the apartment. The momentum slung her past him and across the floor.

"Oh ... help ... don't hurt me ..." she whimpered, dragging herself upright and scrambling to reach the phone that had skittered a few feet away.

He shut the door and snapped at Rick. "Keep her quiet." Time was ticking now. Someone might expect her to return.

Rick flipped her on her back and pressed a gloved hand across her mouth and nose. Her blue eyes streamed tears as she flung her gaze between them and clawed at his hand.

Terrance scooped up the phone she'd dropped and kneeled beside her. "If my officer friend lets you up, will you scream?"

She tried to shake her head, but Rick's hand was too tight for her to move.

"This is your only warning." He motioned to Rick. "Put her on the couch."

In one swift movement, Rick hoisted her up and half-dragged, half-carried her across the room.

A pained sound escaped her throat.

"Silence," Terrance snapped.

Her whimpers subsided into quiet gasping, and she perched on the edge of the cushion, her body curved forward, cradling her arm.

Tossing the phone beside her, he glanced at Rick. "Did you break her arm?"

Rick shook his head. "Must've happened when she fell."

Terrance made a tsking sound and settled on the couch. "Mrs. Griffin. Aren't you the nosy neighbor? If you'd minded your business, you wouldn't be here. But, since you are, I have some questions for you." He twisted more fully toward her, and hot pain knifed through his side. Fuck. He'd probably pulled a stitch handling her fat ass.

"What questions?" she asked in a trembling voice.

He needed her to calm down if he was going to get any information out of her, so he spoke as gently as he could. "If you answer nicely, we'll call someone to take you to the hospital and get that arm checked out. Sound good?"

"Yes," she whispered.

He presented the Polaroid photo and pointed at the dark-haired girl. "Marissa Parker. That's her, isn't it?"

"Y-yes," she breathed.

He pointed at the photo again. "Can you tell me where she went?"

"Umm." Tears streamed over Mrs. Griffin's wrinkled face, and her body quivered so hard the cheap springs in the couch wobbled.

"If you piss yourself and it gets on me, I'll rip your fucking throat out. Now tell me where I can find Marissa."

"I-I'm not … I don't know." Mrs. Griffin shook her head frantically.

Terrance tapped the gun against his leg, and her gaze locked on the motion. *Progress.* "I need you to give me more than 'I don't know.' Tell me something useful if you want medical attention. You're Marissa's good neighbor who came to check on her. You must have an idea where she went."

Mrs. Griffin panted. "She came home yesterday. I watch her daughter when she works nights. She-she came in at three in the morning." Realization dawned on her face. "I spoke to you."

Now they were getting somewhere. "Yes, I thought that might've been you on the phone. I need to locate Marissa. It's important, you understand?"

Tears dripped over Mrs. Griffin's cheeks. "Please … can I go home? I won't tell anyone I saw you here."

Terrance pushed the barrel of the gun into her breast, pressing hard enough to make her moan. "Where. Is. Marissa Parker."

"I'm sorry. Please … I don't know," she said, rocking her head back and forth.

"I think I believe you." Relaxing against the flimsy cushion, he laid the gun on his knee to pick up the photo again. "Do you know this blonde woman?"

"No." She paused. "Yes, I think so."

Terrance rolled his hand in a keep going motion. "Tell me more?"

"She—she's her friend. They went to school together, but she's never come here. Marissa told me about her before." Mrs. Griffin hugged her injured arm tightly.

He inclined his chin. "That's good information."

"Can I go?"

"One more question. This is important. Do you have a number for Marissa's mother?"

"Her mother? Y-yes. I never met her, but Marissa gave me her number for an emergency contact. It's on my phone." She hesitated. "They don't get along."

Terrance extended the phone for her to unlock.

"If I do this, can I go?" she asked through trembling lips.

He continued holding out the phone.

"Okay." Her finger shook when she pressed it to the phone.

Terrance patted her leg and rose. "Evonne Parker and I are old friends. We lost touch." Then, for the fun of seeing her reaction, he added, "I'm Marissa's father."

Mrs. Griffin didn't acknowledge his words, which was disappointing. Instead, she curled her body farther around her arm.

"I ... I'm going to be sick. Please, I won't tell anyone if you let me leave."

He scrolled to the contact he wanted on the phone. "Do you have any more information for me?"

"No." She keened the single word.

"Then it's time to go."

"Go?" Hope filled her eyes. "Thank you!" She made to rise, and he held up a hand.

"Wait a minute. Rick?"

She never saw it coming. Rick whisked a wire garrote around her neck, and it was over in seconds.

CHAPTER 12

Burn closed one eye, lined up his trajectory, and threw the dart with a satisfying whoosh, landing it in the exact center of the red circle. His friends erupted in cheers, congratulating him and slapping him on the back. Friday nights at Cicadas drew a big crowd, and tonight was no exception.

"Who's up next?" he called out with a broad grin as he scanned the crowd gathering to watch the game. Then he paused and did a double-take. He must've had one too many beers, because his dream girl was making her way across the crowded room toward the bar.

Burn craned his neck for another glimpse. As much as he wanted it to be Rissa, no way she had returned to Cicadas after three years. He'd searched for months, asking everyone he knew, yet no one could point him in her direction. His heart thumped faster. What if it were Rissa? A thrill of anticipation zinged through him.

"Burn," Pan said, nudging him with a handful of darts. "It's you and Greg for this round and—"

"Nope. I'm out." Burn handed Pan the darts he still held. "I see someone I need to speak with."

"How will we get our money back?" one of the guys complained.

"Next time, boys. Next time." Burn arched a brow at Pan, and his friend gave a slight nod. "Pan will take my place. He's way better than any of you."

That met with guffaws and laughter, but Burn paid no mind as he weaved through the crowd.

If it really was Rissa, she might be meeting someone else tonight. But he needed to see her mesmerizing green eyes again, if only for a minute. Burn's pulse surged at the memory of Rissa's dark hair tumbling around her beautiful face.

His gaze zeroed in on two women standing at the bar. A tall blonde standing next to a much shorter dark-haired woman. The blonde raised an arm to catch Patrick's attention. Rissa had been with a blonde woman the night they met. Burn desperately wanted to rush over and confirm it was her, but he held back. He needed to be certain, so he found a place farther down the bar where he could get a better view.

A few minutes later, Patrick, one of the bar's owners and his good friend, lifted his head to scan the crowd near the dartboard. He frowned and said something to the women, prompting them to twist toward the players. Then Patrick's gaze connected with Burn's, and he gave him a get-your-ass-over-here chin lift.

Hell yeah. Burn moved as swiftly as the crowd allowed, his chest tightening at the sound of the voice he'd dreamed of so many times.

"I don't see him. Do you have a way to contact him if he's already left?" Rissa asked.

Patrick's lips twitched, and he gave Burn a full-on smile. "I expect I can, because Master Chief Cruz is standing right behind you."

The women whirled so quickly that they bumped into each other. Burn reached out to steady Rissa. The blonde looked as though she'd land on her feet without any assistance.

"Burn," Rissa breathed, her voice catching.

"Hello there, gorgeous. It's been too long." He grinned, drawing closer.

"I'm so happy to find you," she said, her eyes sparkling with happiness or maybe tears.

He took that as a sign she was glad to see him and gently gathered her into his arms. She clung to his shirt, her entire body quivering with emotion.

Concerned, he attempted to pull away, but she moved with him. "Rissa. Are you okay?"

Nodding against his chest, she slowly released him and moved back. "I'm glad I found you," she said with a shy smile.

Blondie angled her head close to Rissa's. "Why don't you two find a quiet corner to catch up? I imagine you have things to talk about. But Riss, if you need me, holler. I'll be on the dance floor."

"Okay," Rissa said to her friend, although her gaze remained fastened on him. "I can't believe you're really here."

"Same," he said, smoothing a hand over her soft hair and scanning her from head to toe. Three years had passed, and she had only been twenty-one the last time they met. Somehow, she was even more attractive than his memories. "I might've spent way too much time in this bar, hoping you'd make another appearance. Or your blonde friend."

"Liesel?"

"Liesel. I forgot her name," Burn said. "Please tell me you're here alone … other than Liesel. And that you don't have a boyfriend, because if he let you out of his sight tonight, it's his loss."

She rested a tentative hand against his chest. "No boyfriend. I returned here to find you."

"Damn. Then I'm the luckiest guy in the room." He reeled her back into his arms, pressing his cheek to the top of her head. "Coconut. Your hair smelled like coconut last time."

"I can't believe you remember that," she murmured against his shirt. "I still smell Rolos on you."

Patrick cleared his throat, catching Burn's attention. "Now that you two have said hello, can I get you kids anything?"

"I have everything I need right here," Burn said.

"Then hit the dance floor or something. You're clogging up my bar." Patrick winked to take the sting out of his words and moved away to serve another customer.

Burn cupped her chin. "Do you want to dance first or find a corner to talk? Because I'll warn you now, I'm not letting you out of my sight."

Rissa cast a glance toward the stage. The band was between sets, but canned music played through the speakers. "Let's dance first."

He guided her through the crowd, keeping a firm hand on the small of her back. She'd agreed to dance with him, nothing more, so he needed to rope in his libido. A few people acknowledged him as they passed, but he didn't pause to chat. The only person who mattered was with him, and he intended to keep her by his side for as long as possible.

At the edge of the dance floor, he twined his arms around her waist, and his heart soared when she pressed closer as they swayed to the music.

He inhaled her sweet scent. "You never gave me your number. Say it now, and I'll memorize it."

"Burn, I ... I've regretted that we didn't exchange numbers," she admitted. "But you said that night was just for fun. I didn't want to put any pressure on you."

"Pressure me now," he said, his throat resonating with low laughter. "No. I'll pressure you. What's your number? And your email and your home address. I'm not about to lose you again."

She turned liquid green eyes to his. "I live—lived in Texas and went back the day after we met."

"Lived? Not anymore?"

"No," she said, pressing her lips together and dropping her gaze.

He maneuvered them to the edge of the dance floor. "You don't have to tell me where you live now, but I'd like to see you more than once every three years."

The surrounding people began clapping, and he noticed the band had returned to the stage. The Forget Me Nots were an excellent group, but it wouldn't be easy to talk over the music. "Let's go sit in the back where it's quieter," he suggested before leading her toward the booths along the back wall.

All four were occupied, but Styles and another team guy were sitting together in one of them.

"Styles, do me a large and let me have this booth," Burn said.

"No problem, Chief." Style's eyes were alight with curiosity as he popped to his feet. His friend followed more reluctantly.

"Thanks, and one more thing. Rissa's friend, Liesel, is that tall blonde over there," he said, gesturing with one hand. "She needs a dance partner."

"Happy to help." Styles dashed off toward the busy dance floor.

"Are you sure they don't mind?" Rissa asked.

"It's all good. Have a seat," Burn said, encouraging her to slide in first. He followed, partly to gauge her reaction to his proximity. Was she the same innocent he'd met before? It was none of his business, but imagining her with anyone else twisted his gut, which was foolish. She wasn't his. Not yet.

"I'm glad you were here tonight," she said, not looking at him.

"Am I making you nervous? There's no need." He reached for her hand and threaded their fingers together. "Is this okay?"

"Yes," she said, her eyes wide enough to drown in.

Burn had convinced himself that he'd imagined the pale green hue and her thick, brown hair, but his memory didn't do her justice. Only her glasses were different from before. "Your glasses are new. Well, of course, they are. It's been a few years."

"I haven't had them long. It's my first red pair. They're a little crazy, but my dau—I picked them out on a whim," she said, using her free hand to adjust them.

"The color suits you," he said, propping his elbow on the table. "It's been a long time since we met. I've thought about you a great deal and wondered ..."

"Wondered what?"

"You left an impression on me." Burn drank in the sight of her. She was as gorgeous as he remembered. More so. "You seem changed, but in a good way. What have you been doing for the last two and a half years?"

"It's been a little more than that." She let out a shuddery breath. "I have a question. Should I call you Bernie or Burn?"

He ran his thumb over her knuckles, glad to see no ring in sight. "Doesn't matter. My mother calls me Bernie, but most people say Burn. I know you're changing the subject, but you should know I'll be harder to shake this time. I still need your number. You also promised to let me see your license." One minute with the license, and he'd memorize her full legal name and address.

Her gaze darted to the side. "I'm not sure if you're being funny."

"Rissa," he said, lowering his head. "I'm very serious about anything to do with you." He gave her plenty of time to retreat before he brushed his mouth over hers.

The surprise on her face was unmistakable, but she didn't recoil. Instead, she leaned into him, and her leg pressed more firmly against his. He wanted to wrap her in his arms, but instead pulled back with a quick, indrawn breath. "Damn, woman. We'd better not start that here, but I'm more than willing to take this somewhere else. Now, what was that phone number?"

•   •   •

"I, um ..." Rissa began, her words tripping over the way his kiss had turned her brain to mush. The only phone she had was the cheap one from the train, but she didn't know that number by heart. "Why don't I text you?" she offered, opening the small purse she'd borrowed from Liesel and sliding out the cheap device.

He rattled off his number, and she plugged it into a new message.

The truth was, she didn't want to talk to him on the phone. No, she wanted to stay tucked right here beside him. The past forty-eight hours had been hell, and here she was safe for the first time since the murder. Maybe staying near Burn was enough to keep that madman at bay, but ... what if Terrance were nearby? She was being paranoid. If he'd somehow found out she was in California, he didn't know about Cicadas.

"How long are you visiting?" he said, cupping her cheek in one big hand. "My team just got back from a long mission, so I'm due some days off. Tell me you'll spend time with me."

She blinked at the heat she saw in Burn's gaze. Did he want a reunion bedroom tour? A frisson of excitement twirled in her belly, and she squirmed in her seat. He'd been her first and only, which was a little pathetic, but she'd had a baby and worked all the time to stay afloat. Besides, in her memory, Burn had become the perfect measure for other guys, and no one else came close.

"Rissa," he said, his brows tilting down as he regarded her.

She blinked. Had he asked a question? "I'm sorry, what?"

His golden eyes pinned her in place. "Have you already been drinking?"

"Nothing yet," she whispered. Her thoughts momentarily drifted to him, so broad, so solid, so unmistakably masculine. A flicker of lust zinged down her spine, and she had to lick suddenly dry lips. She was officially losing her mind. Today was not the day for her sex drive to override her mommy drive. She had to think of Shelby.

"Hey." The bartender, Patrick, deposited a pink cosmopolitan and a tall mug of foamy beer on the table. "Drink delivery for you."

"Thanks," Burn said.

She reached for her purse. "I have money."

"No, I got it." He covered her hand and addressed Patrick. "Put these on my tab."

"No need. They're from Styles." Patrick flashed a grin and flipped a curl of hair off his forehead. "Her friend suggested the Cosmo, and I knew your flavor of beer. I gotta get back to the bar. Raise a hand if you need anything."

Rissa took a small sip of the pink beverage—tart and delicious and filled with memories. "Liesel knows I don't drink much, but I like these. I haven't had one in a long time." Not since that night three years ago.

She glanced away from him and noticed the crowd had doubled in the last hour. A man bumped their table as he passed on his way to the bathroom, and Rissa gasped. He wore a white shirt and cowboy boots, but he wasn't Terrance Simmons. Her breathing changed to short, nervous bursts, and she struggled to get herself under control. She swung her gaze toward the dance floor. It wasn't visible from their booth, but she knew Liesel wouldn't desert her.

"Is everything alright?" Burn asked.

Now was her chance. She told herself to start talking, but when she peeked up at this face, her brain fogged, and the words left her. "I, uh …"

He studied her, then pushed his beer forward and switched to the spot across the table. "Let's try again. My name's Bernard Cruz. My friends call me Burn, or Bernie, and I live in San Diego," he said, holding his beer in a salute.

She blinked, unsure what he wanted and missing his warm bulk at her side. "Cheers?" she said, lifting her Cosmo to tap against his beer.

His mouth hooked up on one side. "That's your cue to introduce yourself to me."

"But we know each other."

He rested his elbows on the table. "I want more. What's your full name?"

"Ah," she said. He wanted the details they'd missed before. "Marissa Parker. My friends call me Rissa. I'm a nurse's aide, and I live—used to live—in San Antonio. I just moved here." She gulped a big swallow from the Cosmopolitan and immediately coughed.

"You drink those too fast. We should get you something else for the next one," Burn said.

"Next one?"

His smile was a slash of white against his dark bronze skin. "We're going to stay here and talk, learn more about each other. If we leave now, we won't be doing much talking."

"I don't—" She wanted to deny that she'd go with him, but was it true? "I only have until midnight." Jack and Andy expected her back to pick up Shelby.

He huffed a laugh. "Glass slippers, huh?"

"What?"

"Cinderella. Didn't you learn your fairy tales as a kid?"

Her parents hadn't been big on reading for fun. They'd wanted her to study and had written her off as stupid when she failed to reach the potential they required. "I know who Cinderella is. I'm not stupid."

"What? I never said that." He reached for her hands. "What's going on here?"

She opened her mouth, then closed it. He'd been sweet and kind to her. Was it fair to drag him into all this? A killer was after her, and oh yeah, she'd had his kid a couple of years ago. Did he want to be a dad?

Burn needed to know everything, but not right now. She wanted to dance. If they danced, he'd put his arms around her, and she could forget Terrance Simmons and the murder for a little while. His arms would keep her safe and protected, even if it were only a temporary illusion.

"I want to talk, but can we dance again first?" she asked.

His brows furrowed, and lines appeared on his forehead. Instead of asking more questions, he slid out of the booth and extended his palm. "We'll likely lose our booth, but will you dance with me, Rissa Parker?"

"Yes, please."

For her, the next few hours were a lovely dream. He held her as they danced, laughed, and even stole a few kisses on the dance floor. Much later, they sat with his friends and their dates at some tables pushed together, eating late-night bar snacks. Liesel had the chair directly across from her, next to one of Bernie's friends. Burn's friends. Everyone called him Burn. She hadn't spoken to Liesel since they arrived, and her eyes were filled with questions.

Rissa was sure Liesel wanted to know what she'd told Burn. Well, she hadn't told him anything yet. She needed to talk to him alone, but everyone was having fun. It wasn't right to ask him to leave all his friends, and she sure wasn't going to spill her secrets in front of so many people.

"What's on your mind?" His warm breath fanned over her cheek.

She'd been staring at her drink and turned to find him watching her. "Hmm?"

"What's going on in that pretty head of yours?" he said, gently running his hand through her hair and giving the long strands a playful tug.

"I ... can we talk?"

"Sure," he said, though he didn't move.

"Alone. I want to talk alone." She had to tell him about Terrance. And about Shelby.

He kissed her cheek, his face so close that her world shrank to the two of them. "You seem nervous, Rissa. I don't want to make you uncomfortable, but is something wrong?"

She whispered, "I'm in trouble and I need your help."

"Legal trouble?" he asked.

"No, not—maybe." She shook her head, her gut doing nauseating flips and twists. If he didn't help her, what would she do?

"I'll help any way that I can," he promised. "Come on. Let's get out of here."

CHAPTER 13

Terrance flicked the button to mute the yapping announcer on the screen. It was well past midnight, and he still hadn't heard from Juan Ravago, his contact in Los Angeles, who was supposed to give him an update. His own drug network lacked connections in San Diego, but Ravago's had plenty, and he'd assured Terrance that someone would check on the address linked to the Zolan woman. He just wasn't sure how much he trusted Ravago.

The wait was maddening. Every minute meant another chance for the girl to unravel everything about Amelia, and if the girl wasn't in San Diego, he still had to locate her.

Rick had found out that the Montano woman still lived in San Antonio at the same address noted in the correspondence. Unfortunately, he couldn't talk to her yet, as it seemed she and her husband were away for the holiday weekend. Unwilling to wait until Tuesday for a conversation, Terrance had dispatched two of his men to track their whereabouts. If Rissa weren't in California, her mother might know where she went into hiding.

He refilled his drink from the nearly empty decanter beside his chair and took a long swallow. The bourbon was sharp and bitter and burned slightly as it went down, but he welcomed the numbness it provided. Terrance pondered the future once his daughter joined his household. She should be eager to work for him; his wealth would secure her the best opportunities the city could offer for her child. Of course, the money already belonged to Marissa, though she was unaware of that fact.

The past few days had been grueling, and his bullet wound seemed to be worsening rather than healing. After questioning Marissa's neighbor, he'd had to meet with the fire marshal at his mother's house in San Antonio, a process that consumed hours. All that time spent driving, talking, and walking while pretending every little movement didn't fucking hurt. When it came time to make the drive back to Austin, he'd nearly stopped at a hotel, but he needed a visit from Doctor George.

Clumsily, weakened by exhaustion and alcohol, he forced himself out of the recliner.

In the kitchen, he rattled a few remaining painkillers into his hand and washed them down with bourbon before limping into the living room to sink back into his chair.

After the funeral on Tuesday, if Ravago found the girl, he might head to California. His schedule was packed, but he could make time. But not tomorrow. Tomorrow, he had to finalize the details on a shipment overseas and vet a potential buyer.

His cell vibrated against the marble-topped table, interrupting the silence. He snatched it up, sloshing part of his drink over his hand in the process. "Rick. What've you got?"

"Nothing on my front, but have you seen the news?"

"Yeah. The Fire Marshall played ball."

"He did," Rick said. "It all looked good. What about Amelia's funeral?"

"There's no need to wait since there isn't a corpse. What's left of her will be cremated, and we'll hold a service on Tuesday at the funeral home. Same one that took care of *Papi*." He set his drink aside and squeezed the armrest of his recliner, trying to find a comfortable position. "I'll handle tomorrow's meeting with the buyer. You keep up appearances at the station."

"What time do I need to be in San Antonio on Tuesday?"

"Ten." A wave of nausea washed over Terrance, and he sucked in air through his mouth. "Wear your uniform and bring a few other officers. Pay them if necessary. It'll look good in photos."

"Got it covered. Two guys will be with me." Rick paused, then continued, "Do you have word on your other thing?"

"The girl? No. And nothing else of note in the boxes," Terrance winced at the pain stabbing through his side. His vision blurred, and he ground his teeth to keep from moaning. "Send the doc around here. Tonight, if you can."

"Problems?"

He despised revealing any weakness, but this was Rick. "I need more antibiotics. And painkillers."

Rick was silent for a long moment. "I texted him. We'll be there in an hour."

•   •   •

Early Saturday, Rissa watched out the window as a blue, four-door truck slid beside the curb. Somehow, she knew it was Burn, so it didn't surprise her when the driver's side opened, and he stepped out holding a large white bag. Standing over six feet tall and built like a linebacker, he was unmistakable even from a distance. His tight black curls and the way his muscular chest strained his forest green shirt left no doubt about his identity. She pressed a hand to her fluttering stomach and checked the time. He was thirty minutes early.

Burn didn't owe her anything. She knew that, yet somehow his presence at the apartment gave her an irrational sense of security, as if everything would be okay because he was here.

Last night, outside of Cicadas, he'd offered to rent them a room, but thankfully, her brain had prevailed over her body. No way could she sleep with him again until she told him everything. Besides, she worried that her daughter might be frightened if she woke up in the night without her. After she refused to stay at a hotel, Burn had suggested bringing her back to the apartment for more time to talk, but she didn't want to introduce Shelby under those circumstances so late at night.

Then Liesel had joined them outside of Cicadas. Rissa told Burn she'd ride home with her friend and invited him to breakfast so they could talk. He agreed and even volunteered to bring the food.

Nerves tightened in Rissa's gut. She had no idea how he would react when she told him about Shelby. It may be wiser to wait until they got to know each other better. She needed his help to keep both her and Shelby safe. Not telling him was a lie of omission, but what was a few more days?

Shelby was tiny, so Rissa could effectively shave a few months off her age. Then again, she'd recently celebrated her second birthday. Though she couldn't talk well yet, she was smart enough to know she was two. They had shared a cupcake at Mrs. G's, and Liesel had treated them all to birthday ice cream sundaes at the zoo.

Rissa exhaled deeply. The alternative of telling him Shelby was older wasn't an option, because Burn already knew she was a virgin. Telling him Shelby was younger meant she'd left his bed and gotten pregnant a few months later.

Yay, me. Tramp of the year.

"Mommy? Juice?" Shelby asked, her eyes wide.

"Sweetie, you're up." Rissa kneeled to hug her. "Good morning."

Shelby tugged at the scarf on her head. "Off."

Rissa slipped off the silk scarf she put on Shelby's curls at night to help keep them from tangling. The pink princess nightgown was cute, but she should dress her before Burn came upstairs. "Let's go potty."

"Me wen' potty." Shelby giggled and rubbed her bunny against her cheek.

"You're such a big girl. Good job. Want to watch some cartoons while I get your juice? After that, I'll get your play clothes, and we'll go downstairs to meet my friend."

Shelby giggled and danced on her tiptoes, her bunny dangling from her fingers as her eyes roved around the room. "Auntie?"

"Auntie Liesel is still asleep, so we have to be quiet." Rissa picked Shelby up and angled to peek at the street. Burn remained by his truck, staring at the building.

"I'm awake," Liesel said in a sleep-roughened voice behind her.

Rissa spun to see her friend slumped in the kitchen doorway. "You could've slept in."

"I've got to work today," Liesel said, lifting both hands to twist her hair in a loose knot.

Rissa frowned at the thought of being alone with Burn. "I thought you were off. It's Sunday."

"My agent texted me. It won't take the entire day, but it's for a good client. Flip side, if I don't go, they'll pick someone else, and I lose the account." She yawned. "That's how my business works. Did I mention I have a job in LA in a couple of days?"

"You have to leave?"

"Only for about three days, but you and the munchkin will be fine here. You can even use my car if you need it. I can't remember if I'm leaving on Tuesday or Wednesday."

Rissa gave a jerky nod, the flutters in her stomach moving into her throat. "Thanks for letting us stay here."

Liesel shrugged and pointed at the window. "Is he outside?"

"Yes, he's standing on the curb, not doing anything. I guess since he's early?"

"Go get your guy." Liesel yawned again before kissing Shelby on the cheek. "Good morning, munchkin. How about an Auntie Liesel morning? I'll get you juice, and then you can pick out your clothes."

"Yes!" Shelby eagerly reached for her, and Liesel took her from Rissa.

"We'll be fine," she tossed Rissa a grin and turned toward the kitchen with a chattering Shelby.

"Could I ask a favor?" Another one. Heat rushed to Rissa's cheeks. She'd already asked for so much, and Liesel wouldn't be thrilled by this request.

Halfway across the room, Liesel pivoted. "What do you need?"

Rissa swallowed hard, pushing down the bile in her throat. "I'm going to tell Burn that Shelby won't be two for three months."

Liesel's mouth flattened. "Really." Not a question.

Rissa could see she was annoyed. "I can't tell him the truth," she pleaded, stepping closer. "Not yet, but I will."

"Down." Shelby pumped her legs to be put down.

"Why not?" Liesel placed Shelby on the couch and crossed her arms.

"I—"

"Wait. Never mind." Liesel held up a hand. "It's your decision. I'm not a liar, though; if he asks me, I'll be extra blonde." She motioned to Shelby. "He might ask the munchkin."

Rissa glanced out the window, but Burn wasn't visible on the street anymore. "I know. Let's see how things go."

"Your call." Liesel disappeared into the kitchen. She returned with a juice cup under her arm, a box of cereal in one hand, and a bowl in the other. "Can she have cereal again?"

"Just the juice. Burn is bringing breakfast." Rissa rushed over to hug Liesel. "Thank you. I'm sorry to be such a trouble."

"Stop apologizing and get the man. I have to leave soon."

"When will you be back?"

"Not sure. Sometimes, these things go on for a long time. I can't give a definite time, but hopefully your guy will stick around till I return."

She hoped so too, and not just because of the danger they faced.

CHAPTER 14

Burn had never parked on this street before, but he was familiar with the area because Styles owned a house a few miles away. Liesel's apartment building reached ten stories with eight units per floor. High-end rent or perhaps condos. Definitely not a place he'd choose to live himself, even if he could afford it on his salary. Seeing this place had him wondering what Liesel did for a living.

Shifting the bag of food in one hand, he surveyed the street in both directions. Hardly anyone was around at this early on a Saturday. Had he been foolish to come this morning? Last night, Rissa had asked for help, then promptly clammed up when they walked outside Cicadas. He needed to know exactly what kind of trouble she was in to know how to help.

He pushed open the glass door to the marble-floored lobby.

"Good morning." An older man with a sprinkling of very short, pure white curls and deep brown skin scrutinized him from behind a polished wooden desk.

Burn would bet a month's salary that this guy was former military. "Good morning." He stuck out a hand. "Warrant Officer Bernard Cruz. Everyone calls me Burn."

"Marine?"

"Navy SEAL."

A broad grin stretched the man's cheeks as he shook Burn's hand. "Sergeant Rafferty, Marine Corps. What brings you here today?"

"I'm visiting a young lady." Burn held up the white bag. "Even brought breakfast."

"Who's the lucky lady?" Rafferty asked.

"Rissa Parker. She's staying here with a friend, Liesel Zolan." He paused, then continued, "I'm curious."

White eyebrows shot up. "About what?"

"How many entrances and exits are in this building?"

Rafferty crossed his arms, his clear brown eyes fixed on Burn. "Is there a reason you're asking?"

Burn considered his answer. He wasn't sure what was happening with Rissa, but she'd asked for help. "Sergeant, I'm going to trust my instincts about you." He placed the bag on the counter. "Rissa Parker is in some trouble, the kind that had her moving from Texas to San Diego with no job and no apartment. That's all I know. So far."

"Doesn't sound good," Rafferty said, pursing his lips.

"No, sir, it doesn't. I'll get the rest of the story today and apprise you if necessary."

"Roger that."

"You mind?" Burn pointed at a stack of Post-its on Rafferty's side of the desk.

Rafferty dipped his chin. "Take 'em."

He grabbed the little square of paper and a pen, wrote his contact info on it, and passed it back. "In case you need to reach me, that's my number. I also put my commander's number on there if you want to check my credentials."

"I'll be calling him."

The elevator chimed, and Burn turned to see the doors slide open. Rissa stood in the lift, her dark hair cascading around her shoulders, makeup-free, and dressed in shorts and a T-shirt emblazoned with "I Love San Diego." Something rolled in his chest. He had it bad for this woman.

"Hi," she said, her lips tipping at the corners.

"Good morning, ma'am," said Sergeant Rafferty. "I don't believe we've met."

She paused in the opening, not allowing the elevator doors to shut. "I'm … I'm staying with Liesel Zolan."

"Good to know." Rafferty's craggy face relaxed into a friendly expression. "Call the desk if you need anything from me."

"Thanks." Her head bobbed, but she didn't move any closer.

Burn stepped beside her and held the door open with a hand above her head. "Catch you later, Sergeant."

"Have a nice breakfast, Chief."

When the doors sealed them inside, he focused on Rissa while she looked anywhere but at him. Did she regret her invitation? "Good morning."

"Morning," she said, peeking at him through her lashes.

"If you're having second thoughts about having me over, wait until you taste these bagels." He gave the bag a little shake. "They bake them fresh daily."

"Sounds and smells great." She adjusted her glasses before adding, "Thank you for coming." Her mesmerizing eyes finally latched onto him, and he grinned like an idiot.

"What is it about you?" he asked.

Her dark brows arched. "I don't know what you mean."

He chuckled and opened his mouth to reply, but the elevator doors slid open again and she darted out ahead of him. Well, he could follow.

She led him to the last unit on the hall, then spun to face him before squaring her shoulders. "Burn—" She gulped in air as if she was about to leap from the high dive.

"Rissa, it's okay. If you aren't comfortable with me being here, we can find a restaurant."

"No." Her gaze dropped. "It's not that. There's something I haven't told you."

He figured there was a lot she hadn't told him, but this something seemed to disturb her. "That's why I'm here."

Her cheeks flushed, and she looked away and back. "I didn't tell you I have a daughter."

From her expression, she thought he was going to run crashing away. *What's the underlying message here?* It would take more than a kid to make him run. "Okay."

"Okay." She repeated the single word and turned to put a key in the lock. "I didn't want you to be surprised. She's twenty-one months," she added as she swung the door inward.

Twenty-one months. His brother had kids, but it was odd that she was being so specific. "Wait. Are you saying we—"

"No." The color drained from her cheeks, and she wouldn't meet his gaze. "I met you in November ... almost three years ago."

He did the math in his head. "This is September. I get it," he said as realization dawned. The woman who'd blown his mind and taken over his dreams since their night together had left him and gone into the arms of another man in a matter of weeks.

Well, shit.

"Are you coming inside?" She watched him from the open doorway, her eyes shimmering with uncertainty.

It wasn't his place to judge. Did it matter if she'd slept with someone else? They weren't in a relationship. Not then or now. She'd left too fast for that. He straightened his spine and ignored the uncomfortable ache in his chest. "I hope you're hungry."

"Yes—"

"Hi, and bye. My ride is waiting to take me to work," Liesel said, breezing past Rissa, only to pause and give him an unreadable look. "You'll be here until I get back this afternoon, right?"

An odd question. "Yes. As long as I'm welcome," he said, glancing toward Rissa.

"Good." Liesel patted his arm before hugging Rissa. "Love you, honey. Sorry I didn't get the munchkin dressed, but we couldn't agree on an outfit." She gave a little wave as she rushed toward the elevator.

"Mommy?" A tiny girl spoke from a few feet beyond Rissa. She wore a princess nightgown and held a bedraggled bunny in one chubby little hand.

Fucking adorable.

Burn eased onto his haunches. "Rissa, you didn't tell me a princess was visiting."

The child scrunched her nose and wrapped her arms around Rissa's leg.

"Shelby, this is mommy's friend, Burn," Rissa said, lifting her.

Burn found himself caught between pairs of identical, vibrant green eyes. Such an unusual color, clearly mother-daughter. Shelby's skin was darker, and her hair was different, with a halo of black-brown curls, whereas Rissa's hung in long, mahogany waves. Shelby had Rissa's features, but her hair and skin must've come from her father. A father who shared some of the same genetics as him.

"Hello, Princess Shelby." Burn pulled the door shut behind him and cleared his expression. "Anybody hungry around here?"

The little pixie hid her face in Rissa's neck, but she whispered a single word. "Me."

Rissa laughed. "Me too, sweetie. This way, Burn."

Shelby peeked at him over her mother's shoulder. He winked and waggled his eyebrows and was rewarded by a tinkling giggle. Rissa glanced over her shoulder, and he shrugged. When she looked away, he made another funny face, and Shelby chortled with glee.

At the Formica kitchen table, Burn opened the bag and shook out a half dozen bagel sandwiches. "You won't believe how good these bagels are."

"Wow. That's a lot of food," Rissa said, pulling out a chair and sitting with Shelby on her lap.

"I didn't know what you liked, so I got some of everything."

"Thanks," she murmured while unwrapping the waxy paper around one of the sandwiches. She lifted the bread to test the egg's temperature, and Shelby snatched the fried egg off the top.

"Me." Shelby said, nibbling on the prize in her little fingers.

Rissa clucked her tongue. "You can have it, but we don't grab food, Shelby. You need to use your manners."

He pushed another sandwich closer. "I'm glad she likes it."

A smile twitched at the corners of Rissa's mouth. "She isn't a picky eater, but there's not much she likes more than eggs. Maybe cheese pizza."

"Pizza?" Shelby asked around a mouthful of egg, her eyes wide and hopeful.

Well, he was the bringer of food this morning. "We'll do pizza another time. The eggs are good for breakfast, Princess." He winked at the kid again, eliciting another giggle. She watched him with wide green eyes as she chewed. Really cute kid. His nieces were cute, but he'd been promoted to Chief about the time they were born, so he didn't get to many family events those first few years. Shelby had good communication and motor skills for such a young kid.

Burn finished his sandwich and unwrapped a second one. The bagels were warm and chewy, with a hint of honey and sesame seeds, and the bacon was cooked the way he liked it—crispy, even underneath the buttery fried egg and cheese slice.

When Rissa finally pushed away the last bit of her sandwich, he did the same with his and asked his question. "Are you ready to talk?"

She paled, and concern rippled through him. That kind of immediate physical reaction disturbed him. He uncrossed his knee and leaned closer, turning his body toward her. "I can see you're frightened. Tell me what's going on so I can help."

She pressed her lips in a flat line and let out a thready breath. "I want to tell you, but I could be putting you in danger."

He had to work to keep from demanding she immediately tell him everything, because using his Master Chief voice would only frighten her more. When he had his mouth under control, he said firmly, "Tell me all of it."

Her shoulders lifted fractionally, and her gaze flitted around the room before resting on him. "I saw something terrible happen back in San Antonio."

"Go on."

"I'm a nurse and I was hired to sit with an elderly woman. It was like two in the morning when—"

The doorbell buzzed, interrupting her.

CHAPTER 15

Burn glanced at the door, then swung his gaze to her. "Were you expecting company?"

She shook her head, and the stark terror on her face spoke volumes.

"Too tight Mommy." Shelby twisted, pushing at Rissa's arms.

Whoever was out there hit the doorbell a few more times.

"Impatient, aren't they? Wait here." Burn strode across the room, edged himself against the wall, and leaned forward to peer through the peephole. In the hallway, he glimpsed a skinny, olive-skinned man holding an oversized, flowering green plant similar to the ones in the downstairs lobby. The man's face wasn't visible, and he wore jeans and orange high-top athletic shoes. The view in the peephole was narrow, but Burn was pretty sure another man hovered behind the delivery guy. Since when did it take two people to deliver one plant?

Burn retreated a step, absently rubbing his neck, which was tingling the way it did before a firefight.

The doorbell buzzed again.

Something wasn't right. The guy didn't have a uniform, and Rafferty should've called before sending someone up. This could be bad news. Or maybe not.

Burn motioned to Rissa. "Go to the bedroom."

She popped to her feet with Shelby in her arms. "Did you see who's out there?"

He wanted to reassure her, but he didn't know what they were facing. "It could be nothing. There's a guy out there with a plant, but I don't like that Rafferty didn't notify us. Is your phone on you?"

"It's on the charger by the bed."

"Show me," he said. When she rushed through the kitchen to the bedroom beyond, he followed. "Grab the phone, take Shelby into the bathroom, then lock the door and be ready to call 911. Can you do that for me?"

"Yes." She pushed her shoulders back and hitched Shelby higher in her arms.

Burn nudged her inside the bedroom and reached for the door handle. Then it dawned on him. "Does Liesel have a landline?"

"No, only her cell."

"Maybe Rafferty did try to call—"

A pounding at the front door interrupted him.

"What do we do?" Rissa whispered, her eyes wide as saucers.

"I'll keep you safe, lock this door, and call 911 right now."

"But—"

"Don't come out till I give the all clear." Satisfied to hear the lock engage, he moved to the edge of the kitchen to wait. It wouldn't be long. With a wedge and a few well-timed blows, at least one man, probably more, would be inside in seconds.

Time slowed as he readied for battle.

He texted Styles one-handed to call in the cavalry. Handling one or two guys was no problem, but if there were more, he'd need help. Thankfully, Styles lived only a couple of miles away. The text said 'read.' Good, Styles had seen the text. Burn could rely on his teammate.

He tapped the icon on his phone to switch to video mode and tucked it into his shirt pocket. All he had to do now was hold position and wait for reinforcements. He pulled his K-bar from the sheath on his boot. A gun would be nice, but his was locked under the seat of his truck.

His mind sifted through the apartment's layout and possible scenarios. If it were only two guys, most likely they'd pick opposite directions. There was a single door on the other side of the living room, but he didn't know what was behind it. Bathroom maybe?

The kitchen didn't have a door separating it from the living room; instead, it had a wide arch. However, it was rectangular, and he was able to stand at one side of the arch without being immediately seen in the living room.

Another thud and the loud crack of splintering wood.

Here we go.

He braced as a man barreled through the arch into the kitchen. The amateur move surprised him, but Burn stepped into the charge, using his arm to flip him onto his back. The fool had a Glock in one hand and zip ties in the other. While he tried to get his wind back, Burn disarmed him, secured his wrists and ankles, then grabbed a dishtowel off the counter to stuff into his mouth. Now he had a weapon.

This one wore leather boots. Now, where was orange sneakers?

"Liesel?" A voice called from the living room.

What the hell?

"I heard a loud noise—Liesel? Your door is open. Is everything okay?"

The roar of gunshots reverberated through the apartment, followed by hysterical screaming.

Burn dove and rolled, searching for a target, but only glimpsed the splash of orange sneakers on the man dashing from the apartment. When he ducked into the hall to follow, it was empty. *Shit.*

"Oh! Help me!"

Burn spun back to the man writhing on the floor. The bullet had struck high on his thigh, and blood gushed in a crimson fountain. If he didn't do something fast, the guy would bleed out.

"Andy! Please, get Andy," the man screamed, thrashing in agony.

Burn set the borrowed gun aside to yank off his belt. "Easy there."

"Burn?" Rissa called. "What's happening?"

"We're clear. Tell whoever you have on 911, we need an ambulance. Also, there's a man on the floor in the kitchen. Stay away from him." Burn attempted to calm the injured man. "Buddy, I'm gonna help you, but it'll hurt like a mother." As he spoke, he strapped his belt high on the man's thigh. "We have to stop the bleeding," he said, cinching it tight. The metallic scent of blood filled Burn's nostrils as he worked.

"Ahhh ..." The man's eyes were glassy, but he ceased his flailing.

"Help is on the way," Burn said, relieved when the fountain of blood stopped. There was no way to tell how badly the artery was affected, but the tourniquet did its job.

Rissa appeared beside him with a handful of towels.

Burn twisted to cast his gaze around the room. "Where's your kid?"

"In the closet with Liesel's iPad. She's okay for a few minutes." Rissa checked the pulse on the man's neck.

"Take care of Shelby. I've got this."

"No, I want to help." Rissa's head whipped up, her eyes challenging him. "I'm a nurse."

Burn figured there was no sense arguing. "Your call." He rocked back on his haunches, angling to keep an eye on the kitchen archway. The kid didn't need to see all this blood, and he worried she might get close to the man he'd left in there.

"Jack, I'm sorry. The ambulance is coming. Please be okay," Rissa murmured as she rolled a towel under Jack's neck and wiped blood with another. "Was he only hit in the leg?"

"I think so." Burn had to admit she was efficient.

"Andy ... call him ..." Jack pleaded.

"I'll call him." She turned her head and whispered to Burn. "Andy is his boyfriend, but I don't have his number. We've got to reassure him to calm his heart rate."

Burn squeezed Jack's shoulder to get his attention. "Tell me your apartment number. I'll get your phone and call Andy."

Jack mumbled unintelligibly, and his eyes closed.

"Stay with me, Jack." Rissa checked the belt. "Tourniquet is holding, but there's so much blood. I think he's in shock. Grab one of those blankets on the couch."

"Got it." Burn reached for the white blanket and realized they were kneeling in a puddle of blood. Blood was also on their hands and clothes.

"Watch ..." Jack groaned.

"What's he saying?" Burn asked.

Rissa snatched the watch off Jack's wrist. "Smartwatch. That's great, Jack." She held it up to Burn. "We can use this to call Andy."

Jack clutched her wrist, his face pasty white. "Shelby?"

Tears dripped down her cheeks, and Rissa clung to his hand. "Oh, Jack, she's safe. You did it. You kept us safe. Please hang on. Andy will be here soon."

CHAPTER 16

Officer Manny Dalton was tall and slim, with sharp cheekbones and a hawkish nose. His dark hair was clipped short, and he exuded a clean-cut appearance that struck Rissa as the ambitious, career-oriented type. The kind of guy who believed he was more seasoned than his age implied—and perhaps he was.

He exhaled a long breath while studying her. "I'll need to consult with my chief about the incident you described in San Antonio."

Clearly, he believed her to be lying about the murder, and she had no way to prove anything. "I'm not making up any of this."

"Yes, I understand," said Dalton.

Even his pen sounded skeptical to Rissa's ears as it scratched against the notebook.

"Mommy." Shelby poked at the iPad.

"We can't turn it up any louder right now," Rissa murmured and shifted Shelby to a more comfortable position. Burn's chair was close enough that their thighs pressed together, a staunch presence between her and whatever else might happen. This was a man who wouldn't back down, and she was glad to have him at her side.

"Are you okay?" Burn asked softly.

She glanced up to see his mouth set in a flat line. "What's wrong?"

Burn wrapped an arm around her back, tugging her closer to his side. "Do you need a break?" he whispered, his breath tickling her cheek.

She allowed herself to relax against him for a moment, but then she straightened. It was essential to remember that she was only with him until the danger had passed. She couldn't let herself depend on him, not on anyone but herself. "I want to keep going, for Mrs. Iglesias."

He nodded slowly before shifting his arm to rest on the back of her chair. A possessive gesture, but she didn't mind because today had been pure hell, and being tucked against him was the safest place around. First, the men broke into the apartment; then she had to watch the EMTs leave with Jack. Thank God she'd managed to reach Andy on the smartwatch.

She had wanted to go with Jack to the hospital, but as soon as the gurney left the apartment, the police began questioning them. Burn got her enough of a reprieve to wash and change clothes. But now they were all in the kitchen, and Officer Dalton had spent the last hour taking both their statements. At first, there had been three cops in the apartment, but two had gone into the hall and not returned.

Dalton asked a few more questions, but they were variations of things she'd already answered. Then he took down her San Antonio address and a few other things before Shelby interrupted.

"Mommy?" Shelby pushed the iPad aside and twisted to curl her arms around Rissa's neck. "Juice?"

"I'll get it in a minute, I promise," Rissa said. She could use a glass of water herself.

Dalton ruffled the pages on his pad. "Let's go over the events in San Antonio again."

Rissa sighed. They'd been over this several times. "Don't you have a database or something? Look it up. I spelled Mrs. Iglesias' name and gave you the address."

"That you did, and I'm sure you believe it to be true. All that aside, the person we arrested here is a known gang member," he tipped his chin at Burn, giving him credit for the takedown. "We have multiple warrants on him, none related to San Antonio, Texas. The idea that he was here specifically for you...well—"

"I don't know about this guy," she interrupted. "But Mrs. Iglesias was murdered. I was there and I saw it."

"I hear what you're saying. Rest assured, we'll investigate," he said, his tone placating. "Another thing, you stated that your roommate is a model. It's plausible that she was the intended target today. I want to ask her a few questions. When will she be home?"

Still standing on Rissa's lap, Shelby whined and bounced a few times.

"I'm not sure." Rissa tamped down her frustration. "Liesel is working today and doesn't have her phone on her during photoshoots. I haven't spoken to her yet." She had finally told an officer everything that happened, and he didn't believe her. Well, not everything. She hadn't mentioned the cash.

He jotted something down, then pulled a card from his pocket. "Here's my information. Please call me if you notice anything or if anyone approaches you. I'll get back to you with my findings."

Burn cleared his throat. "We good to clean-up?"

Dalton tucked away his notebook. "Sure. We have what we need for now. Be available at the numbers you gave me, in case I have follow-up questions."

Relieved that the questioning was over, Rissa cleared her throat. "I want to check on Jack and Mr. Rafferty." Her stomach clenched at the thought of what could've happened to the security guard. "How badly was Rafferty hurt?"

Dalton shrugged. "EMT said he dislocated his shoulder and got a few bruises is all."

"That sounds painful." She shivered, and Burn wrapped his arm round her shoulders again. However temporary, she was grateful to have him on her side.

"We'll have a car drive by every hour," Dalton said, pulling out his cell. "Excuse me, I need to take this." He stepped away, murmuring into the phone before tucking it back into his pocket. "You have my card. I'll file a report with the chief this afternoon and check into that San Antonio incident."

"Sit tight," Burn murmured to her before following Dalton to the door.

She watched as they examined the handle together. Shelby drooped against her, thumb in her mouth, neither asleep nor fully awake. She rubbed Shelby's back. "Do you want your juice now?"

Shelby nodded before withdrawing her thumb with a pop. "Cartoons?"

"Okay, honey." Rissa crossed to the sink and gently set Shelby on the counter. "I'll fill your cup, and you can snuggle with your bunny on the couch. Stay right here while I get the juice from the fridge."

After filling the cup, she turned back to find Burn leaning against the counter, tickling Shelby's feet. The sight of her little girl chortling with laughter and clinging to her father's arms made Rissa's chest ache. It was unfair that he'd missed so much of Shelby's life.

She moved closer. "You're good with her."

He gave an amused snort. "I have nieces, and Shelby's a great kid. Hey, is there a TV in the bedroom?"

She handed Shelby her juice without taking her eyes off Burn. "Both bedrooms have televisions, why?"

He gently tucked a strand of hair behind her ear, letting his fingers trail over her cheek before dropping his arm. "Why don't you watch a little TV with Shelby in there while my buddy and I fix the door and clear the mess?"

She should offer to help, but the thought of all that blood made her stomach in knots. What she really wanted was a good cry, but moms didn't have time for self-indulgence.

•   •   •

Burn surveyed the chaos around him before springing into action. Within minutes, he had bundled all the bloody items into a garbage bag. He couldn't risk the kid seeing any of this. Or Rissa. Shelby was a sweet kid, and the urge to protect her, protect both of them, overwhelmed him.

"I got the stuff," announced Styles from the open doorway. He held a paper sack emblazoned with a hardware store logo in one hand and a toolbox in the other.

"Thanks, man. Wait—how did you get up here?"

Styles lifted a shoulder. "An officer was chatting with the desk clerk. I told him I was the handyman, and he waved me past."

"Security is shit around here," Burn muttered. "Thanks for bringing the new handle. I'll finish the cleanup, and you work on installing it."

"Sure thing, Chief." Styles dropped to one knee to examine the door mechanism.

Burn retrieved a mop from the kitchen. The only sounds in the apartment were the occasional clinking of tools and the rustling of trash bags as the men worked. Styles focused on his task and Burn thought it odd for him to remain quiet this long. "You got something to say?" he prompted.

Styles shot him a sidelong glance. "I'm wondering what you've gotten yourself tangled up with."

Burn tossed the disposable mop pad in a trash bag and tied the top. "Aside from this break-in? Rissa told the officer she witnessed a murder in San Antonio and believed that those responsible were after her. The cop disagreed."

"Shit. Tell me about this morning."

Burn shrugged. "I told you most of it on the phone. As I said, there were two in the apartment and a third in the lobby. I took one down in the kitchen, but the neighbor heard the noise and interrupted before I could engage the second guy. Rafferty, the lobby security guard, nailed the third with a stapler before they knocked him out."

"Walk me through it. You got one inside and the other ran off? You didn't follow?"

Burn shook his head. "The neighbor took a hit in the thigh, and I had to stop the bleeding."

"He's alive?"

"Was when he left here, but no updates."

Styles scooped up his tool bag. "The lock is fixed. What else do you need?"

Burn exhaled in relief. He wasn't in this alone. "My go-bag is in my truck. Will you stay here while I get it? You armed?"

Styles tapped his side and pointed to his boot.

"It won't take long, but let me talk to Rissa, since she doesn't know you."

He left the trash bags and knocked on her bedroom door. When there was no response, he cracked it a fraction. Rissa was curled up next to Shelby on the king-sized bed, a white afghan draped over them. His heart tripped. If something had happened to them today … But nothing had. They were safe.

He gently shut the door and returned to Styles. "They're asleep. I'll hurry, but I need the passkey if they stop me at the desk when I return." Hopefully, they'd at least ask who he was and not let just anyone into the building. He had to do something about the security here.

Styles held up a key with an orange tag labeled PASSKEY. "This was in the bowl over there." He gestured toward a small table at the entrance.

Burn slipped the key into his pocket, gathered the trash, and found the garbage chute before boarding the elevator. He preferred to take the stairs, but they were on the sixth floor, and he wanted to be quick.

Once outside, he scanned the street in both directions but spotted nothing suspicious. He unlocked his truck and retrieved his gun, then rifled through the glove box while watching the street. Nothing triggered his radar. He needed more information. Burn couldn't help his desire to protect Rissa and Shelby, but deep down, he knew they weren't his responsibility. The baby's father should be here.

Burn entered the apartment and tossed his bag behind the couch. "Nothing going on outside."

Styles gave a slow nod. "What's your plan?"

"The officer isn't convinced Rissa was the target, but this hit was intentional. Poorly executed but intentional."

Styles smirked. "Thank your lucky stars for incompetent criminals."

Burn made a *pff* sound.

"Have you spoken with the roommate?" Styles asked.

"No, Rissa texted her. She said her friend can't keep a phone on her when she's working."

"Alright then," Styles said. "Where do you need me?"

Burn touched his friend's shoulder, silently conveying his thanks. "General recon outside."

"Will do. I'll text Butter, and we'll swap off."

"Thanks."

On his way out, Styles whipped his head back. "Tell me one thing. Who's this woman to you?"

Burn's mouth twisted down. "Remember the woman I mentioned on the way back from Germany? The one I haven't been able to get out of my head?"

"No shit?"

Burn's mouth pressed in a line. "Makes no sense, but she's important to me."

Styles gave a sideways salute. "Sure, Chief. We'll keep her safe while you figure things out."

CHAPTER 17

Rissa blinked awake, taking a moment to orient herself. She was in Liesel's guestroom, and Shelby lay curled into her side. How long had she been asleep? She twisted toward the clock and squinted, but it was no use. She couldn't make out the numbers without her glasses.

A rush of memories rushed back—men breaking into the apartment, Jack nearly dying, and poor Mr. Rafferty. Today would've ended very differently if Burn hadn't been there.

Was he still around? Drawing in a trembling breath, Rissa sat up and reached for her glasses. Careful not to disturb her daughter, she slid off the bed and tiptoed to the bedroom door. She opened it a crack to listen and faint voices drifted in from the living room beyond the kitchen. The words were indistinct, but it was clear Burn was speaking with another man.

She needed to go out there and face whatever came next.

Hurrying back to the bed, she tucked the knitted afghan around Shelby. Her daughter lay curled in a tight ball, her thumb in her mouth and wild curls spread across the pillow, her hair reminiscent of Burn's if his were longer. Lucky for her, men didn't notice that type of detail.

Would he resent her once he discovered the truth? Rissa doubted she could forgive him if their roles were reversed. She hadn't intentionally hidden Shelby from him, because she hadn't known how to reach him. Now, by some stroke of fate, they were together, and she couldn't bring herself to tell him about Shelby, because she didn't know him well enough to know how he'd react. And wasn't that selfish of her?

She kissed her daughter's cheek and slipped into the kitchen. The lights were off, and the windowless room was dark, but everything was in its place, as if a man had never been tied up on the floor. Rissa shivered and quickened her pace into the living room. Burn had his back to her, peering out the front windows, and the second man was nowhere in sight.

He pivoted to face her. "Hey."

She bit her bottom lip, unsure how to thank him for saving their lives. "I can't believe I fell asleep."

"It was a tough morning." After a slight hesitation, he gathered her into his arms, resting his chin on top of her head.

"I—" She wasn't a child who needed to be held, but oh ... she needed his powerful arms around her. He was so ... present. She pressed closer, and the words she wanted to say clogged her throat.

Burn stroked a hand up and down her back in big circles. "Are you hungry? I planned to fix something to eat after you woke, but then I checked your friend's cabinets."

Mirth bubbled in her throat. "Let me guess. Protein cookies, broth, or jar spaghetti sauce?"

He snorted. "Don't forget the two cans of chicken noodle soup. I've never tried salt-free, low-fat, gluten-free, chicken substitute."

"Sounds awful." She grinned, then realized she was enjoying herself and pushed away. Two good men were hurt because of her.

"What is it?" He reached for her, and she stepped back.

"I forgot. For a minute. Any word from the hospital?"

He shook his head slowly. "You didn't sleep long. I'm hoping Andy will update us on Jack, but then he might only have Liesel's contact."

"Nothing from her either?"

"I don't think she has my number."

Rissa pulled her phone out and checked for missed calls. "No text or anything on my phone." Her stomach rumbled, reminding her it had been hours since their interrupted breakfast. "How about if we order pizza?"

"Pizza is the perfect food. Just ask my nieces."

"That's right. You have nieces. Are you close to them?"

"I'm gone a lot with my job, but our family is tight. I spend as much time with the girls as I can. Twins. They're great kids," he said, returning to the window. "I guess we barely know anything about each other."

"No. We don't." Guilt slithered through her belly. Her fault. "What do you like on your pizza? I'll order it, and then you can tell me about your family."

•   •   •

He was glad they'd ordered pizza, and even better, Rissa liked Supreme. Nothing beats a pie loaded with every topping. The Supreme had red and green peppers, chunks of different kinds of meat, and slices of mushroom, while the plain cheese they'd ordered for Shelby was a simple blanket of yellowish goo. Way too much for her to eat, but at least she'd have leftovers for another meal.

Instead of sitting at the table, they camped in front of the sofa with the big screen playing a farm animal cartoon. Rissa was more relaxed than he'd ever seen her. Well, other than that night years ago. How could he remember every detail of that night as if engraved on his soul? They'd had one night. An encounter that hadn't meant as much to her as it had him, if Shelby's existence was anything to go by.

His mother was a firm believer in fate and soulmates. She claimed that the moment she set eyes on his father, her heart was stolen. His dad, on the other hand, recalled that the first thing he noticed about Mom was her thick, black curls, draped like silky ropes to her waist. Burn had his mother's dark hair, and his dad's Venezuelan features, and light-brown eyes.

He didn't consider himself shallow, but truthfully, Rissa's physical appearance had first attracted him. She was stunning, and her eyes—damn, they were something else. They were an unusual shade of green, burning right through his defenses. Rissa should be the supermodel. Sure, her friend Liesel had a more classic kind of attractiveness, but nothing compared to Rissa's petite, curvy figure and warm brown skin.

"Burn," Shelby said.

He switched his gaze to Rissa's tiny lookalike. "What do you need, Princess?" The kid smiled at him, her almost black curls a messy cloud around her face. He reached out to wrap one springy curl over his finger.

"Tank yoo." Chubby fingers gripped a piece of cheese pizza in each hand. Or maybe just cheese. He couldn't tell.

"You're welcome." He grinned at Rissa. "I scored with your kid."

"She loves pizza."

Rissa smiled at him, and his heart stuttered. Could there be something to his mother's theory of love at first sight? He could fall into those eyes.

He had to ask. "Riss, you both have such unique eyes. Do they run in your family?"

"What?" Rissa's expression blanked.

"Did I say something wrong?"

"No. My parents and I don't have a good relationship. I don't favor either of them." Rissa put Shelby on the floor and knelt to clear the mess. "Only child. No grandparents or cousins. No relatives."

He lightly held her arm to slow her down. "You told me they kicked you out, that you made it on your own. I'm sorry if my question upset you. You're a beautiful woman; it was merely an observation."

Her gaze softened. "It's okay. Thank you."

Someone banged on the front door, and she shuddered.

"Stay here," Burn ordered, springing to his feet.

"Wait," she said. "It's probably Liesel. She doesn't have a key." Then, she covered her mouth, but not in time to suppress a squeak of laughter.

Confused, he paused. "Are you laughing?"

"Sorry. Not funny." But then she hiccupped another giggle. "She doesn't have a key to her apartment."

Burn grinned, relieved that Rissa was relaxed enough to laugh. Wasn't humor supposed to have a unique healing quality? Although he didn't see the humor quite yet. "Stay here till I check the door." He looked through the peephole to find Liesel typing on her cell with Styles beside her.

Rissa called from behind him. "It's Liesel. She sent me a text."

He glanced back to see Rissa sitting on the sofa with Shelby. "Good to know." Then he unlocked the door.

Liesel rushed past him in a hurry to get to Rissa. "Are you guys okay?"

Rissa hugged her, and Shelby bounced on the cushions, still holding fistfuls of pizza.

Burn said to Styles, "Secure the lock. I need to rescue the couch."

Catching Shelby, he blew a raspberry on her tummy to distract her as he pried the pizza from her fingers. Then he tucked her on his hip and carried her to the kitchen. After turning on the water, he put her bare feet in the sink and let her splash around while he used paper towels to clean her hands and face. The little girl babbled, a cute mix of unintelligible words, as he tidied her up. Her shorts got a little wet, but that didn't matter.

"Come on, little mischief maker. Let's go see Mommy." He dried her with paper towels and returned to the living room, where he halted in the doorway. Rissa and Liesel were staring at him as if he'd grown a second head. Were they mad that the kid got her shorts wet? "It's only a little water. It'll dry."

"Thanks for cleaning her up," Rissa spoke in a barely audible voice. She reached for Shelby, and the kid protested.

"No. Want Burn." Tiny, clean hands dug into his shirt, and she shrieked "no" again when Rissa attempted to pull her free.

Burn pressed one hand over Rissa's and winked. "She's fine. Other than her octopus' tendencies."

For half a second, Rissa leaned against him. Then, she retreated to stand beside Liesel. "Okay. It's okay."

Then, for some inexplicable reason, Liesel put an arm around Rissa. What's going on here? Did they think he'd hurt the kid?

Styles broke the awkward silence. "Any pizza left for a starving man?"

Rissa pulled away from her friend to finish straightening the remains of their dinner. "Burn ate most of it."

"Hey, now. Call me out." He plopped down on the ottoman with Shelby on his lap. "She was telling me something in the kitchen, but I don't have a clue what she said."

Seeming more relaxed, Rissa joined him on the wide seat, close enough that their legs pressed together. This worked for him. He should've picked the kid up sooner.

Styles sighed dramatically. "Guess I have to order my own food."

Liesel thumped his arm. "You poor baby. Do you want me to fix you something else?"

"Like what?" Burn and Rissa said in unison and burst out laughing.

"What's funny?" Liesel asked.

"Well—" A cellphone on the coffee table rang.

"That's mine," said Rissa.

Burn reached for it. The caller ID was a local area code. He turned it around to show Rissa and she shook her head.

"I don't know anyone here."

He raised a brow and waited for her to nod before he swiped to accept the call and put it on speaker. "Hello?"

"Hello? Whose this? Is Rissa there?"

"This is Burn. She's here with me."

"Good—I'm Andy." The man's voice hitched, and he exhaled a shuddery breath. "The EMTs told me what you two did for Jack today. Thank God you were there."

Burn lay the phone on the table to make it easier for them all to hear. "You're on speaker. How's Jack doing?"

"He's going to be fine. Dammit. He'll be fine." Andy gasped, his voice cracking. "The bullet nicked his femoral, and he lost a lot of blood. They did transfusions and emergency surgery to repair, but if you hadn't used the tourniquet and done what you did, my boyfriend wouldn't be alive now."

"I'm glad he's okay. He's the one who saved us today. We were outnumbered and outgunned. Jack surprised them."

CHAPTER 18

Rissa watched as Burn slipped his phone into his back pocket and repositioned Shelby to accommodate his movements. Her daughter clung to him, her busy fingers examining the watch on his wrist. Most people said Shelby looked like her, but that was likely because of their eyes. Her daughter's resemblance to Burn was ridiculously apparent to Rissa. How can he not see that?

"We're going out to eat," Liesel announced, interrupting Rissa's thoughts.

"Don't worry, Chief," said Styles. "Butter had some things to handle, but Cam Nelson is watching the perimeter."

"Will you pick up some sandwich stuff while you're out?" Burn asked, pulling out his wallet and glancing at her. "What does Shelby need?"

"I'll make a list." Rissa jumped to her feet. "I have money. Let me get my bag."

"Sure, honey. Take your time," Liesel said.

Rissa dashed into her bedroom and returned with a handful of cash. "I'll text you, okay?"

Styles gave an exaggerated wink and draped an arm around Liesel's shoulders. "Grocery shopping is a hardship, but we'll manage. Together."

Liesel laughed and nudged him toward the door. "Come on. You said you were fainting from hunger."

Burn set Shelby on the couch and followed them to click the deadbolt. He turned back to Rissa. "I could've paid for the groceries."

"You shouldn't have to do that," Rissa said. She hadn't told the cop about the cash, but maybe she should tell Burn.

"Does her dad help you at all?"

She was still thinking about the bag of money and whether she should tell him about it, and his question momentarily confused her. "Her dad?"

"Shelby's father. Does he help pay for her care?"

Rissa gulped. "No. I ... he's not been involved in our lives." Her cheeks heated, and she pulled out her scrunchy to let her hair tumble around her shoulders. "It's not his fault, though."

When Burn didn't say anything, she darted a glance at him. Any minute now, he would start asking questions she didn't want to answer. Her mind raced and came up with the quickest distraction.

"There's something I didn't tell the police officer."

Burn arched a brow and waited for her to continue.

She rolled back her shoulders and looked straight at him. "Mrs. Iglesias had a purse filled with money in the secret closet. Over four thousand dollars, and she told me I should take it. It's mine."

He dipped his head in agreement and took a seat next to Shelby on the couch. "No one is harmed by you keeping that money." The side of his mouth tipped up in a wry grin. "If you're wondering, I agree that you're justified in keeping it to yourself. The cops would probably stick it in an evidence room to collect dust."

"Thanks for saying that. I've stressed about it, but we needed the money to leave San Antonio quickly," She knelt by the coffee table to brush crumbs from their pizza onto a napkin. Admitting she needed the money exposed just how little she had. Heat flooded her cheeks as she stared at her hands, wishing she could disappear into the carpeted floor. This was one reason she hadn't told him about Shelby. He was in a much better place than her to provide for their daughter.

"Rissa? Something wrong?"

She picked up the smaller pizza box with Shelby's leftovers and did her best to clear her expression. "Earlier, Styles said that Cam would be outside. Who is he?"

"Cam is a friend and I've known him for years. I trust him. Right now, he's temporarily assigned to Whiskey team." Burn paused, then added, "If you see a tall, skinny guy with red hair and way too many freckles, that's Cam Nelson."

She rose and propped the pizza box on her hip. "Do we—do I need to pay him for watching over us?"

He shook his head. "It's not like that with the teams. We look out for each other."

Guilt knifed through Rissa. Her current crisis was disrupting so many people's lives ... even people she'd never met. "Please tell him thank you for me."

"Rissa—"

She interrupted, "I'll double-check the kitchen and text Liesel about what to get from the store." Needing a moment to compose herself, she rushed out of the room. When she returned, Burn and Shelby were settled together on the floor, their dark heads close together, studying Shelby's ragged bunny.

Her daughter was chattering away, and Burn's expression said he was taking in everything she said. She'd noticed that when Burn focused on something or someone, he dialed in completely. Rissa had been the focus of that attention once. A long time ago.

Pausing in the open doorway, she watched their interaction. It wasn't right that he didn't know Shelby was his daughter, but she needed Burn's help to keep them both safe. If only things were different.

"Join us, Rissa. You can translate for me." He motioned her forward.

She settled cross-legged on the floor beside him, and Shelby immediately climbed onto Burn's lap.

"No, Mommy." Shelby squinched her nose at her and pressed back against Burn.

Mirth bubbled in her chest. This wasn't funny, though. Unaware of their relationship, Shelby clung to Burn, and his hands cradled her as gently as the most caring father. Rissa nestled against his side, wanting to be a part of something this important.

Burn grinned and wound an arm around her as they all snuggled on the floor before the couch.

"Watch cartoon?" Shelby asked.

"I got it," Burn said, manipulating the remote. "Are we searching for that farm animal thing that was on earlier?"

"It's about a talking pink pig." Rissa giggled, realizing that sounded like nonsense to someone who didn't watch children's cartoons.

"Hmmm ... riveting." He kissed the top of Rissa's head.

Shelby wiggled until her back was against Burn's stomach, then pulled his arm across her middle. Her daughter was a tactile child and loved snuggling, but she'd never been this affectionate with anyone but her.

"Should we move to the couch?" he asked.

"In a minute," Rissa said, resting her head on his chest above Shelby's and considering what she wanted to say. "Today has been—"

"It's in the past," he said, briefly squeezing her closer.

She sighed. "If you hadn't been here, I don't know what would've happened to us."

"I'm here and I'll stay as long as possible."

"As long as possible?"

"If I need to leave for work, I'll make sure you have backup. Tell me something. Is there a chance those guys could've been after your roommate?"

Something flopped in her belly as she twisted to peer at him. "Do you believe me about the murder?"

"Yes, I do," he said, smoothing a hand over her hair. "I'm only asking if there could be more to this."

Her breath rushed out in a heavy sigh, and she lay her cheek back down. "That officer didn't believe me."

"Cops are trained to be skeptical until they verify the facts. If no murder was reported, it makes it complicated," he said.

She turned everything over in her head for a few minutes. Mrs. Iglesias had been a very wealthy woman, and it stood to reason that with her gone ...

"The murderer was her stepson, and if he has her money, he's wealthy. I guess he twisted things around."

"My brother is in law enforcement. I texted him earlier and asked him to check into it. Let's see what he finds." Burn shifted Shelby to one arm and extended his free hand to her. "Couch?"

Rissa had been clinging to him the same way as her little daughter. She should put distance between them. It wouldn't do for her to get too dependent on someone who might not always be there. "I ..."

"Come on, Riss, it's only a couch."

"Okay," she said, letting him tug her to her feet.

He sank back onto the plush red couch, urging her beside him and propping his feet on the coffee table. "This is more like it."

She tucked her feet under her and relaxed against his side. "Definitely softer seating." Shelby remained draped over his lap, mesmerized by the cartoon.

"After this morning, I like having you both where I can touch you," he said, trailing his hand over her shoulder to stroke her bare upper arm.

Shelby giggled at something on the screen.

Burn cleared his throat. "Can I ask you something?"

"Ask away," she said in a light tone, but her stomach clenched with dread. Had he figured out the truth?

"It was a long time ago, but will you tell me what I did wrong that night?"

She braced against his chest to meet his gaze. "You didn't do anything wrong. I left because it was supposed to be a fling. You said, 'We'll have fun.' I didn't want things to get awkward."

"It was fun, but also more than that to me." He cupped her jaw with gentle fingers. "Touching you and being with you was special. I've never forgotten you—never wanted to forget our time together."

Every detail of that night was etched in her memory, not just because it had been special, but also because her daughter was a living reminder of him. She glanced at Shelby, "I could never forget you."

"Look at me."

When she did, he slid his fingers into her hair and pressed his lips to hers in a soft, undemanding caress. "You taste so good," he said, licking along the seam of her lips. Coaxing her to part for him, and when she did, he delved in with a sweet, tender exploration that left her breathless.

"Burn," she whispered, tangling her fingers in his shirt. "We need to talk first." She needed to tell him everything.

"Mommy no," Shelby said, waving her arm to push Rissa back so she could see the television.

Heat streaked to her cheeks as she pulled away from Burn to sit upright. She'd forgotten her daughter was right there as soon as Burn kissed her. She was a mother first and foremost, but when she reached for Shelby, her daughter was already climbing off the other side of Burn's lap to move farther down the couch with her bunny.

"She's fine," Burn said.

And she clearly was. Shelby rested her head on a pillow at the end of the couch, her little arms wrapped around her bunny and her eyes drooping.

"Now, where were we?" Burn said, winding an arm around her back to lift her against his chest.

She moaned and closed her eyes, tilting her head to give him better access to her throat for his kisses. When his mouth claimed hers again, the room shrank to the sensation of his lips. She could've stayed here for hours, pressed against his hard body, but her daughter was only a few feet away.

"Burn, we shouldn't ... let's take a moment," Rissa twisted to check on Shelby and her daughter was fast asleep.

"She's good," he said with a grin, cupping her face in his big hand. "My green-eyed beauty. You slipped into my head and heart that night, and I can't get enough of you."

She nuzzled his palm, then lay her cheek against his chest. "Believe me, I've thought of you often," she whispered. How could she not? Ten weeks after their one night, she discovered he'd given her the gift of a new life. Although when the stick had turned blue, she'd been more scared than excited. It hadn't seemed like a gift then. But now she couldn't imagine her life without Shelby. Her baby was a joy and her reason for everything. It wasn't fair that he couldn't share in that joy.

"Let's explore this thing between us. We don't have to rush, but I want to get to know you, before you disappear on me again," he said.

"I'm sorry. When I left, I thought I was doing the smart thing for both of us." She tilted her face to meet his gaze. "Do you believe me when I say I definitely would've returned to find you if my finances had allowed it?"

He cupped her jaw, his thumb tracing her bottom lip. "Sweetheart, if I'd known you wanted to see me, I would've bought you a plane ticket."

"I called," she said, resting her cheek against his heart.

"Called?" he echoed.

"The Navy base. I called, but they wouldn't give me any information because I didn't know your full name. All I knew was that you were a Navy SEAL named Bernie. The woman on the phone told me to call back when I had more details." Remorse tightened her throat as she thought about the time they'd missed—about all the time he'd missed with his daughter.

His hands wove through her hair, gently massaging her scalp. "All in the past. You're here now, and I plan to convince you to stay."

She met his gaze. "You want me to stay?"

"Never doubt it." He peppered a few kisses over her face. "I was serious when I said I went to that bar every time I was in town, hoping to run across you again."

Her eyes welled with tears. "I was back in San Antonio and Liesel flew to Japan that next week for a contract. She ended up staying there more than she was home for a couple of years."

"I guess I never stood a chance of finding either of you. Cicadas liked the team's patronage, anyway." He tugged her back against his chest.

Silence fell between them, punctuated by singing barnyard animals on the television. Weariness swept over her, and she could barely keep her eyes open.

"Rissa?"

She sighed but didn't lift her head. "Hmm?"

"Can I ask you something else?"

Something else? Those words zapped away her lassitude. "I guess. I mean, sure. What do you want to know?"

He hesitated, then said, "I'm grateful to have found you again and thrilled you came to me when you needed help. Your trust means a lot. I do have one question I need you to answer."

"What question?" Her blood chilled, and she held her breath, waiting.

"Why isn't Shelby's father helping you? You didn't answer when I asked before if he was supporting you. Is he in San Antonio?"

Her stomach dropped as if it had fallen through the couch cushions to the floor. Lies compounding lies. She didn't have a good track record of trusting people or people following through on what they told her they would or wouldn't do. "Shelby's father hasn't been part of our lives."

"He's a deadbeat."

"No!" She jerked upright and put some distance between them. "It wasn't his fault that things didn't work out for us. The timing was wrong."

Burn scrubbed a hand over his face. "Last question. Do you love him?"

Rissa opened her mouth, closed it, and carefully considered her words. She didn't want him to believe her heart belonged to another man, but she didn't want to lie anymore. "I loved him from the first kiss. But ... we never had what you would call a relationship. I love my daughter. Can we leave it at that?"

"For now." He reached for her hands. "I care about you, for more than one night or week. But we need to consider Shelby. I'm already getting attached to the kid. If another man showed up to claim her, I would have a problem with that. Even now."

Rissa swallowed past the lump in her throat. "Don't worry. No other man will claim her. We don't have any family that wants us, and her father ... he won't be a problem for you. I swear it."

Her answer seemed to satisfy him, and they were quiet for a few minutes.

"I'm glad you're here. Glad we're together," Rissa whispered.

"Being with you like this makes me want things you aren't ready for," he said before gently brushing his lips over hers.

Something warm unfurled deep in her belly. "Things like more kisses?"

"That and more."

"Burn," she murmured, biting her lip, "what if I don't want to wait any longer?"

A low chuckle rumbled in his chest. "You are tempting, my green-eyed dream girl. But what about her?" He tilted his head toward Shelby.

Her daughter lay curled on her side at the end of the couch, sound asleep.

"Since her morning nap was short, I expect she'll be out for at least an hour—maybe longer," Rissa said.

His eyes crinkled at the corners. "No guarantees, huh?"

CHAPTER 19

Burn rose and pulled Rissa to her feet. "The lock on the front door is too high for Shelby to reach, and we'll hear her if she wakes up."

Rissa glanced toward the window. "What about…"

"Cam is on the street. He'll let me know if anything seems off."

"Okay," she said. "I'd love to have some time with you. But we should put cushions on the floor in case she rolls."

"I got it." Burn quickly tossed down the cushions, then extended a hand to Rissa. It was her choice, but he hoped she didn't change her mind. Styles and the roommate would return soon, but Burn would take anything he could get.

She gave him a shy smile. "Let's go," she whispered.

In the bedroom, he pressed her body close and kissed her as thoroughly as he knew how. The chemistry between them was electrifying.

"Wrap your legs around me," he murmured, and satisfaction surged through him when she obeyed without hesitation. Her hot center burned his stomach through his t-shirt, and his dick was an iron rod jammed behind the zipper of his jeans.

He kissed her while walking backward, and when the edge of the bed bumped against his knees, he lay down, pulling her over his chest. "Will you let me see you?"

She propped her elbows on his chest. "We probably only have an hour." Her pretty eyes were wide orbs as she flicked a glance toward the door. "If that. There are no guarantees with a kid."

"We'll redirect if we get interrupted. But it's been a long time. Can you trust me?"

"I trust you." Her tongue darted out to wet her lips.

He rolled them, so she was on the bottom. Then he whisked off her shirt, revealing her smooth skin and perfect curves. His heart did a double thump as he eased her bra straps off her shoulders.

Magnificent. Her breasts were flawless globes, high on her chest with nipples the same dusky rose as her lips. "You're so beautiful," he murmured, trailing kisses down her neck before settling his mouth on one luscious tip.

Rissa moaned and clung to him, digging her fingers into his back. "Burn, don't stop."

Switching to the other nipple, he used his free hand to flick open the button on her shorts and slide down the zipper. Then he had to release her breast to help Rissa push the shorts down her legs, leaving only her black cotton panties.

"We should get under the covers," she murmured.

"Good thinking." Grinning, he freed the comforter from under their bodies and shook it over them. Then he lay on his side beside her, resting his head on his elbow while his other hand cupped her hip, drawing her close. "I've never forgotten you and our night together. I don't want to rush you."

"Don't you want to do this?"

Shifting his fingers to cradle her cheek, he pressed against her side so she could feel the length of his arousal through his jeans. "Does that answer your question? I want you more than I need air, but you're too important for me to rush you."

"You aren't rushing me. I want this," Rissa said, her hands tugging at his belt.

"You're sure?"

"I'm sure."

He pressed his lips to hers in a lingering kiss, then lifted his head. "Let me take care of it," he said, rising onto his heels. First, he pulled off his shirt, then flopped onto his back to remove his jeans, pausing only to grab his wallet before tossing them off the bed. "Condom," he said as he fumbled with the packet.

In the next moment, her mouth was on his dick. Hot and wet. He'd never last. "Riss ... I want you gorgeous. What you're doing feels amazing, but for this time, will you let me have you?"

She let him slide out of her mouth and raised her eyes. "Okay. Yes." Her hands rested on her thighs as she watched him roll the condom over his hardened length.

"If I don't get inside you soon, my heart might explode," he said before sliding his hands under her legs, lifting her knees to lay her flat on her back. He kept kissing her but moved with her, his dick locking on target, the tip pushing into her entrance even before her head met the pillow.

•   •   •

The sensation was incredible, almost too much to take, as he slid deep inside her. The weight of his body and his deliberate movements, both tender and relentless, quickly brought her to the brink of climax. "I'm going to—"

"Yes, sweetheart, let go for me," he whispered, tracing kisses along her jaw before returning to delve into her mouth, sucking her tongue and consuming her with his breath, his lips, and his need while never stopping the slow, languid thrusts into her body.

His hands clasped her hips, guiding her movements as he quickened the pace, bringing her closer to the edge. He released her mouth, and her name was a low rumble in his throat as he increased the rhythm.

"Burn ..." she gasped when he pressed his thumb firmly against her most sensitive place. Her entire body undulated through the release, and he quickly followed with his climax. She relaxed the fingers clamped to his back and slid her arms up to circle his neck. "Wow."

He nuzzled her cheek. "Wow is right. I'm too heavy," he said, rolling onto his side even as she arched to keep him in place.

"No. Stay inside me a little longer."

"Anytime, dream girl. I'm your guy," he whispered, capturing her lips in a kiss sweet enough to bring tears to her eyes.

This man would be easy to love.

CHAPTER 20

Rissa sprawled on the couch, a half-empty bowl of buttery microwave popcorn between her and Liesel. Shelby sat on the floor at their feet, completely captivated by the singing fish characters in a popular Disney movie.

Liesel and Styles had returned sooner than Rissa liked, but it was for the best. The sex and the orgasm still had her insides quivering, but she didn't need to get used to having Burn in her bed. They'd only made love once. It was fortunate, too, because she had barely zipped her shorts when Liesel rang the doorbell and woke up Shelby.

Five minutes sooner, and it would've been catastrophic. Or at least embarrassing. The more time she spent with Burn, the more she liked him. He was a good man, and she longed to share many things with him, Shelby being at the top of the list.

"Riss. Riss?" Liesel raised her voice.

"What?"

"The guys will be back in a few minutes. Spill it. What happened with Burn after we left?"

"Um …We talked." And had fantastic sex.

Liesel lobbed a piece of popcorn at her. "What does that mean? Did you tell him about Shelby?"

"No," she said, dropping her gaze. "Not yet."

Liesel put the bowl on the coffee table. "You said you wanted to tell him. Has that changed?"

Rissa shook her head. "I don't know why I haven't told him yet." How could she explain her hesitation to Liesel when she herself wasn't sure if it was the right decision? Seeing Burn had reignited that spark of intimacy, but she hadn't come clean when the chance presented itself.

"You don't know?" Liesel crossed her arms.

"Everything is complicated. I lied about Shelby's age, and now he believes I left him and met someone else right away. When I tell him the truth, will he want Shelby and not me? I need him for Shelby, but I also need his help."

"Oh, honey." Liesel patted her leg reassuringly. "I get that you're scared, but it's not fair to keep his daughter from him. That's my opinion. You're my best friend, and it's your choice, but lying is no way to treat someone you respect. Even by omission, it's still a lie."

A frown tugged at Rissa's lips. "Maybe Shelby and I should leave. With the money from Mrs. Iglesias, I could start a new life somewhere."

"Four thousand dollars won't get you very far."

"I could get a job."

"Then that guy Terrance will come looking for you." Liesel gripped Rissa's hand. "You need to stay here with these SEAL guys protecting you— all of us."

"But if I tell him, Burn could get mad and leave. Or worse, what if something happens to him because of me?"

Liesel scowled. "First, I don't think he'd leave because you pissed him off. Second, he's a Navy SEAL; he can take care of himself."

"But he could decide he's a better parent and take Shelby away from me."

"Honey, you're overthinking what could or couldn't happen." Liesel made a humming sound and tugged Rissa into a tight embrace. "I love you, but you need to take that risk. Have a little faith and tell him the truth."

"I want to. Why is this so hard?"

Liesel sighed and released her. "I'm a broken record—but do the right thing."

Rissa let out a shuddery breath. Everything came easy for Liesel. She'd never struggled to put food on the table or faced a shut-off because she couldn't pay the minimum on the power bill. But, she was also right. If telling the truth meant sharing custody of her daughter, she could manage that. More importantly, regardless of what he thought of her, Shelby deserved to know her father.

Rissa nodded. "I'll do it."

●　　　●　　　●

Terrance ended the call and surged out of his recliner to pace the living room. He hadn't expected his men to secure Evonne Montano so quickly, but they'd had a stroke of luck. A discarded travel brochure had led them to a secluded vacation home. Evonne and her husband were on a Labor Day weekend getaway and wasn't that nice for him that they wouldn't be missed until Tuesday.

It was after seven. Terrance paced as he worked out a plan of action. He could wait and drive to San Antonio in the morning, but he wanted answers now. His housekeeper wouldn't return until Monday, so he needed to create an airtight alibi. Officer Windham had too many questions, and he wasn't about to give her a reason to be more suspicious.

He threw a robe over his clothes. Then he poured himself a bourbon and pinged his attorney to connect on Zoom. They spent an hour discussing an investment project, his stepmother's funeral, and a pay-to-view streaming boxing match scheduled for later that night.

After disconnecting Zoom, he purchased the match and made sure the app was open so it would come on automatically. Then he turned off his cell and set his lights on a timer. Once the exterior alarm was armed, he slipped onto the hidden path to the adjacent property.

The dark tint on the truck windows concealed his face as he drove out a secondary gate, looped through the neighborhood, and merged onto the highway. His side ached, although the steroid and antibiotic treatment from Dr. George had dulled the pain to a manageable level.

The vehicle's GPS was turned off, but the old-fashioned Garmin on his dashboard directed him on a two-hour-long circuitous route that ended on a dirt road cutting through a stand of trees. After exiting the vehicle, he turned in a full circle, pleased to find no other lights to indicate nearby dwellings.

The house Evonne rented was a two-story cabin with vertical cedar siding, a silver metal roof, and a traditional wrap-around porch. It was also built on thirty-six-inch piers. Terrance gently pressed his side. Damn. That was a lot of stairs.

One of his men stood on the porch. "Good evening, Mr. Simmons. They're in the kitchen."

This man had been in his employ for more than ten years, so Terrance easily recalled his name. "Dave. Any problems?"

"No, sir. This is the only house on this twenty-acre lot, and no cameras."

"Good," Terrance said as he struggled to keep his expression neutral while climbing the steps. The long drive had aggravated his wound, and he was forced to pause at the top to catch his breath. He nodded at Dave and walked through the long foyer and into a brightly lit kitchen.

In the center of the room, Evonne and her husband were strapped to chairs. Although he needed her to talk more than he needed to scare her, he was gratified by the terror in her eyes and the muffled exclamation around the cloth stuffed in her mouth.

One of his crew lounged against the far wall, and another in the gap between the kitchen and the big den, ready to assist him.

He moved closer to Evonne. It was difficult to tell if she'd retained her looks because his men had delivered a few blows to her face. No doubt she'd fought them. "Evonne Montano, how nice to see you again after all this time."

Evonne ducked her head and screwed her eyes shut.

He glanced around and, seeing another chair, dragged it in front of the pair. Even the light weight of a single chair had him breathing like a sprinter.

Fucking Amelia and her fucking gun. Suppressing a groan, he eased onto the seat. "I'm going to remove the rag, but no screaming. Do you understand?"

Her eyes flashed defiantly, but she offered a quick nod.

As soon as he tugged the cloth free, she coughed and spat. He recalled Yvonne had spunk, although he was in no condition to take advantage of that. A shame, really.

"Why are you doing this?" Her voice was shrill, and her eyes wide. "We did everything your mother asked, and she promised to leave us in peace if we kept our mouths shut." She kept glancing at her husband, who hadn't lifted his head. The room reeked of sweat and fear, mingled with the scent of burning wood from the fireplace.

Terrance folded his arms and shifted most of his weight to one side of the chair to ease the pressure on his side. "I'm sure Amelia made promises to you."

"Then why didn't you leave us alone?"

He went to cross his legs but thought better of it. "I need some answers."

"Please," she whimpered. "I'll tell you anything." She glanced at her husband again, and her voice broke. "They hurt him."

Mr. Parker's head lolled sideways, but his chest rose, so not dead.

Terrance decided to let her stew for a bit, to see if she would volunteer any information. He pulled out the pocketknife he always carried and began cleaning under his fingernails.

"Please. What do you want?" Evonne asked in a plaintive voice. "I have some money, you can take it all, and we won't tell anyone. Please let us go."

"Let you go?" He tucked the pocketknife away and focused on her. "There are questions you need to answer. For starters, tell me about my daughter."

Evonne sputtered. "Your mother and I had a deal. I sent her annual updates as she requested."

Terrance waited, not taking his eyes off her.

Her head bobbed uncertainly. "I took care of Marissa, as agreed. But ... she moved out when she turned eighteen. We don't see her often. She's got a daughter now."

He studied the trembling woman. "Tell me about my granddaughter. Who is her father?"

"I don't know," Evonne whispered through trembling lips.

"Then you're of no use to me." He made to rise, and Evonne began babbling.

"Wait! He's a Navy SEAL, and Marissa met him in San Diego. She came to me afterward and wanted my help."

"Your help?"

"She'd been to visit a friend from school, and that's when she hooked up with the guy."

"His name?"

Evonne frantically shook her head. "Marissa didn't know. That's the truth. She wanted me to give her money so she could go back and find him. She fucked him, but only got some nickname—Burn. I remember that because it sounded so stupid. Please, I've told you all I know, let us go."

He shushed her with a raised hand. "Did you help her find her lover?"

"What?" Evonne's eyes went wide.

"You are an idiot," he said. "Did. You. Help. Her?"

"No." Evonne shook her head. "She wasn't living with us and I —"

He cut in sharply. "You didn't think Amelia would pay for news of a grandchild?"

She licked her lips. "Amelia and I cut ties. I didn't want to involve her again."

"I suppose my stepmother threatened you about future contact," he said, tapping his fingers on his knees. "Let me see if I have it straight. Your only daughter told you she was pregnant, and you turned her away. Is that correct?"

Evonne bared her teeth at him. "Marissa is your daughter. Amelia always made it clear that she wasn't mine. My husband never wanted kids, and Amelia forced me to keep her."

"And paid you too much to dispose of her," he added coldly.

"You hurt me. How could I love a child that was a result of the pain you caused me?" She glowered at him, the fire back in her brown eyes. "She received an education, food, and a roof over her head."

Steepling his fingers, he thought about what he'd learned. Was his daughter unintelligent? How could she not know the name of her child's father? More likely, she hadn't wanted to tell Evonne.

"If you have nothing else for me, I have a long drive home, and I'd like to be there before daylight," he said, slowly unfurling from the chair so as not to reveal his infirmity to his men.

"No, wait." Evonne panted. "Marissa said she regretted leaving him and that she loved him."

"That's interesting but not helpful."

"You have to let us go," she shrieked.

Pointing at the nearest man, he said, "Plug her mouth."

Evonne mumbled behind the rag as she rocked her chair violently on the wood floor.

It was a pity he wasn't up to enjoying that fire one last time. He turned to leave, speaking as he walked toward the front. "Make it look like a car accident and clean everything here."

The Navy SEAL's identity had become his highest priority.

•   •   •

Back at the apartment, Burn hesitated across the alley from the building, staring at the back entrance. It was a metal door with key card activation. He could get past it, but he was a SEAL. His cell buzzed with a text from Cam saying he was parking his truck.

Rissa was secure inside the apartment, but he was eager to join her. It had been nearly three years—no, more precisely, they had met at the end of November, and now it was September, which amounted to roughly two years and nine months. The realization hit him hard. Shelby? Could it be?

Though Burn had no reason to doubt Rissa's honesty, his mind raced with what-ifs. The kid had been talking about birthdays and dinosaurs when he'd been washing her off in the sink. The thought sent a flutter of anticipation through him.

Another buzz on his phone signaled that Cam was ready to take over the exterior. To buy himself more time to think, Burn took another loop around the back of the building. Whether Shelby was his daughter or not, his immediate priority was managing this situation. He couldn't expect his team to stay indefinitely, so he was borrowing some of Style's gear. Surveillance would be much easier with cameras in the right locations.

Tomorrow, the Whiskey Team was joining his brother's DEA guys for a pre-Labor Day gathering at his brother's house. If Rissa agreed, he'd bring her, Shelby, and Liesel along. They could stay with his friends while he made a quick trip to the base to request leave. His nieces would be there too, giving Shelby some playmates.

It was after midnight when Burn headed for the elevator. He could go for long stretches with little sleep, and he had some steam left. Inside the apartment, Rissa and Liesel were curled at opposite ends of the couch. Shelby was nowhere in sight.

Rissa blinked sleep from her eyes. "Is everything okay?"

"All good," he said, kneeling beside her. "I sent Styles after some equipment." He gestured toward the sleeping Liesel. "Whether those guys were after you or Liesel, I'll keep you safe till the cops figure things out."

"I'm ... thank you," she whispered. "What should I do?"

He pulled her to her feet, gently kissing her before stepping back. "You should head to bed. I'll set up the tech with Styles. No one will surprise us again."

"Don't you need to rest?"

"I'll grab a couple of hours on the couch after we're done." He didn't plan to sleep, but he wasn't telling her that.

Rissa smoothed her hands over the front of his sweatshirt. "You can come to the bedroom."

He arched a brow at her. "Shelby?"

Rissa looked away, then met his gaze. "I mean to sleep. Shelby has a pallet on the floor. It's better for her there, so she won't roll off the bed."

He cupped her cheek. "Sweetheart, there's nothing I'd like better than to be in your bed. Ask me again tomorrow or the day after."

The phone in his pocket vibrated, and he checked the screen. "Styles," he said, kissing her forehead. "Send Liesel to bed, and you get some rest. You're safe."

"Why are you helping me? Really?"

He wanted her to understand her importance to him, but she might run for the hills if he told her he was in love with her. He'd play it cool, but he didn't plan to lose her again when this was over. Shelby either. "There's something between us. Something real, and I will make sure you stay safe so we can explore it."

CHAPTER 21

The next morning, Burn convinced her and Liesel to join him for lunch at his brother's house. He led them into the two-story brick home without knocking, and, after a quick pit stop for Shelby, they stepped onto the redwood deck at the back of the house.

The scent of barbecue chicken, mixed with the earthy smell of fresh-cut grass and blooming flowers, tickled Rissa's nose. She adjusted her glasses and lifted Shelby higher on her hip. Her daughter was uncharacteristically quiet as she took in the new place.

"Lunch smells good, I can hardly wait," Liesel said. "There are a lot of folks here already. I thought we were early?"

"Are a lot of people coming?" Rissa asked.

Burn moved closer and slung an arm around her shoulders. "A few of Paul's DEA folks and some team guys will be here. If you aren't comfortable, we can leave anytime."

"Before we eat?" Liesel blinked wide-eyed at Rissa. "I'm hungry and I'm not counting calories today."

Rissa chuckled, "I'm okay. We'll stay."

"You made it!" called out a man carrying a large tray of wrapped corn and wearing an apron with 'Chef Dad' in bold, dark letters.

"That's my brother," Burn said before releasing her to give Paul a manly side hug around the tray of corn.

"You must be Rissa Parker," Paul said with a face-splitting grin. "My little brother thinks a lot of you."

"Ah … thank you," she said, glancing from Paul to Burn. The brothers looked so much alike, they could pass for twins.

"Me down," Shelby wiggled, her eyes glued to a fat little Corgi.

"Is your dog friendly?" Rissa asked.

"Reecie? Absolutely, wouldn't hurt a fly. You need to meet my girls. Mera! Vera!" He called across the yard where the girls played corn hole with Styles.

Rissa set Shelby on the grass and extended her fingers for the dog to sniff. Shelby chortled with glee and clapped her hands. One day, when she had an actual place to live and they weren't on the run, Rissa would get her baby a puppy.

"Play!" Shelby hopped up and down.

"You brought a kid!" The twins skidded to a stop in front of them.

"Can we play with her," asked one of them.

Rissa had no idea which one was which.

"Girls, this is Uncle Burn's friend Rissa and her daughter Shelby," Paul said, glancing up to introduce Liesel, but she'd already headed across the yard to join Styles. "And that is their other friend, Liesel."

Paul went down on his haunches to catch Shelby's eye. "These are my daughters, Mera and Vera. Do you want them to show you how to play fetch with Reecie?"

Shelby nodded vigorously and the twins each grabbed one of her hands to tow her into the yard, the chunky dog racing along behind them.

Burn laughed, "I knew the kids would get along. Where is Clare with my favorite nephew?"

"Still upstairs, she'll be down soon. I'd better get these on the grill."

"Hey, Paul. I need to pop over to the base to get some signatures."

"Lunch won't be for another hour. You can go now if you want. We'll keep your girls occupied," said Paul before heading to the grill.

Burn rested his hands on her shoulders. "Will you be okay here for an hour or so?"

"Yes," she said, trying to exude confidence she didn't have. She only knew a couple of people here, but everyone had been friendly, and she couldn't think of a safer place for her and Shelby, what with all the DEA agents and Navy SEALs. "We'll be fine. Shelby is having fun."

"There's shade over there if you want to sit and enjoy the nice weather while you keep an eye on the kids," he said, gesturing toward a glass table under a tan umbrella.

"I'll be fine. Can I have something cold to drink? Not beer."

"Sure. I'll grab you a soda," he said.

Rissa slid into a chair and took in her surroundings. The yard was completely enclosed and had a swing set, fire pit, and outdoor grill area. No pool, but that was fine with her since Shelby didn't know how to swim. At one time, she'd dreamed of a home like this, but it seemed so far out of reach.

"Here's a soda," he said, dropping a kiss on her cheek. "I'll be back as quick as I can."

She could tell his mind was already working out what he needed to do next, so she said, "Go. We'll be fine here until you get back."

"Save me some food," he said, taking off at a jog.

Rissa rubbed her fingers over the glass table. Shelby was in heaven running around the backyard with the dog and Burn's two nieces. Liesel had joined Styles at the cornhole game on the opposite end of the lawn.

This morning, when Burn asked her to come to this party, she'd been nervous, but the small crowd and bright sunshine lifted her spirits. She looked forward to meeting his sister-in-law, Clare, and maybe getting to hold little Jackson. It was good the baby had a whole family to help care for him.

Her memories of Shelby as a newborn were bittersweet. Rissa had lived hand-to-mouth, with only Liesel's financial support as her lifeline. That first year had been a relentless cycle of trying to make ends meet, and it wasn't until she met Mrs. G. and started working overnight shifts that she began to cope.

"You must be Rissa," said a woman with a friendly smile as she pulled out a chair at the round table. "Would you mind if we joined you?"

"Uh, sure." Rissa said.

"I'm Anita, and this lug is my boyfriend, Pete."

Pete gave Rissa a thousand-watt smile. His brown hair curled around his ears, and he wore dark sunglasses. "I'm part of Whiskey Team," he said, settling on the opposite side of Anita.

Rissa tried to remember all the names she'd learned today. "How many are on the team? I've only met Cam and Styles."

"There are eight on Whiskey Team. Cam is the ninth, filling in for Mack until he's back on his feet." Pete cleared his throat and continued. "Burn's brother is DEA, so a few of the men and women out here work with him."

She straightened her glasses again. "I met Paul when we arrived. He's nice."

"Wait till you taste his barbecue chicken and grilled corn. He's a magician with the grill," Pete said.

Anita laughed, a tinkling musical sound. "Yes, we all say Paul should have his own food show. We never turn down an invite to one of his barbeques." Anita was very petite, with nut brown skin and darker eyes—clearly of Hispanic heritage, like Rissa's own.

Rissa crossed her arms and uncrossed them, trying to come up with something interesting to say. "Do you live nearby?"

Anita smiled. "I live a bit further north, only about twenty minutes, and Pete's on base, like Burn. The guys have been out of the country so much that we haven't all been able to get together." She stuck an elbow in Pete's direction and stage whispered, "I'm glad we arrived before the food got ready. You won't believe how much these guys eat, so get your share quick or you'll get nada."

"I feel judged," Pete joked, pushing back his chair. "Speaking of food, I'm off to hunt for snacks."

"You do that, big guy," Anita teased, swatting his butt as he passed, and he snagged her fingers to bring them up for a kiss.

After Pete moved away, Anita slid her chair closer. "It's sweet that you and Burn met years ago and have reconnected. Will you tell me how it happened? Styles claims he was there in the beginning, but I can't tell when he's kidding."

Were they a topic among his friends? She wasn't good enough for Burn, or for these attractive, confident people. Even if they were friendly now, Rissa worried they'd despise her when they discovered her lies. She took off her glasses to nervously clean them on the edge of her T-shirt. "What do you want to know?"

Anita bounced a little in her seat, and her eyes sparkled. "Everything, don't you know? This is juicy stuff. Besides, I'm naturally nosy, and Pete wasn't with the team that night. Styles told him you guys met at Cicadas, but you didn't live here and didn't speak again until you returned a few days ago."

"That's all true." Rissa shrugged and picked up her empty soda can before realizing she'd already finished it. "I've moved here now." She guessed she had, because she couldn't return home unless they locked up Terrance Simmons. On top of that, Shelby was getting to know her father. And, after seeing Burn with his nieces, she was confident he'd want to be part of Shelby's life.

"Is your daughter's father in San Antonio?" Anita asked.

Rissa shifted awkwardly. Nosy was an understatement. This woman cut right to the chase. "He's not been involved in our lives." That much was true. "We like San Diego."

"I'm glad," Anita said. "Burn is a terrific person."

Was there a warning hidden in there? Rissa wished he were here now. "Yes, he's great. He had to go to the base to sign some papers."

Burn was using his vacation days and talking about her with his friends. He was also treating her like a priority in his life ... like she mattered. It was unsettling. When had anyone rearranged their lives to help her?

"Most of the single guys don't use all their leave." Anita waved as a woman with flaming red hair and a girl of about five or six who looked exactly like her stepped onto the deck. "That's Coal's wife, Maggie, with her daughter, Chelle."

Chelle squealed and dashed toward the other three girls.

Rissa considered excusing herself to get a soda. Everyone was nice, but she didn't know anyone, and so many questions made her uncomfortable.

"Your daughter is adorable," Anita said.

Rissa breathed through her tension. Shelby was her favorite topic. "Shelby's having an absolute blast. She rarely gets to play with other kids because I work at night. Or I did. I appreciate how sweet Burn's nieces are to her."

"Chelle's a good kid, too," Anita said, her eyes fixed on the other side of the deck. "I wonder who that blonde woman is with Styles."

Rissa followed her gaze. "That's my roommate, Liesel Zolan."

"She's gorgeous and so tall!"

"Yes," Rissa chuckled. "Liesel is a fashion model."

"I wish I were taller. People assume I'm a kid until I start talking." Anita smiled at her. "We didn't exactly hit the height jackpot. You know, I'm really glad you moved to San Diego. You and Burn will be perfect together."

"I don't—"

"Snack time!" Pete announced, arriving with a plate of watermelon slices which he placed on the table with a flourish. "I have hunted and brought back food for my woman."

"A regular Tarzan." Anita snickered and reached for a piece before nudging the plate toward Rissa.

"Thanks." Rissa's mouth watered at the sight of the juicy, red watermelon. She picked up a slice and took a huge bite about the same time as the red-headed woman, Maggie, approached the table,

"Would you mind if we joined you?" the pretty redhead asked.

The man with her had military-cut jet-black hair and dark brown eyes, which were slightly tilted at the edges. He was drop-dead gorgeous ... not that Rissa was interested in anyone but Burn. She wasn't, but she couldn't help noticing the man's movie star looks.

"Wait. You and Coal can't sit here," Anita insisted, holding up her hands.

Maggie's perfect brows lifted, and she propped her hands on her hips. "And why not?"

"Because only people who didn't elope and cheat their friends out of a fun wedding party are allowed at our table."

"Don't be ridiculous. I promise, once our deck is finished, we'll throw a huge party. Right?" Maggie elbowed her husband.

"Sure. We can have a fall get-together in a couple of months. You'll all be invited," Coal said, taking a seat and reaching for a watermelon slice.

Rissa barely resisted hunching her shoulders. She wasn't sure about tomorrow, much less a month from now.

Maggie plopped down before fastening her gaze on Rissa. "Hello. I'm Maggie, and this is my husband, Rockford. You must be Burn's friend?"

Hadn't Anita called him Coal? These nicknames were confusing. Rissa set her watermelon rind on a napkin. "Yes, I'm with Burn."

Anita gently nudged her arm. "You should definitely come to Maggie's house for the party. Not only is their place beautiful, but Maggie makes the best pies you've ever put in your mouth."

Rissa gave a slow nod, at a loss for words. Her stomach turned jittery at all the attention. Everyone was friendly, but they all knew each other. Why were they automatically including her? Her gaze settled on Maggie's husband. "I'm sorry, do I call you Coal or Rockford?"

Maggie and Anita laughed.

A grin sprang to his lips. "Either is fine. My given name is Rockford, but my team name is Coal."

Anita patted Rissa's hand gently. "We all know what that confusion is like. When I met Peter, it took me ages to get everyone's names straight."

"Okay," Rissa said, not knowing what else to say. Then it hit her. What if, by being here, she was putting these people in danger? Like poor Jack and Mr. Rafferty. The thought was a hard rock in her belly.

"What do you think?" Anita asked.

"Umm ..." She'd asked her a question. Rissa gripped her empty soda with both hands. "I'm sorry, I didn't sleep much last night and—"

Everyone chuckled.

Maggie gave her a conspiratorial grin. "We've all had sleepless nights. Wink-nod."

Did they mean ...?

"Oh." The flush that rushed to her cheeks would be a neon sign confirming their assumptions, only Burn hadn't slept in her bed last night.

"Don't overthink it." Anita threw an arm around her shoulders in a sideways hug. "The rest of you, stop picking on Rissa. She's new to our group, and I like her. Let's not scare her off when Burn's not even here."

Now, Rissa wanted to cry, but she didn't want to embarrass Burn in front of his friends. To Anita, she said, "I need to go inside for a minute. Would you mind watching Shelby until I get back?"

"We'll keep her safe."

Safe? Tears blurred Rissa's vision as she bolted through the sliding glass doors. Burn said his SEAL team was his family, and they were including her. She didn't understand how they could accept her. She was nothing special.

The living room was empty, so she quickly crossed to the short hallway containing the half-bath she'd brought Shelby to when they arrived. She locked the door and splashed water on her cheeks. Then she took a few steadying breaths while lecturing herself to pull it together. Burn would be here soon, and everything would be fine.

After drying off, she went in search of another soda. The sugar would help restore her equilibrium. But was the cooler on the deck or in the kitchen? Burn had handed her the first one, so she had no idea. She took a few steps toward the archway that connected to the kitchen but decided against snooping any further. It was best to go back outside.

"*Hola.*"

Rissa spun to find a middle-aged woman wearing an apron and standing at the edge of the hallway. The corners of her lips tipped up, but there was no welcome in her eyes.

"I wasn't snooping. I needed to use the restroom, but I'll go back outside now," Rissa stammered.

The woman clucked her tongue and stepped closer. "Wait. It's hot out. Let me get you something to drink. What would you like?" Her brown eyes met Rissa's, and her thick salt-and-pepper hair was secured in a tight knot at her nape.

Rissa licked her dry lips. "Do you have any more lemonade? I saw someone else drinking it."

"*Si*. Come, come. I'll pour you a nice, cold glass. I'm Nia." She motioned for Rissa to follow her.

"Are you family? Or part of the ... other group?" Rissa asked, moving farther into the spacious kitchen.

Nia barked a laugh as she opened the fridge. "None of those. My cousin works here, but she's been sick. I'm lending a hand. Have a seat at the counter. What's your name?"

Rissa didn't want to stay in the kitchen, but it seemed rude to leave now, so she leaned on the high counter instead of sitting. "I'm Marissa, but everyone calls me Rissa."

"And the tiny girl is your daughter? *Si*?"

"Yes." Rissa assumed the woman had seen her carrying Shelby earlier.

Nia placed a very full glass of lemonade on the counter. "Is her father here?"

Rissa bobbled the glass, nearly dropping it. "She's my daughter. I recently moved here." The way Nia's gaze sizzled with interest was unsettling. What did she care about Shelby? "Why do you ask?"

"I'm a bored old woman. Pay me no attention," she said, and began slicing some bright red tomatoes with a long, serrated knife.

Rissa's heart pitter-pattered, and she fought the urge to run from the room. Nia was acting very strangely. Or maybe she was a strange person. "I better go back outside."

Nia reached forward and grasped her wrist tightly. "No need to rush, *niña*. Please sit with me and I'll fix you something to eat."

Rissa didn't like the tight clasp of her fingers. It reminded her of another woman's long, manicured nails. Then relief made her lightheaded when she heard Burn's voice from the living room. "I hear my boyfriend. Thanks for the offer, but I should go."

CHAPTER 22

Burn was admiring Jackson, the newest family member, when a wide-eyed Rissa burst out of the kitchen and sprinted into his arms.

"Hey, beautiful." He was glad he hadn't demanded to hold his nephew because now he had an armful of a warm, welcoming woman.

"I'm so glad you're back," Rissa said breathlessly.

He was gratified that she'd missed him. "I was only gone an hour, but that's a nice welcome."

She pulled back, but not away. "Sorry ... I ..."

He cupped her cheek to catch her gaze. "Did you have a problem while I was gone?"

"No, but I need this," she said, winding her arms around his neck and leaning on her toes to kiss him.

That was an invitation that he wasn't going to turn down. He pulled her closer and slid his hand into the hair at her nape to slant his mouth more firmly over hers.

"Let's keep this PG. The baby is watching," said Clare, smirking at him from where she stood with Jackson on her shoulder.

Burn chuckled and gently tucked Rissa against his side. "Give us a break, Clare bear. We've been apart all afternoon."

"More like an hour, Bernie Cruz," Clare said, pointing a long finger at him. Then she shifted her gaze to Rissa. "Don't let him bully you."

Rissa straightened. "Burn wouldn't do that. He's kind, and I'm here because I want to be."

He liked that his little Texan was ready to come to his defense. "Easy, Tiger. My sister-in-law is an attorney and has strong opinions regarding male testosterone."

Clare arched a dark brow, "As long as everything is consensual and safe, I have no problem with it."

Burn chuckled. Their little PDA had probably already given Clare plenty of ammunition for the next family dinner lecture, but damned if he cared. "Rissa, this is my sister-in-law, Clare, and my nephew, Jackson. Clare, this beautiful woman is my *girlfriend*, Rissa Parker," He grinned at Rissa when he said girlfriend, wondering how she would react.

She didn't pull away or even look annoyed. *Okay then.*

"Hi," Rissa extended a hand to Clare.

At that moment, the baby began to fuss.

Clare snorted. "Jackson's timing is questionable. Sorry folks, I need to change him. Rissa, I'd love to talk if you'll find me outside," she said before hurrying away toward another part of the house.

Burn turned Rissa to face him, but this time she stepped back. "What? Are you mad I called you my girlfriend?"

"No ... not that. I need to check on Shelby. I left her outside with the other kids."

"She's okay. My friends are out there."

"Right," Rissa said, her lips trembling slightly. "They promised to keep her safe."

His heart clunked at the sheen of tears in her eyes. "Is this too many people for you? Do you want to leave?"

Her mouth opened, and he expected her to agree, but she shook her head. "Shelby is having fun, and everyone is great. It's me," Rissa said, looking across the room.

He followed her gaze. A Hispanic woman stood in the doorway leading to the kitchen. She held a glass of lemonade in one hand and a phone in the other. Burn automatically shifted to put his body slightly in front of Rissa. The hairs on his neck rose to attention. "Who are you?"

Her mouth stretched in a toothy grin. "*Hola.* I thought the young lady might want her lemonade. We were chatting in the kitchen earlier. I'm Nia," she drawled, crossing the room to extend the glass. "My cousin Marcia works here, but she broke her hip, and I'm covering while she is out."

That explained why he'd never met her. However, something about the woman put him on alert. He knew his brother, a DEA agent, would have vetted Nia before allowing her into his home. "I'm Paul's brother, Bernie." he said.

Rissa reached around him to accept the lemonade. "Thanks."

"You look like Mr. Paul," Nia said, tucking her phone in an apron pocket. "I should get back to work. When your brother gets the meat off the grill, he'll want the other things ready."

·   ·   ·

Terrance flipped through the stack of mail, and, finding nothing needing immediate attention, he tossed all of it on the end table beside his recliner. He picked up his drink and the television remote, but then his phone vibrated with a blocked caller ID on the screen. The ice in his glass clinked when he set it down to accept the call. "Hello?"

"I have news, *buen amigo.*" Juan Ravago's wheedling voice came through the speaker.

He wanted to point out that they weren't good friends or friends at all, but he got to the point. "Did you get the woman?"

"*Aún—no.* Not yet."

"Then why are you calling me?"

Juan snickered. "My news is interesting."

"Tell me," Terrance growled out.

"We've been watching the apartment building and attached a tracker to the boyfriend's truck. He took her, the roommate, and the child to the home of someone we've been monitoring."

Terrance was sick of trying to extract information from Juan. "This helps me how?"

"Relax. The good news is we have an ear inside the house. A housekeeper."

Settling into his recliner, Terrance said, "Let me understand. You followed them, and he went to a place you were already watching? If you're lying to me—"

"No, no. It's true. I replaced the housekeeper in the home of a DEA agent we haven't been able to compromise. Nia is loyal to me and useful in tracking the agent's movements. According to my housekeeper, the boyfriend is the agent's brother. She even snapped a photo of your target with the Navy SEAL."

"Send it to me," Terrance demanded.

"One moment," Juan said, clearly covering the phone to speak to someone else. "The boyfriend is called Bernie Cruz. Now tell me, do you want just the woman, or do you want the child also?"

"I want both."

Juan clicked his tongue. "Hmm. Now that we see the DEA is connected, it will be more complicated."

"I assume you mean more expensive. Tell me your price and get it done. I want them alive."

"It's a delicate balance. We'll get your woman, but it will take more time. My people can't be tied to this pickup."

Terrance's pulse hammered and his fingers dug into the arm of his recliner. "You say that, but you're already involved. Your guy was arrested at the woman's apartment."

"That fool won't talk. We have his family, and he'll rot in prison before risking them."

"I hate delays," Terrance said, thinking about his schedule. After the funeral, he'd have a small window of time. Perhaps he would handle the problem himself.

"You must understand, my—"

"I'm coming to San Diego," Terrance interrupted.

"*Que sorprendente.* Send me your flight times and I'll arrange for someone to pick you up at the airport. My home is in L.A., but I'll visit while you are in San Diego. It'll be good to see you, *mi amigo*, but ..."

"But what?"

"I can't bring you to where I'm staying, because the DEA watches me, same as I watch them. I don't want my name connected either, if you are linked with the girl later, *¿lo entiendes?*"

"Yes, yes, I understand. Give me a safe house to use."

"I will see—"

"No." Terrance grunted, sick of this man and his irritating voice. "Have somewhere ready, or the price of any product you get from me will triple."

Juan fell silent for a long moment. "I'll have a place."

"I fly out Tuesday," Terrance said. He'd leave after the funeral. And maybe after another visit from Doctor George.

"Very well. In the meantime, my people will watch for an opportunity. Perhaps, if they believe they are secure, something will change. Are you bringing anyone with you?"

Terrance preferred having his own backup, but given his current limited funds, he'd be flying commercial, and traveling with his security guys might attract more unwanted attention. "Not this time. Give me a few of your men who know the area."

"That will be done," Juan said.

Terrance ended the call and poured himself another drink. This occasion called for a celebration. His daughter and granddaughter had been found, and most likely, the child's father. Now he had more chess pieces on the table to play with.

CHAPTER 23

Rissa cringed at the irritation on Liesel's face. Everything had been going so well that she'd conveniently forgotten about promising to tell Burn everything.

They'd all had a wonderful time the previous day at Clare and Paul's house. When they returned, Burn had rushed outside to check on things, and Shelby had been exhausted. Rissa barely managed to get her in and out of the bath before she fell asleep. Burn hadn't returned inside till this morning when he'd woken her up with sweet kisses before leaving yet again.

"We talked about this. We spent the entire day together yesterday. How much time do you need to mention, 'Oh, by the way, Shelby is your kid?'" Liesel demanded.

Rissa removed her glasses to avoid seeing the disappointment in Liesel's eyes. "I can't tell him yet," she said, rubbing the lenses against the bottom of her shirt.

Folding her arms over her chest, Liesel scowled. "Why the heck not?"

She jammed on her glasses and crossed her arms. "For starters, he didn't stay inside long enough last night. As soon as we got back, he left to check the cameras. I only saw him for a few minutes this morning." When they'd been kissing.

"Please," Liesel said, resting her hands on Rissa's shoulders. "You need to do the right thing by that good man and by your daughter. She deserves to know him."

Rissa blinked back tears and sucked in a steadying breath. Liesel couldn't understand how difficult it was to trust someone completely. Her friend had never been deserted by people she loved. "I will tell him, in my own time."

The energy in Liesel deflated. "Please don't wait too long. He needs to hear it from you. Okay, that's settled," Liesel declared, pulling Rissa in for a quick hug. "By the way, my agent called a little while ago. That job I mentioned when you first got here came through. I'm going to L.A."

"What job?"

"Don't you remember? I told you I had something in the works when you called from the train. I'm leaving in a little while. Do you want something to eat?" she asked, walking toward the kitchen.

Rissa was accustomed to Liesel's rapid subject changes, but she wondered where this left her and Shelby. If Liesel was leaving, did they have to go as well?

"Mommy. Cartoons." Shelby patted her leg with a sticky hand.

"Sure, honey. Use your spoon for the cereal, okay?" Rissa clicked buttons, changing channels, but not to the right thing. She glanced toward the kitchen but didn't hear her friend in there. "Liesel?"

There was no answer. "Liesel?" she called louder.

Shelby chimed in. "Auntie Leee!"

"What?" Liesel poked her head out of the kitchen.

Rissa held up the remote. "Can you help me find cartoons?"

"Pleeeeease," Shelby added.

Liesel's expression softened, and she returned to scoop Shelby up in her arms. Propping the child on her hip, she took over the remote. "There you go, munchkin."

Shelby planted a smacking kiss on Liesel's cheek. "Tank you!"

"You're welcome," Liesel said, stretching away from the sticky fingers. "My stylist will have a fit if that stuff gets in my hair."

Rissa tugged Shelby away. "I'm sorry."

"Don't worry. I'll use dry shampoo or rewash it. What's she gotten into?"

"She poured her apple juice into her cereal." Rissa's gaze went to a wet spot on the couch cushion. "Oh no."

Liesel shrugged. "No biggie. Come into the kitchen. We can talk while I make coffee."

Rissa's chest tightened. Would Liesel tell her to leave? Her feet dragged as she followed behind her.

Liesel took a chair and pointed at the one opposite. "Now. Tell me the truth right now. Are you secretly planning to walk away from Burn when this is over?"

"No." Rissa shook her head vehemently. "I would never do that. I told you I'm going to tell him."

"I'm glad, because he's good for you both." Liesel tilted her head, her blue eyes intent. "There's something else we need to talk about. Those guys breaking in? It's not safe here right now."

"I'm sorry—"

"No," Liesel said, jumping up to retrieve coffee mugs. "The break-in wasn't your fault. I'm saying this place used to be my safe place and now it isn't," she said, slamming a cabinet shut.

"Are you angry?" Rissa asked.

Liesel pointed a finger at her. "Quit with the puppy-dog eyes. I'm not mad at you. I have to go to L.A. for work, and you are welcome to stay here. But maybe it isn't safe?"

"Burn will take care of us." Rissa was certain he'd do everything in his power to keep them safe.

"Fine. Stay here and consider this your home for as long as you want. When I go to Japan in a few weeks, you can be my house sitter." Liesel reached over the table to clasp Rissa's fingers. "Spend this time getting to know Burn. Have some grown-up fun."

•   •   •

Burn plugged in the final wire with a satisfied grunt. "Done. Now you have access to all three cameras. Toggling this switch enlarges the images."

"Impressive," Rafferty said. "You've covered the front, back, and hall by Ms. Zolan's apartment."

Was it enough? It would have to be for now. These were Style's only three cameras. They could get more from the base, but that would require a lot of red tape or outright theft. He'd work with what he had for now. "Listen, man, if you have any problems, anything hits your radar, you call me. Day or night."

Rafferty dipped his chin. "I'll be on alert. Now get some rest. You're dead on your feet."

Burn let slip an enormous yawn. He hadn't slept more than a few minutes in the last thirty-six hours. "I could use a couple of hours. Who is that?"

A silver Lincoln had pulled to the curb outside the glass doors. The man who emerged from the back wore an aqua blue fitted suit. He took a minute to straighten his jacket and smooth his blond hair in the reflective windows, then he charged toward the entrance.

Rafferty rose to greet him. "Can I help you?"

The man paused, his lips tilting up in a practiced smile. "Call Liesel Zolan for me. She isn't answering her cell."

Rafferty set his shoulders back and swept his gaze over the man. "If you'll give me your name, I'll check if she wants to see you."

The fake smile disappeared, and lips flattened. "Tell her Todd Krug is here to pick her up. Get her on the phone."

Rafferty glanced at Burn before reaching for his handset.

Burn noticed motion on the upstairs camera and tapped Rafferty's arm. "Might not need to call." He indicated the image on the screen. Liesel was exiting the apartment with a small duffel over her shoulder. The cameras were visual only, so he couldn't hear what Liesel was saying to Rissa.

Todd leaned over the counter. "What are you looking at? I'm on a schedule here."

"She's on her way," Rafferty said, crossing his arms and glaring at the smaller man.

"What do you want with her?" Burn asked.

"Not that it's your business, but I'm her agent."

"You do realize you could be putting her in harm's way by taking her out of here?"

Todd pulled out his phone. "She'll be fine with me. No one knows where we're going."

The elevator opened, and Liesel stepped out. "Good morning. I guess Todd told you I had a job out of town. I'll be back in a few days."

"Morning, ma'am," Rafferty said.

Todd tapped his watch. "Let's get out of here," he said, walking back outside without bothering to hold the door for Liesel.

She paused by the desk. "Burn, will you tell Styles I hope to see him when I return?"

"He'll be glad to hear that."

After Liesel left, Rafferty plopped back into his chair.

Burn stretched. "I'll leave you to it. Call if you have problems. My buddy is on the street keeping watch."

"Good friends you got there."

"They're my team." *And my family.*

CHAPTER 24

Rissa's phone vibrated, and the display showed a message from Burn.

Be there in five.

When she heard the key in the lock, she rushed to greet him. "Is something wrong?"

"No. Everything's good," he said, re-locking the deadbolt. "I need something to eat and a couple of hours of sleep. Then I'll be good."

She was glad he was back. The apartment felt more secure with him in it and besides, she was ready to tell him everything. "Liesel left for a job," she blurted.

"I saw." Burn squinted at her. "Something wrong?"

Rissa returned to the couch and sat heavily on one end. On the other side, Shelby dozed in front of the television. "Liesel had a job, but she also said she didn't feel safe here anymore." She hated that her voice faltered. "It's my fault for bringing the trouble to her doorstep."

He crouched at her knees. "We'll get through this. You can depend on me not to let you down."

She sniffed. "Thank you. We need to talk about something—"

"Sit with me," he said, settling on the couch and dragging her half over his lap in a tight hug, his arms wound firmly around her. He buried his face in her hair and sighed in contentment. "I'm starting to love this couch."

She breathed in his scent. It felt so good to have him hold her, but guilt pricked at her conscience. He deserved the truth. "I need to tell you something," she murmured, trying to push away, but he tightened his hold.

He yawned. "Give me a minute." His body went lax when he exhaled the next long breath.

She stroked the front of his shirt. "It's important," she said, her throat tight.

"Sure, honey. I'm listening," he said, but then his cell buzzed, and he jerked upright to get it out of his back pocket. "It's my CO. I've got to take this."

"Sure, okay."

He answered the call and walked over to peer out the window, murmuring in low tones.

Rissa rose and kicked herself all the way to the kitchen. She'd been so close to telling him about Shelby. As soon as he got off the phone, she would do it. Come clean.

He'd said he wanted food, so she decided to fix something for him to eat. She opened the fridge and stared at the sparse shelves. They'd need to make another run to the store. Liesel and Styles had brought milk and cereal for Shelby, but not much else. Someone had finished off the pizza leftovers.

"Anything to eat in there?" Burn wrapped his arms around her from behind and kissed her neck.

She giggled and grabbed a mostly empty package of deli-sliced turkey from the shelf. "We have bread and this turkey. We need things from the store."

He kissed her cheek and brushed his lips over her ear affectionately. "Styles and Liesel must've finished the lettuce and tomatoes. I've got to go to the base for a few hours tomorrow. I can pick up some groceries after that."

"I thought you had time off," she replied, wondering why he sounded so irritated.

"This is different. I have to handle someone else's problem because they lied to me."

"They lied? What—what did they lie about?" Rissa stammered.

"Not your problem." He reached around, shut the fridge door, and took the turkey from her. Turning to the counter, he opened the loaf of bread. "You should know that nothing will set me off quicker than dishonesty. Tell me if I do something you don't like. I'm a hard-headed SOB, and I'll piss you off at some point. Let me know, and I'll respect your boundaries—but don't lie to me."

Her mouth opened and closed like a catfish thrown on the dock.

He had his back to her as he continued. "You'll be safe while I'm gone. Cam, or someone else, will hang here with you."

"You don't have to do that. We have Mr. Rafferty in the lobby and the cameras." Rissa wrapped her arms around her middle, watching as he loaded the few remaining slices of turkey on the dry wheat bread. She retrieved mustard and mayo from the fridge and placed them on the counter. "You've done so much for us. I hate to be more trouble."

He shook his head as he slathered on the mustard. "It's no trouble. You and Shelby mean a great deal to me."

"We do?" Her heart thumped erratically.

"Yes," he said, angling toward her. "I don't know what it is about you, but in almost three years, I've never stopped thinking of you, Rissa Parker." His fingers trailed over her cheek. "I care for you. Probably more than you're ready to hear right now." He craned his neck toward the living room.

"Are you looking for Shelby? I don't think she'll sleep long. She'll want lunch or a snack soon."

"But not right now," he said, shifting closer. "I'm happy Liesel gave us the place to ourselves."

The kiss that followed was barely there, making her ache for more. "Burn ..." She tilted her head for him to trail a line of kisses down her neck.

"Could we share one bedroom tonight? With Shelby in the other one?" Burn asked, fastening his gaze on her.

"Yes," she said, desire coiling in her belly. "That would be nice."

"Nice?" He stroked a hand over her back. "I need to work on my moves if all I've got is nice."

She loved being with this man. If a relationship involved laughing and holding each other, she wanted more. But wasn't that stupid? He wouldn't want her when he found out the truth.

"Rissa, did you hear me?"

"I'm sorry, what?"

He paused, his golden eyes inches from hers. "I'm falling in love with you."

She jerked out of his arms, bumping her back against the refrigerator. "Don't say that."

"Why not?" The hurt and confusion on his face were easy to read.

"You can't." Her heart thundered in her chest.

"I can. I didn't ask you to return the sentiment, although I hope that one day you will," he said, reaching for her again.

She sidestepped because letting him touch her right now would muddle her brain. "You don't know me. Maybe you don't want to know me."

He went still, his gaze intent. "Tell me what I don't know."

Could she bolt to the other room or say that Shelby needed her? He loved her. That was crazy. Worse, did she love him? That was a dumb question. Of course, she loved him. She'd loved him since their first dance and seeing him in their little girl every day only made her love him more.

He held up his palms and retreated to lean his butt against the counter. "No pressure. It's the truth, that's all."

She twined her arms around herself. "I'm sorry."

"Don't apologize." His eyes crinkled at the corners. "How about this? I'll make my rounds and check in with Cam. After that, I can pick up something for lunch for us from that Chinese restaurant on the corner. Will Shelby eat that?"

"Yes. She loves rice and chicken. There's a menu on the fridge." She hesitated. "But you fixed a sandwich and said you wanted to take a nap."

"The nap can wait. And I'll eat the sandwich," he said, rolling one shoulder, then the other. "It'll be my appetizer."

Liesel had told her to trust her heart, and her heart loved this man. It wasn't the right time to tell him that, not until she told him about his daughter, but it was true all the same. "Thank you," she whispered.

•   •   •

Three hours later, she was searching for a new cartoon on the television and considering a bowl of Shelby's cereal. Where was Burn? Something might've happened to him. Should she go down and check? She didn't want to text him constantly, but it wouldn't hurt to send one more message. The door opened at the same time as she pulled out her phone.

"What took so long?" She wanted to be cool, but it was hard to be the one waiting for things to happen and unable to do anything.

"When I got downstairs, a camera was out, and it took time to fix. But lunch is here," he said, holding up a large brown takeout bag. He held a white plastic bag in his other hand. "I also picked up cereal cups and milk from the newsstand."

Burn went out again after they ate, leaving her to keep a restless toddler occupied all afternoon. He didn't return for dinner, and Rissa let Shelby eat the rest of the rice before putting her to bed in the guest room.

After that, she settled on the couch to wait for him.

CHAPTER 25

Early morning light streamed into the bedroom through slightly parted curtains. Rissa couldn't make out the time on the clock without her glasses, but knew Shelby would wake soon, and she didn't want to be caught naked in Burn's bed. He'd gotten in late the night before and scooped her off the couch. Her intentions had been good, but they never got around to talking because she had been caught up in all the things he was doing to her.

She had to reposition his arm before sliding onto the side of the bed. The mattress dipped as she stood, and his eyes popped open.

"Time to get up?" he asked, his voice husky with sleep.

She leaned over to press a kiss to his cheek. "Not yet. It's early. Go back to sleep," she whispered, then patted around on the nightstand to locate the plastic edge of her glasses. Finally, she could make out the numbers on the digital clock—it was after seven.

"Hurry back," Burn said, stretching and folding his arms behind his head.

She opened her mouth to respond, but his eyes had closed again. Getting back into bed wasn't an option. She needed to shower before Shelby woke. In Liesel's bathroom, she found a robe and searched the drawers for a hairbrush.

Last night had been incredible. She traced a finger over her swollen lips, and her tummy did a little shimmy as she thought about all the ways he'd used his mouth on her. He'd been tender and passionate, exploring every inch of her. Burn had said he loved her. The only people in her life who truly loved her were Shelby and Liesel. Of course, he'd only said it once and could've been saying what he thought she wanted to hear.

Rissa puffed out a breath. What did she know about love? She'd only dated a few guys after high school and never long enough to fall in love. Post-Shelby, she'd spent all her time in survival mode with no time for romance. Burn's sense of humor and loyalty to his team and family made her long to be included in the list of people important to him. The list of people he loved.

In the movies, love was instant and effortless, but it wasn't easy in real life. She couldn't afford to make a mistake, not when Shelby was involved. Besides, he might permanently kick her out of his life when the truth was revealed. In that aspect, she was screwed, and not in the good way of last night.

Time to be a mom. She flicked off the light so as not to wake Burn before tiptoeing to the door. He lay in the same position, so she slipped across the hall to the room she shared with Shelby. Her daughter slept curled in a ball in the center of the pallet. Good. She still had time to shower.

Twenty minutes later, clean and refreshed, Rissa exited the bathroom to find an empty bedroom with a wide-open door. Crap. Her daughter was curious. No telling what she'd gotten into.

Rissa rushed through the kitchen, drawing up short at the sound of Burn's rumbling laugh and her daughter's high-pitched giggles. She peeked around the corner to find Shelby hunched over something on the coffee table. Burn sat on the sofa behind her, meticulously dividing her curls into high ponytails.

He's fixing her hair.

She must've made a sound because Burn glanced up.

"Join us." He motioned her forward with his head.

Her brain had trouble absorbing this scene. Shelby had on clean shorts and a Barbie T-shirt and Burn was braiding her hair while she played with a nesting doll on the coffee table. "You know how to braid hair?"

"One of my superpowers. But don't be impressed. I have two nieces, and I babysit for them sometimes. They are great kids, but you know ... There can be hair emergencies, and a man has to be prepared."

"Navy SEAL, babysitter, and hairdresser. What can't you do?"

His face split in a wide smile. "Don't tell the guys about the hairdresser thing, but feel free to be awed."

"Your secret is safe," she said, kneeling on the floor by her daughter.

"Mommy." Shelby blew her a kiss.

"You dressed her too. Thank you." Rissa turned to peer up at him. "How about breakfast? There aren't any more eggs, but we have protein cookies."

"Crunch, Mommy."

"Crunch cereal, I know." Rissa pushed to her feet. "She loves those cereal cups you picked up at the newsstand. Do you want coffee?"

"Coffee sounds good."

"Okay." She puffed a breath and continued, "Burn ..."

He arched a brow over those amazing golden eyes. "Yes?"

She twisted her fingers together, stumbling over the words. "Before I came here ... I had no one to help with Shelby. Not unless I paid them."

A smile spread slowly over his face. "I'm exactly where I want to be, and I'll stay for as long as you let me."

"Thank you."

He shrugged and finished putting three little braids in the second ponytail. "I found your package of hair ties but didn't see any beads. The sides might not be level, but it'll at least keep the hair out of her eyes. She did well this morning. Went potty and brushed her teeth."

Shelby whipped her head around to shine her teeth at Rissa.

"Good job, baby girl."

"Play Mommy?" Shelby held out the nesting doll.

"Don't you want cereal?"

The toddler clapped two halves of the wooden doll together. "Play."

Burn unfurled to standing. "You stay with her. I'll start the coffee brewing and jump in the shower. Then I'll bring breakfast in here to you guys. Actually ... hang on. I've got an idea." He disappeared into the kitchen and returned with a handful of metal measuring cups. "Stacking these will occupy her for a few minutes if she tires of the wooden doll."

"You're amazing." Rissa beamed at him.

"Secure that thought in your head." He rested his hands at her waist and brushed a kiss over her lips. "Back in ten."

While he showered, she helped Shelby stack and re-stack the doll and the metal cups. Her stomach growled, but nothing in the kitchen sounded enticing. Rissa moved up to the couch and turned on cartoons for Shelby. Liesel had a few romance novels and mysteries on the bookshelf in the bedroom, but she didn't have the energy to search for one. Maybe Burn would let them order DoorDash.

Burn emerged wearing a fresh pair of cargo pants and a clean blue T-shirt. "How are my girls?"

Her heart leaped and wasn't that silly? He'd only been gone a few minutes. "We could order something to eat. I have money."

Burn plopped down and tugged her against him. "If we eat cereal now, we could walk to the ice cream parlor later this morning. They open at ten-thirty."

"Really? Where is it?" She straightened.

"It's only a couple of blocks away. You guys can stretch your legs, and we'll pass that newsstand I went to before. Pick up more cereal on the way back."

"Shelby would like to go out. We both would. If it's safe."

He lifted a hand to smooth his thumb over her cheek. "I won't let anything happen to you. Not today, not ever."

A jumble of emotions overwhelmed her—affection, guilt, and fear—all of them weighed on her mind. She pushed his hand away and slid over on the cushion. "You say that, but what happens when you leave? You won't always be with us."

Shelby patted his knees. "Up. Up."

Eyes glued to Rissa, he settled Shelby onto his lap. "Where'd that come from? I'm here, Rissa, and I don't plan to go anywhere. If I have to leave for work, I'll have someone watching over you."

"You're here now," she said softly, pressing her lips together, not sure what to do with the hot burn of her temper. Rissa knew she was being unreasonable, but she couldn't help it. He wouldn't be here forever. When it really counted, had anyone ever stood by her?

"What did I say?"

She rose and shook her head. "Nothing. It's okay. There are two cereal cups left for you and Shelby. I'll wait for ice cream."

"Mommy?" Shelby's eyes were round green orbs.

"It's fine, Shelby. Watch your cartoons. I need some coffee, then I'll bring you crunch cereal," she said, rushing into the kitchen.

She headed straight for the sink and splashed some water on her face. Every time she needed help, her best friend Liesel had sent her money, but she'd always had to ask. When she found out she was pregnant, Liesel hadn't dropped everything to come and help, and Rissa understood that. She hadn't expected her to, but oh, how she'd longed for someone, anyone, to care about what she was going through.

Burn was offering that, and it scared her. She was accustomed to solitude, self-reliance, and taking care of her daughter, Burn's daughter. Things were changing too fast. Was she ready? Burn was here, and he hadn't asked for anything. Still, there might come a day when he would ask for Shelby.

She filled a tall mug with hot coffee and added sugar-free, fat-free creamer. The creamer smelled much better than it tasted. Leaning back against the counter, she closed her eyes and sipped the coffee.

"You should eat something," Burn said from the doorway.

Since her stomach was currently doing the mambo, that wasn't a good idea. "I'll have one of those protein cookies."

He came toward her, and when she sidestepped his embrace, he asked, "What did I do?"

"Not anything. It's not you. I'm stressed. Here," she said, setting down her coffee and offering him the crunch cereal cups. "There's a little milk left. You go ahead and take it to Shelby. I need to plug in my phone."

"Call out if you need me." He took the plastic tubs and half-gallon container and returned to the living room.

Something like grief rushed over her, and she had to cover her face with her hands to prevent a sob from escaping. Now was not the time to fall apart. She had come to California seeking help from her friend and her baby's father, yet she hadn't anticipated the emotional toll it would take. Burn had missed the first part of his daughter's life, and now that he was here, she craved his presence not only for Shelby but also for herself. It was unfair to him, but if she revealed herself now and he withdrew, stopping his desire, his touch, and his closeness, her heart would shatter. She didn't think she could put it back together again.

Rissa inhaled sharply through her nose and grabbed the box of protein cookies. She opened one, broke it in half, and tossed one piece into the trash before picking up her coffee and heading into the living room. There, she found Shelby nestled in Burn's lap, engrossed in cartoons.

"Shelby, sit on the floor and let Burn eat his cereal."

"Me!" Shelby wiggled down to get to her bowl.

"Don't worry. I won't eat yours, princess." Chuckling, Burn picked up his plastic cereal cup.

Rissa could tell by the rattling sound it made that he'd given Shelby all the milk. She raised the half cookie, took a tiny nibble off the edge, and chewed enthusiastically. "I'm having one of these."

His lips quirked. "I've had worse than those things, but they're not good."

"It's sufficient." She tossed the cookie on the table and sat, tucking her feet under her. "Sorry about earlier. I'm stressed and stir-crazy." Definitely a little crazy.

He shrugged. "Understandable. It'll be good to go outside, if only for a few minutes. I need to make some calls first, and we'll go after that."

She relaxed into the couch and sipped her coffee. Going outside should scare her, but with Burn they'd be safe. In less than three minutes, she'd switched from furious to sad to ridiculously excited about walking in the sunshine. Yep. She was losing her mind.

CHAPTER 26

An hour later, while Burn made his calls, Rissa browsed Liesel's bookshelf and picked out the newest steamy military romance by J.M. Madden. Back home, she'd had to wait until the good books reached the library, but Liesel had all the newest releases.

Everything that had happened this past week had been awful, but Rissa was thankful to be in San Diego, in this apartment and safe with someone she cared about, with Burn.

Had Mrs. G. figured out they were gone? She had mentioned going to her daughter's house for Labor Day, so she wouldn't look for Rissa and Shelby until after their family gathering. But since today was Tuesday, Mrs. G. was likely home again and she'd be expecting to watch Shelby tonight. Rissa needed to call and tell her she was out of town and also warn her to avoid her apartment. In case Mrs. Iglesias's son showed up there.

Burn returned to the living room. "Officer Dalton checked in, nothing new to report, but he wants to set a time for you to come to the station for a statement."

She swallowed hard. "But we told—"

"About San Antonio."

"Okay, sure."

"He said he'll call us, but likely not before tomorrow. I'm going to check with the front desk. Rafferty is off today, and a new woman is down there. I'll make sure we're good and come back to get you guys."

"We'll be ready." Rissa placed the paperback on the coffee table and clambered to her feet.

"Ready?" Shelby asked hopefully from her seat on the couch.

Rissa lifted her. "First, let's wash your hands. Burn is taking us to get ice cream. Doesn't that sound fun?"

"Me!" Shelby chortled and patted Rissa's cheeks with both little hands. "Choco-late?"

Rissa's heart melted, and she glanced at Burn. He was staring at his phone with a scowl on his face. "Is everything alright?"

"Yes. Styles is on the street," he said, and then shrugged. "I'm covering all the bases."

"But we can still go, right?"

"We can. I'll be back in ten to ride downstairs with you."

Perfect. Better wash Shelby's hands and face before he changes his mind. They'd been snugged up in the apartment for too long. The only day they'd gone out was the team barbecue on Sunday, and not only was she not used to all this inactivity, but Shelby didn't have much to play with in the apartment.

The newsstand might have a toy or something. Rissa grabbed her small wallet and tucked it into her pocket. Less than five minutes later, she had Shelby's hands and face clean of the sticky cereal. When they returned to the living room, Burn waited for them by the front door, phone in hand.

"Choco-late," repeated Shelby, rushing over to wrap her arms around Burn's leg.

Rissa's lips tilted at the corners. "You know she had sugar cereal last night and this morning, and now ice cream. We need to get her some real food."

"We will," he reassured her as they headed out of the apartment. "For all of us."

"What time do you have to leave for the base?"

His brows bunched together. "As soon as we get back. It's a training exercise, so I can't say when I'll be done. Could be late."

Rissa nodded, latching on to another excuse to wait to tell him about Shelby. What was a few more hours? She glanced up to find him watching her. "What is it?"

"I need you to promise to stay inside while I'm gone."

"Why would you say that? I know we have to stay inside."

He cupped her chin, drilling his gaze into her. "Your word?"

"Yes," she said, throwing out her arms and stepping back. "We'll stay inside till it's safe. Now let's get that ice cream."

"Up! Up!" Shelby demanded, her arms raised.

He picked her up with one arm while texting with his free hand. Rissa assumed he texted his guy outside. Had he said Styles was out there?

After exiting the apartment, Shelby demanded to be put down and raced ahead to mash the elevator button. Burn tucked away his phone and reached for Rissa's hand.

They shared a smile, and her stupid heart thrummed in her chest.

"Go!" Shelby shouted, racing back to them, hyper as a new puppy, and tried to swing from their joined fingers.

The new lady was behind the desk in the lobby, but Rafferty stood beside her wearing a sling on his injured arm.

"Good morning, Chief. Ms. Parker."

"Mr. Rafferty. I thought you had a few days off," Rissa said.

Rafferty blew out a breath and grinned.

Burn chuckled. "Yeah, I told him earlier that his doctor better not catch him at work."

"I'm only here a couple hours. This is Jeannette and it's her first day, so I dropped in to check on her."

"Nice to meet you," Rissa said.

"You too," The pretty, middle-aged brunette gave her a friendly smile.

Shelby bounced around them, pointing at the door. "Go."

"Hey, Shelby," Rafferty said, raising a brow at Burn. "Are you taking them outside?"

"Ice cream." Shelby giggled and pointed at the door again.

"Be patient, honey. We'll go in a minute. How's your arm, Mr. Rafferty?" Rissa asked.

"Healing well, ma'am. I'll be out of this thing in a few days," he said, although his focus was on Burn.

"We won't be gone long. They need to stretch their legs," said Burn.

Rafferty frowned. "Stay sharp."

"Always." Burn reached for Rissa, but Shelby was already between them, tucking her hands in both of theirs.

"Swing!" Shelby demanded as they stepped into the sunshine.

The sky was cloudless, and the sun shone bright, knocking away the chill of the spring night. Enjoying the warmth, Rissa tilted her face to the sun. "This is so nice."

"Jimbo's Creamery is a block and a half away. Let's get going," Burn said, his eyes scanning the street in both directions.

His attention wasn't on her, so Rissa didn't speak, just fell in step beside him, Shelby swinging between them all the way down the block. Jimbo's Creamery was a glass-fronted ice cream shop with dark, tinted windows.

Burn swung the door wide, and cold air blasted out. The rich aroma of baking waffle cones had Rissa's mouth watering. Shelby darted straight past the four round tables to a long glass counter filled with tubs of ice cream.

"Choco-late! Up!" Shelby demanded, throwing up her arms to Burn, and he immediately obliged. He held her against the glass to examine all the flavors, and with Rissa's help, Shelby eventually chose a smooth, soft-serve chocolate yogurt cup with colorful sprinkles.

Rissa chose a chocolate-dipped waffle cone with a whole banana and a scoop of vanilla ice cream. Burn picked strawberry sherbet in a cup with fresh-cut strawberries on top.

"I can pay for this," Rissa said, pulling out her wallet.

Burn held out a twenty to the cashier. "This is my treat, and I think Shelby needs a hand over there."

She spun to find her daughter climbing onto a stool at a tall table with her ice cream precariously balanced in her little hands. By the time Rissa had her situated and claimed the stool beside her, Burn had joined them. He dragged a third seat to Shelby's other side so all three of them faced the entrance.

He hummed in appreciation after his first bite. "This is good. We should get a to-go carton and take it back with us."

Rissa broke off a piece of waffle cone to use as a spoon with her ice cream. "It's delicious, but we need healthy food, too."

"Choco-late," Shelby chimed in, her face and shirt now sporting dribbles of the sweet treat.

Rissa laughed at her happy child. Who cared about the mess? She could wash the clothes later, and Shelby had been good these last few days. Tomorrow would be one week since their whole lives had been uprooted. Wasn't that a sobering thought? She had no idea what the future held or how much longer they would be forced to hide out in Liesel's apartment. "Burn?" She cut off a piece of banana and offered it to Shelby.

"Yeah?"

"Thank you for bringing us here. We needed an outside break."

His mouth flattened, and he dropped his chin. "Wish I could take you to the base with me, but I'll be doing the training exercise, and I can't leave you to wander around. I'm sorry. It's best if you stay at the apartment while I'm gone."

"No, it's fine. We'll manage." She had to learn to exist without him at some point.

"Me?" Shelby held a drippy spoon toward Burn's cup of sherbet.

"You want to try mine?" he asked, immediately lowering it to the table.

She gave him a toothy grin, dug out a strawberry, and carefully transferred it to her cup of chocolate.

Rissa laughed. "Glad you don't mind a little slobber with your ice cream. You spoil her."

He winked and continued eating. Shelby was the last to finish, and Rissa mopped her hands and face as best she could with the dry napkins. When they stepped outside, Shelby tried to tug her hands free.

"Me run?" Shelby asked.

Rissa glanced at Burn, and he shook his head. She knelt beside her daughter. "Not right now, Shelby. But I have a good idea. We're going by a store and maybe we can find you a toy. What do you think?"

"Me!" Shelby hopped and clung to Burn's hand, lifting her feet to dangle off the ground. "S'wing," she demanded.

Burn was texting with one hand again, his eyes flicking up the street and over his shoulder.

"Everything okay?"

"Yes," he said, leaning in to brush his lips over hers as he tucked away his phone. "I was checking in with Styles. Nothing to worry about."

"Do you think I'm wrong?"

"About what?"

"About thinking we're in danger?" Her heart clunked in her chest as she waited for his reply.

"I'd rather be careful until we're certain who those gang members were after. You're safe with me, Rissa."

CHAPTER 27

Terrance winced as he shifted his weight on the SUV's leather seat. His gunshot wound wasn't healing. Perhaps he simply needed a more competent physician, and if his associate, Juan Ravago, had bothered to greet him, he could've arranged better medical care.

Ravago had insisted the DEA was watching him. Yet he proposed solving Terrance's problem with a sharpshooter, a solution he couldn't accept, seeing as his entire future hinged on keeping Marissa Parker alive, all because of his damn stepmother. Clenching his fists, he harbored a vengeful desire to grip Amelia's throat again, this time prolonging her agony before ending her.

The burly man in the passenger seat turned his head and pointed toward a mirrored high-rise apartment building. "This is the place."

"Drive past and then come back this way. If you see an opening, park on the street," Terrance ordered, exhaling slowly as he observed the building.

The intriguing piece of this puzzle was his daughter. Why hadn't she gone to the police? Was she hiding something? His lips curled at the thought of how differently things might have turned out if he'd known about the will. If he'd had that information, he could've framed her for the murder. Problem solved. He could've managed her fortune while she rotted in jail.

Walt, the SUV's driver, said, "There might not be any place good—"

"We won't stay long," Terrance interrupted. "I need to see the building."

Walt grunted acknowledgment.

The other man texted someone.

Terrance straightened his jacket before folding his hands in his lap. He didn't care who the fuck was on the other end of the phone. This was his target, and he was in charge. Things would've been easier if he'd brought his own men from Texas. But this was Ravago's territory, and his men were locals. It made sense to utilize the tools available.

After a short distance, Walt pulled into an office parking lot. He circled around and emerged the opposite way, remaining in the right lane until he merged behind a line of cars parked by meters a couple of blocks from the apartment.

"Put some money in," Terrance ordered the larger man.

"We don't need to be seen around here. The boss won't like it," he grumbled.

Heedless of his injury, Terrance leaned forward to clasp the big man's shoulder at the base of his neck. "Shut your trap. I'm your fucking boss right now," he hissed before reclining again, his agony matching his simmering anger. How dare this fool question his authority?

Walt cleared his throat and glanced over his shoulder. "Sorry, sir. Grant wasn't arguing. Mr. Ravago doesn't want our faces caught on camera. Be quick, Grant. Pull your cap down," Walt directed.

Grant cursed under his breath but added a quarter to the meter before climbing back in the SUV. "We have ten minutes."

There wasn't much of anything to see. People on the street and no one entering or exiting the glass-fronted building. "I've seen enough," Terrance said.

"Fuck me," breathed Grant.

"What?" Walt demanded.

"Over there. Isn't that your girl?" Grant tapped a knuckle on his window.

Terrance shifted his gaze toward what had caught Grant's attention, scarcely believing his eyes. Marissa Parker held a giggling toddler beneath a pink sign for Jimbo's Creamery, an ice cream store. He reached for the door handle but stopped himself.

"They're not alone." Walt tapped the window again.

Grant shot Terrance a meaningful look and stated the obvious. "Sitting here is suspicious. We need to go before we draw attention."

The idiot was right. Terrance's gaze fixed on the man who'd joined Rissa on the sidewalk, and he took a photo with his phone. The man's gaze appeared fixed on the SUV, but he wore very dark sunglasses, so it was hard to tell. "Get us out of here."

Their SUV slowly pulled away from the curb and into the crawling traffic. As Marissa Parker and her SEAL ambled up the sidewalk, Terrance watched the little girl swing between them.

"It's fine. He's looking this way, but no way can he see through the tint on the back windows. The front isn't as dark, so smile at me, Grant." Walt gave Grant a wide grin and exaggerated nod. "No one will ever recognize you with a friendly expression."

"I'd rather punch your face." Despite his tone, Grant's mouth twisted in a caricature of a smile as they passed the trio.

Terrance twisted to catch another glimpse of his adversary, and the movement made him grunt in pain. The boyfriend was a tall, well-muscled man with a square jaw and short hair. He looked different in sunlight than in the photo the housekeeper had provided, but at least his daughter had good taste. Terrance hoped his granddaughter would be just as attractive.

The errand had been productive. He'd glimpsed his quarry and had her location. Still, as long as she remained free, there was a chance she'd go to the authorities. The best option was removing her from the gameboard and taking her back to Texas.

His head throbbed as he rubbed his temples, yearning for a drink. He wasn't willing to expose his relationship with the girl to Ravago, and because of that, he couldn't ask him for help with transportation. He'd have to come up with another plan. And what if Marissa left the apartment and relocated? He'd have to find her all over again.

"Does Ravago have men watching the building around the clock?" he asked.

Grant pulled out his phone. "I'll text the boss. We ending her?"

"No," Terrance snapped, his fingers digging into the armrest. "I need to know if she leaves the apartment for any reason."

"Understood," Grant muttered.

Terrance had more pain pills stashed in his suitcase but hadn't wanted to carry them on the plane. Rick should've taken time off and come along. He'd call him later when he didn't have these two listening in on their conversation. If Ravago found out everything at stake, he might try to leverage the girl against him.

The large man turned to him. What was his name again?

"No one's here now, but the boss is sending backup. He wants to meet you for lunch." He addressed Walt. "You're staying here till someone arrives. I'll drive him to Mr. Ravago."

The driver scowled as he pulled onto an off-ramp to circle back. "Fine, but if she drives away, there won't be much I can do on foot."

CHAPTER 28

Rissa strolled along the sidewalk beside Burn, enjoying Shelby's mostly gibberish monologue. The scent of hot pretzels wafted from a nearby food cart, mingling with the smell of car exhaust and cigarettes. She stole a glance Burn's way, and the heat in his eyes set her insides on fire.

"What are you thinking?" he asked when they paused inside the newsstand.

A ribbon of desire twirled in her belly. "I'll tell you later. Right now ... look, they have toys!" Rissa scooped up a few Matchbox cars and a small package of plastic dinosaurs and held them aloft. "Score."

"She likes dinosaurs?" Burn asked.

"Everyone likes dinosaurs."

"Birthday, Mommy," Shelby said.

Rissa's heart sank. They had been to the zoo to celebrate Shelby's birthday. They'd all had dino-themed ice cream, and she'd played on a prehistoric playground.

"What does she mean?" Burn asked. Fortunately, his eyes were trained on the street, and he didn't see the dismay on Rissa's face.

She'd lied about Shelby's age, and her daughter was on the verge of giving her away. "We went to a dino ice cream place at the zoo, and someone was having a birthday," Rissa said lamely.

Burn didn't press the issue. "What else do you want for her? We need to go."

Relieved he hadn't caught on, she handed Shelby a package of cars and picked up bread, cheese, and some other essentials. "They don't have any pull-ups."

"The night pants?" Burn asked.

"Yeah."

"I'll get some later today and bring them back." He steered them to the checkout.

Outside, Burn lifted Shelby, still holding her bag of little toys and quickened their pace to the apartment. Rafferty was still behind Jeannette at the desk, and Burn reassured him he'd be back down in a few minutes. Upstairs, Shelby dashed to the couch with her new toys.

Rissa carried the milk to the kitchen, and Burn followed with the rest. He swung the fridge door wide to put all the cold stuff inside, then he turned to her.

"It's time for me to head to base, but I'll return as soon as possible." He ran a hand through his hair, clearly troubled by having to leave.

"It's alright," she said.

He slid his fingers down her arms to clasp her fingers. "Promise me you won't leave the apartment while I'm gone."

"I already did when you asked me before, but I promise. We'll be fine." Rissa pulled her hands free and stuffed them into her pockets. Burn wouldn't always be around, and she needed to protect herself from getting too attached. "You can come back tomorrow if you have things to do."

He leaned his butt against the counter and drew her against his warm chest. "I don't want to leave. The thought of being away from you twists me in knots. And it isn't about whatever is happening out there," he gestured vaguely. "I'm all in with you, Rissa Parker, and it's tough to leave you here because I love you."

She was so caught up in her pity party that she had trouble taking in his words. "You need to stop saying that. We're in a difficult situation, and maybe when this is over—"

"I've never said those words to another woman. Only you." He tried to tug her closer, and she pressed her palms against his chest.

"Don't—"

He immediately released her. "Don't what?"

"It's time for you to leave. For the base, I mean." She hid her trembling fingers behind her back.

"We'll talk when I return," he said, never taking his eyes off her.

Desperate to put some distance between them and protect her heart, she replied, "Don't worry about us. We'll be fine. You've put your life on hold for us, and now you can stop. You set up the cameras, and I'm sure the police are looking into everything. Shelby and I will manage. You should get back to your own life and leave us here."

The two of us—the way it's always been—we don't need anyone else. Like her parents, he'd leave once he discovered she was a nobody.

And I'm a liar, so he has a reason to leave me.

·   ·   ·

A few hours later, Burn walked out of the team's briefing room to pick up his dive gear. He was still simmering with anger from Rissa's announcement. He needed to convince her he wasn't going anywhere. The problem was, too many people had let her down. For right now, he'd done all he could to ensure her safety, but guilt at leaving her ate at him.

This training obligation was important, and he'd committed to it a month ago. Without enough hands on deck, newbies could get hurt, and injuries could be critical.

He greeted a few people while making his way to his team's lockers. Rissa had told him to get back to his life, and he'd bet his specialized breathing apparatus she meant it. Her expectations were too low. Shelby's father was fucking irresponsible. If he had a kid, he wouldn't let them walk away. Family was everything.

If he had a kid.

Shit a brick.

Shelby was his daughter. Or maybe not.

He slammed the door to the locker room and stalked over to his cage, repeating to himself that it didn't matter. Whether she was his biological daughter or not, he was going to be in her life, and he was going to be the father that she could rely on. And if Rissa was hiding such a big secret, she must have had her reasons. Burn leaned his forehead against the locker's cool metal surface, allowing his brain to digest this revelation.

As far as he knew, no one else from Whiskey Team had been drafted to assist in this training exercise, so he had the locker room to himself. Normally, the thought of spending ten or twelve hours on the water was something he looked forward to, but not today. He wanted to get back to his girls.

Right now, he needed to put his personal issues aside and focus on his team. He'd agreed to this extra duty before requesting leave, but his buddy, Zach, a.k.a. Beetle, had promised to pick up the shift, then bailed at the last minute.

Burn wouldn't let Tommy down, so here he was, fulfilling the obligation. Tommy was the team leader of the up-and-coming SEALs, the ones who'd gotten through BUDs and were waiting on an assignment. Tommy's idea of keeping them sharp involved lots of water training—in the Olympic-sized pool on base and over open water. Today, they were using two helos for search-and-rescue pickup scenarios. Burn's job was to be an extra set of eyes, ready to jump in if anyone got into trouble.

Rissa would be fine inside the apartment. The cameras were functioning, and Styles was on the street. In addition, local cops were conducting an hourly drive-by. Yet Burn couldn't shake the nagging sensation that something was wrong.

"Chief," came a deep voice from behind him.

Burn turned to see his team's Corpsman entering their gear room. "Kama."

At first glance, people underestimated Kama's six-foot-three inches of muscle and shoved him in the brawn-and-no-brains category. But Kama was brilliant. He'd joined the military to pay for medical school but ended up as Whiskey Team's medic. He was also working on his RN on the side. When he got tired of kicking in doors and jumping out of planes, he planned to go back to medical school.

"Heard you had some serious shit going on with your girlfriend. Got that worked out?" Kama asked.

"Not yet." Burn released a prolonged breath. "Styles is keeping an eye on her today. Beetle was going to cover the swim for me, but something came up."

Kama snorted. "Yeah, I heard he got tickets to the truck pull down south with his buddy from Ace's team." He slung his duffel over one shoulder and locked his cage.

Burn curled his lip. "Good to know he cancelled on me for an emergency."

"I assume you're with Tommy's swim party today?"

"I am. And you? Did you get the short straw?" Burn asked.

"Nope. Owed Tommy a favor. Plus, the woman I've been seeing had other permanent plans."

"Sorry to hear that," Burn said.

Kama shrugged. "Win some, lose some."

Burn thumped him on the arm. "Be honest. You'd choose water training over a date any day."

Kama's lips quirked. "Absofuckinglutely. I'm a water baby, but don't forget the helicopter ride. On a windy day like today, it'll be better than any roller coaster."

Burn picked up his bag. "True that. Let's get on it then."

The glare of the afternoon sun was blinding when they stepped on the tarmac. The blades on the two aircraft spun as the trainees loaded gear. Shit, how many were they taking? This exercise would take hours if they had to drop off and pick up twenty guys multiple times. Burn patted his pockets.

He should text Rissa. Then he recalled he'd left his wallet, keys, and phone in the locker per the training rules. No electronics during the training mission, so all eyes were on task.

It was going to be late before they got back. Well, Rissa had told him not to return today, so that's what he'd do. Sleep at his place on base tonight and get some clean clothes. Then he'd go back to her apartment early tomorrow morning. They had some things to talk about. His daughter at the top of the list.

CHAPTER 29

For Terrance, lunch with Juan Ravago had been interminable. The man had bragged endlessly about his accomplishments, women, and his excessive wealth. Terrance had downed a few drinks to dull the ache in his side, but what he really needed were the pills in his suitcase back at the safe house. He'd avoided taking them while with Ravago, not wanting to seem vulnerable. But damn—it hurt.

The house Ravago lent him was at the end of a cul-de-sac. It shared the circle with two other homes. Each property boasted sprawling triple lots enclosed by various types of boundary fences. Ravago's place was surrounded by a ten-foot-tall wooden fence and secured by a black wrought-iron gate. All it needed was a couple of rottweilers to complete the intimidating picture.

Walt punched the code into the electronic keypad at the gate, and both sides swung open.

"Anyone else here?" Terrance asked.

"Nope," Grant replied.

There were no trees close to the dwelling. Instead, a terraced, rock-lined path bordered by small shrubs led up to an expansive stretch of grass on either side of the approach to the front door. In Terrance's view, it was a bit showy, but at least it was spacious and tucked away from the road. The driveway swung around the side of the house to access a three-car garage in the back, with the other bays remaining unused.

"I'll get the alarm and text the boss," Grant said before exiting the vehicle and jogging up the concrete steps to the connecting door.

"I'll get your bag," Walt said. "There are two bedrooms downstairs and two upstairs."

"I'll take one downstairs," Terrance replied. Climbing stairs was out of the question for at least a few days. The trip out here had been an impulse, one he now severely regretted. He should've left this errand to his counterpart or at least brought Rick along.

If only it weren't so important.

He followed Walt into the kitchen and through the dining room, which opened into an expansive foyer at the front of the house.

"This way." Walt crossed the living room toward another doorway.

Terrance took a moment to orient himself. This room had a big-screen TV which took up a good portion of one wall with a long couch beneath it and two deep cushion chairs which faced the television. Odd that the couch was beneath the television instead of facing it.

Off to the left was a staircase with an ornate banister and twisted wood posts rising to the second floor. In the corner of the dining room, he noticed a bar. "You got bourbon?"

"Should be," Walt replied. After setting down Terrance's single bag, he returned to check the contents of the built-in bar. He poured a generous glass of amber liquid and handed it to him.

Terrance gulped it down and held out the glass. "Another."

Walt poured again and left the bottle on the wooden counter. "I'll leave this for you."

"Good. I'm going to shower, then we can make plans," Terrance said, following Walt through the living room.

He chose the bedroom at the end of the hall. The paint on the walls echoed the warm, golden hue of the stucco outside. A king-sized bed dominated the space, its quilted, all-white bedding piled high with pillows. There was also a nightstand, a dresser, and a small sitting area that included another television.

Walt placed Terrance's suitcase on a bench at the foot of the bed. "Let me know if you need anything."

After Walt shut the door, Terrance retrieved his pill bottle and shook out a few. Halfway through his second bourbon, he'd recovered enough to wander over and flip back the curtain on the back window. The house had an in-ground, lagoon-type pool with a rocky waterfall on one end and a hot tub closer to the house. A stretch of grass extended thirty to forty yards behind the pool house, ending at a channel of rocks beneath the fence. The rocks lined the entire fence with decorative shrubs set at intervals along the perimeter.

He put down his empty glass and unbuttoned his shirt to examine his wound. The edges had puckered, and the deep red color was worrisome. The rippling white scars on his chest made it difficult to determine if the streaks extended over his stomach, but he suspected the infection had spread. A long, hot shower would do it some good.

After soaking in the shower a good thirty minutes, he dressed in clean clothes and took two more pills to knock the edge off his pain. He wished he was home in his favorite chair, but he was here now and here he would stay for a few days anyway.

The sun hadn't entirely set, and he needed something to settle his stomach. Venturing out in search of Ravago's men, he found them sprawled on the two wide chairs facing the television, engrossed in a football game on the big-screen TV. Their comfortable, relaxed posture irritated him.

"Get up. I want to drive by the apartment again," he snapped, his mood darkening even as he contemplated another bourbon.

"What for?" Grant asked.

If he'd had his gun with him, Terrance would've shot the man right between his beady, stupid eyes. That thought must have shown on his face, because Grant lurched to his feet, hands balled into fists.

Walt clambered forward to position himself between them. "We can drive over there. There isn't much food here, so after we do the pass, we'll pick up something at a drive-through. Everyone will be happier on a full stomach."

Terrance nodded.

Ravago's men had failed once to get the girl, and he'd said the building now had additional security. But there was always another way—Terrance needed to figure it out.

•   •   •

After Burn left them, the day had seemed to go on forever. They had sandwiches for lunch, and Shelby refused to nap. Now it was time to eat again, and her daughter wasn't cooperating.

"Please be careful," Rissa rubbed a hand over her eyes. At least Shelby could go to bed early since she hadn't had any naps today.

Shelby knocked her plastic cereal cup off the coffee table. "Acc'dent," she whined, her lips in a petulant line.

Rissa tossed down the clothes she'd gathered and let out a frustrated breath. "That wasn't an accident. Not nice, Shelby," she said, grabbing a roll of paper towels and a can of carpet cleaner from under the sink.

Shelby threw herself on the floor dramatically and sobbed her frustrations. Rissa wanted to pick her up and cuddle her, which would reward bad behavior.

"I know you're tired. I am, too." She knelt beside her crying daughter and handed her a paper towel. "You need to help me clean this up."

Even though she might make more of a mess, inappropriate behavior needed a consequence. Reluctantly, Shelby took the corner of a towel and dabbed her face and hands with it.

"The floor now." Rissa had it mostly cleaned up, but she leaned back on her heels to see if Shelby would try to help.

The little girl crawled over and pressed the towel to the floor before collapsing on Rissa's folded knees.

"Thank you for helping." Rissa rubbed gentle circles on her back before placing her on the couch. "Why don't you watch your cartoon while mommy finishes this and finds her wallet? Do you remember seeing Mommy's pink wallet? I used it this morning."

The small change purse-type wallet she'd taken with her when they'd gone to the ice cream shop. There was a hundred dollars in it, but more importantly, both her license and social security card. If she lost those, it would be extremely difficult to replace as she didn't have a copy of her birth certificate.

Shelby shook her head and stuck her thumb in her mouth before reaching for her bunny. Then she straightened and turned a tear-streaked face up to Rissa. "Ice cream?"

"We had that already. Do you want to play with your cars?" Rissa wiped off the coffee table and leaned close to inspect the damage to the carpet. Maybe it would dry okay. She carried the towels and spray to the kitchen and continued to search for her wallet.

"Want Mrs. G," Shelby whined from the couch.

Rissa took a deep breath. "Mrs. G. is in San Antonio. That's too far away." She'd meant to call Mrs. G. yesterday to let her know they were okay, and she'd forgotten.

"Mommmmmyyyyy—"

"Oh, Shelby. I'm trying. I'll call Mrs. G. now. Let me throw away this trash, and I'll get my phone." Minutes later, she returned to sit on the couch.

Shelby scrunched her nose and reached for the phone. "Me."

"Give me a second. I have to dial the number." Rissa plugged in the number from memory on her burner phone. The call went to voicemail, which was odd. Mrs. G. always answered her cell. "Mrs. G.? This is Rissa. I … uh… have this new number. Please call me when you have a minute. There is something I need to tell you." The nosy woman would surely call back with a message like that.

Rissa placed the phone on the coffee table. "I'm sorry. Mrs. G. didn't answer."

"Mrs. G.?" Shelby stuttered out through hiccupping sobs.

"We can't talk to her right now."

"Meeeeeee," Shelby whimpered, curling into a ball on the couch.

Rissa would've been irritated if Shelby had thrown herself on the floor, but she lay there dripping sad alligator tears. Rissa reached for her, but Shelby wiggled away.

"Want Burn."

Well, Rissa wanted him, too. She leaned back on the cushion and touched her lurching tummy. Why had she told Burn to stay away? Without him here, she was both exposed and lonely. She hoped he would return later tonight. She'd apologize and tell him everything.

"Mommy!"

"Honey, please stop yelling. Mommy's tired, too. Mrs. G. isn't answering her phone, and Burn is at work."

"Work?"

"Yes, he's at work."

"Want Burn." Shelby poked out a lip, then changed tactics. "Ice cream?" she asked with a quivering smile. "Me good girl."

"Honey." Rissa reached for her again. This time, Shelby didn't resist when she pulled her onto her lap. "Burn had to go to work, but you're a good girl. We're both tired." She mopped her daughter's face with a tissue from a box on the end table.

"Toys?" Shelby asked, a hopeful lift in her voice.

Toys. Oh no.

She might have left her wallet in the newsstand when she was looking at the little cars and dinosaurs. She'd had it in her hand, but then Burn had insisted on paying for everything, and she hadn't used her wallet. She must have laid it down. How dumb could she get?

She glanced toward the window. It was dusk outside, but the sun wouldn't set until around seven. They could check the newsstand and grab an ice cream before the sun went down, couldn't they? Burn had a man watching the street. It would be okay if they went out. This was an emergency. She needed her identification if she was ever going to get another job.

She kissed Shelby's forehead. "Maybe we deserve an extra treat."

"Treat?" Shelby gave her a watery smile.

"Yes," Rissa said, checking the time again. She didn't know when he would finish the training. This morning, she'd told him she didn't need him, but that wasn't true. It was more like she didn't want to need him.

As if reading her mind, Shelby asked again, "Burn?"

"No, honey, Burn can't come back yet."

"Mmmph." Shelby grunted and cuddled her bunny. "Treat?" she mumbled around the thumb she'd stuck in her mouth.

"Well ..." Rissa pulled her daughter's thumb out and kissed her hand. She could text Burn and apologize for leaving the apartment. And for this morning. But she needed her wallet.

Her stomach churned with guilt. She'd promised not to leave the apartment, and Burn would be annoyed, but would he even know? Well, the guy outside likely reported everything to him. The upside was that if Burn were mad enough, he'd come here tonight and yell at her. She wanted him to come here tonight.

"Please?" Shelby patted Rissa's cheek.

"Okay," Rissa said.

Shelby scrunched her nose, her brows high. "Me. Choc-o-lat?"

Rissa kissed her forehead. "Yes, we'll get ice cream, but you have to listen to Mommy, and we need to be fast."

"Yes!" Shelby cheered and pumped her legs to wiggle down to the floor.

"Grab a sweater from the chair in our bedroom and find your shoes."

"Wheeeeee!" squealed Shelby as she raced from the room.

Rissa slipped on her sneakers and tossed the couch pillows around, searching for her windbreaker. The temperature dropped in the evenings. It wasn't cold so much as brisk outside, and they'd have ice cream.

Rissa discovered the sweatshirt Burn had worn the night before. It was soft, hunter-green cotton that he'd clearly washed a hundred times. She hesitated a moment before pulling it over her head. It fell past her hips, and she needed to roll up the sleeves, but it was loose, comfortable, and smelled like him. She considered changing into jeans but decided the sweatshirt would keep her warm enough for a short walk.

Shelby tore back into the room with her sweater in one hand and a single shoe in her other. Rissa laughed while helping her into the sweater. "Where's your other shoe?"

"No," Shelby said.

"Wait here." Rissa found the missing shoe tangled in the white afghan in the bedroom. She needed to straighten up, but it could wait until after they returned. If her wallet wasn't at the newsstand, it had to be somewhere in this apartment.

A few minutes later, they entered the elevator and pressed the button for the lobby. She hadn't considered Mr. Rafferty's reaction to them leaving and hoped he wouldn't try to stop them. When the doors whooshed open, Mr. Dean sat behind the desk.

"Hello, Mr. Dean," Rissa greeted him.

Shelby squealed and waved enthusiastically. "Santa!"

"Ladies. What brings you down this evening?" Thick white eyebrows climbed up his forehead as he approached them. "Mr. Rafferty said you were in for the day."

"Choc-o-lat!" Shelby cheered.

Eyes wide, he turned to Rissa for an explanation.

Rissa picked up Shelby. "She's begging for chocolate ice cream. The place down the block is open till seven, so we'll run down fast and come right back."

"Okay then," he said, his bushy brows never lowering. "I'm off at seven; tonight is my anniversary. I have to leave on time, or my wife will skin me alive. Do you have your key to get back in if Mr. Rafferty isn't back?"

"I do." She hesitated. "Have many people been coming and going?"

"Nothing out of the ordinary. Mr. Andy came in a little while ago with dinner for him and Jack. I haven't seen any other tenants in the last hour, but I'm only here until the night watchman returns. It seems they've upped the security since the break-in. It's about time, too."

Rissa bobbed her head. "We should hurry before the shop closes." And before Burn knows they left the building.

She put Shelby down and held her tiny hand. She would let her run there to work off some energy and carry her back. Would Burn's friend come out and yell at her for leaving the apartment? It was only for a few minutes.

CHAPTER 30

Terrance was woozy from the mix of booze and drugs, but he managed not to grunt when he climbed into the luxurious leather seat of the SUV. Walt drove again with Grant in the passenger seat.

"Once we swing by the apartment, I know this incredible Italian place. We can order now and pick it up on the return trip," Walt suggested, his tone hopeful.

"Yeah," Terrance agreed with a tilt of his head. Food might settle his churning stomach. "Get me spaghetti ... and bread."

Walt nudged Grant. "Order it on the app."

Scowling, Grant worked on his phone for a few minutes. "Done."

Walt glanced over the seat. "We're almost there, Mr. Simmons. One more turn, and you'll have an unobstructed view of the building a few blocks ahead."

"What the—" Grant made a sound in his throat and twisted around in the seat. "Jorge, our man watching the building, texted me. Your woman is on the street. She's at the ice cream place again with her kid."

"Fucking kidding me." Adrenaline burned through Terrance, momentarily drowning out the pain and nausea. "Is the SEAL with them?"

"Hang on." Grant clicked on his phone. "Jorge says only her and the kid."

"We need to pull over and wait for them to come out." A spark of triumph lit inside Terrance. Finally, things were going his way. If Marissa were alone, the pick-up shouldn't be too tricky unless … "He's certain no one is with her. No one is waiting outside?"

"There's a man parked farther down who's been watching the building all day," Grant said, still checking his incoming text messages. "Jorge says he hasn't noticed her yet. He will, though."

Terrance leaned forward to peer out the front window. "Pull to the curb. I have an idea." He thumped the back of the seat. "Have Jorge call the cops and report the watcher as suspicious. There's bound to be a foot cop around here. They'll have to question him. If we time this right, this will work."

Grant quickly passed the message. "He'll text when it's done."

Walt maneuvered the SUV close to the curb, and they waited. Terrance figured this was a shot in the dark, but worth a fucking try. How long would she remain inside the ice cream shop?

"He's done it," Grant said.

The entrance to Jimbo's Creamery wasn't visible from their spot, but if they pulled forward, there might not be another place to park, or they could miss her altogether.

"Want me to move?"

Terrance shook his head. "Not yet. Wait."

"For how long?" Grant asked, but then the phone buzzed, and his face broke into a smug expression. "The cops nabbed the watcher, and he was armed. They cuffed him."

Terrance jabbed a finger at the road. "Now. Get us closer."

"Got it." Walt slid the big SUV into the flow of cars.

"There they are." Grant pointed.

Terrance saw them, too. Marissa Parker was there, carrying her child and a large white bag with a pink ice cream cone emblazoned on it. She was focused on keeping the kid out of the bag. How could it be this easy? "Is this vehicle traceable?"

"No," Walt huffed. "The plates are borrowed."

Terrance wasn't looking a gift horse in the mouth. "Pick them up. Grant, grab them and bring them to me."

"I'm calling the boss," Grant said, punching numbers into his phone.

Terrance squeezed his shoulder. "I'll give you fifty thousand dollars—each—if you grab them for me right now."

They exchanged a look.

Walt said, "This vehicle is clean, but even with the fake tag, it's memorable. The boss won't be able to use it again."

"No problem. I'll throw in another hundred thousand to buy Ravago a new one."

Walt shrugged. "I don't know…"

Grant's mouth flattened into a thin line. "Make it seventy-five each and we're in."

Terrance dipped his chin in agreement. "Done. Now get them."

"Let's make some money," Grant said as he retrieved a handful of black cloth from the glove box and tossed a balaclava over the seat to Terrance. "Put this on. Open the door when you see me coming. But cover your face in case the shop has cameras."

"Right." He should've thought of that, but the pain pills and bourbon he'd drunk earlier muddled his thinking.

Walt eyed him in the rearview mirror. "Can you handle her?"

Had they noticed his infirmity? Probably, but who the hell cared. They would never get another opportunity like this. "Bring her to me."

Walt found a gap along the curb in front of the newsstand, about ten feet ahead of Marissa and less than a block from the apartment entrance. The snatch had to be perfectly timed. Terrance's nerves crackled with energy, and he momentarily forgot about his pain.

Grant donned his mask, flicking a glance over the seat. "Be ready."

"Go," Terrance snapped, pulling the balaclava over his head. There was a long opening for his eyes and a smaller one for his mouth. He edged over to grip the door handle.

When Marissa and the kid were level with the vehicle, Grant sprang into action. In three long strides, he seized her from behind, locking his arms around both her and the kid and lifting Marissa entirely off her feet. She fought and screamed as he swung her back toward the SUV.

Walt rolled forward, and Grant only had to take a few steps to reach the open rear door.

Terrance motioned. "Hurry!"

Kicking and screaming, Marissa fought as he shoved her through the open door. "Please, no! Someone help!"

Grant tossed them into the back with Terrance. The SUV was already moving, and he had to leap into the front as Walt darted back into traffic.

"Quick! Masks off and keep her out of sight," Walt ordered.

Terrance's lips curled as he pressed a hand to his side, barely managing a grunt while riding wave after wave of pain, courtesy of Marissa's head colliding with his stomach when Grant threw her onto the seat.

"No. Not you," Marissa whimpered, her eyes wide with shock as she recognized their captor. "How did you find us?"

"Shut your mouth," Grant snarled.

The baby sobbed, and Terrance caught a whiff of urine. His stomach churned so violently he feared he might vomit on his new "family" members.

From the front, Walt said, "Calm the kid down, lady, or I will."

Marissa's gaze darted around the vehicle. She seemed to sense Terrance's weakness as her hand inched toward the door handle.

"No," Grant bellowed. "Touch that, and I'll shoot your kid through the seat."

She pulled the baby close and huddled in a tight ball. "Please don't hurt her."

The kid continued to sob.

The waves of pain receded, and Terrance found his voice. "No. I want them alive. Besides, she isn't stupid enough to jump out in traffic. The baby would be killed in the fall."

The kid lifted her head, saw him, and shrieked a blood-curdling sound. So much noise from such a small body.

Grant twisted to glare at the captives. "You said you only needed the woman."

The child was his insurance policy, and he wanted her alive. However, he didn't have to intervene because Grant's threat prodded Marissa to calm the kid. Terrance struggled to stay upright and maintain a neutral face while waiting for her to pacify the child.

"Marissa—"

"Please, let us go. I promise not to tell anyone."

"Don't say another word." Terrance didn't need her blabbing in front of the muscle guys, or he might have more problems. Right now, he needed their help to control her. If necessary, he could kill her and take the kid, but that meant more work for him in the short term. He had to keep one of them alive, and his patience might not be sufficient for a baby. "Hand me your phone," Terrance said.

"What?" she whispered.

"Don't be stupid. Give it to me. Your shoes, too." His head pounded, and he clenched his teeth. Now that he had his daughter, he only wanted some rest.

She reluctantly handed over the cell phone before removing her tennis shoes, one at a time, and placing them on the seat between them. She wasn't wearing any socks. Terrance used a multi-tool from his wallet to remove the SIM card before lowering his window.

"Don't do that." Walt glanced over the seat. "You can't throw shit out. San Diego has all kinds of littering ordinances."

Unused to being told what to do, Terrance paused.

"I'm serious. The PD is more likely to notice you dropping that out the window than us grabbing the ice cream cones." Walt tilted his head at Grant. "Give him the phone."

Terrance kept the SIM card and handed the rest to Grant.

"I'll toss it later. She got anything else?" Grant peered over the seat.

Terrance studied the shivering pair. The child had stopped wailing and was whimpering into her mother's neck. "What else do you have? Do we need to strip you?"

"Money. I-I have cash." She pulled a few crumpled bills and a small pink wallet from her pocket and tossed them by the shoes.

"Alright. Sit on the floor on that side with your back against the door. Try nothing, or I'll let Grant shoot your kid."

Her eyes never left his face as she slid into the cramped space and curled into a tight ball behind the driver's seat with the kid pressed against her chest.

His *papi* had always said, "Never take your eyes off the snake, or it will get you." He was the snake, but Marissa already had poison in her veins—she just didn't know it yet.

Walt turned onto another road and checked the rearview. "Looks like we're in the clear."

"Fuck yeah." Grant thumped the dashboard with a fist. "I'm hungry. How about we make that other stop?"

Terrance struggled to remember what he was talking about and came up blank. His head throbbed, and his stomach clenched. The food. He needed to eat. "You're sure we aren't followed?"

"No blue lights."

San Diego was their town. He'd have to trust they knew what they were doing. "Fine. Get the food."

"I'll park in the back and switch the plates. It's an old establishment, and they don't have cameras. Keep them quiet while I run inside," Walt said.

They stopped in a dark corner of a parking lot. There were plenty of cars in front of the restaurant, but only a few on this side.

Marissa sang softly to her kid.

"Grant should stay here," Terrance said. In case he passed out, which was becoming a possibility.

Walt murmured something to Grant that he couldn't hear, but it didn't matter; they were a means to an end. He wouldn't need them much longer.

Grant draped his arm over the seat and pointed a thick finger at Rissa. "Not a sound from you or the kid is dead. Got it?"

Marissa gave a jerky nod. "I understand."

"Be right back." Walt exited the vehicle and moved to the back, presumably to switch the plates, before he jogged toward the restaurant entrance.

They waited in silence, the only sound Marissa's quiet singing. Then, a white Chevy Express van pulled into the space next to them. Seven blue-haired ladies piled out, all wearing red hats, most dressed in red. The dark tint on the side windows prevented them from seeing much inside, but Terrance was glad he'd put the girl on the floor.

Walt turned his back to his window and kept his cap pulled low.

"Hello, hello." A woman in a wide-brimmed red hat tapped on Grant's window. "Are you alright in there?"

Marissa's breath hitched.

"Not a sound," Terrance whispered, keeping his gun held low but aimed at her face. "Grant. Don't be rude. Tell the woman you're fine but have COVID."

Grant cursed under his breath before cracking his window a few inches. "I'm waiting for someone. I have COVID. He coughed for good measure and rolled up the window.

The red hat backed away so fast she bumped into the van.

Tears leaked from Marissa's eyes, but she didn't speak. Progress. Maybe he could do something with this girl when they returned to Texas. "We'll get along fine if you follow my orders."

"You should tie her hands and put tape on her mouth," said Grant, handing over a couple of zip-ties and a roll of black duct tape.

Terrance took the items without answering. The girl was compliant now, but she'd escaped him in San Antonio. It might be better to limit her resources. "Grant, I need you to point your gun at her."

"Already is. The seat will muffle the sound."

"Don't shoot unless she tries something. Marissa, put out your wrists."

She moved the child and held her hands so Terrance could secure the plastic ties—not too tight, because she had to manage her kid. Now, how would he put the tape on her mouth without leaning over? She'd have to do it herself.

He tore off a strip of black tape and extended it toward Marissa. "Cover your mouth with this."

CHAPTER 31

The sweet aroma of tomato and parmesan filled the vehicle's interior as they pulled out of the parking lot. Her kidnappers had stopped to pick up dinner like they hadn't a care in the world. Had someone seen them get taken? She should've screamed for help when the woman knocked, but if she made any noise, Terrance—Mrs. Iglesias' killer, would've hurt her daughter.

Rissa's stomach churned. The apartment and safety had been less than a block away. If they'd moved a little faster or not gone for ice cream, they would be safe. Burn had assured her that a Navy SEAL was watching the street. Why hadn't he come to her rescue or at least raised the alarm?

The cashier at the newsstand had her wallet, and the money was still inside. She should've gone straight back after picking it up, but she hadn't. She'd foolishly taken Shelby to get ice cream and now here they were.

Shelby had quieted. Her head rested on Rissa's chest, and her eyes were closed. Maybe she was asleep, or maybe she was shutting out the surrounding terror. Rissa nuzzled her dark curls and prayed that Burn would find them. He would try, she was sure of that. But would he find them before Terrance killed them?

"That van was parked close. Have any problems?" the driver asked as he backed out of the parking spot.

The big man who'd grabbed her chuckled. "Old lady wanted to know if we needed help. I told her I had COVID, and she hightailed it inside."

Terrance bumped her leg. "What do you think, Marissa?" he asked.

She drew back as far as the door allowed, trying to ignore him.

"I asked you a question," he growled, grinding his boot heel into the top of her bare foot. "Look at me."

A muffled groan escaped behind the tape on her mouth, and she lifted her chin to meet his gaze.

Terrance's eyes glittered. "Marissa and I know old women remember things, don't we?"

Is he talking about his mother?

"Was the woman wearing a red hat?" the driver asked.

Terrance answered, "Yes, Walt, all of them had hats. I understand red hats are a symbol of geriatric solidarity."

Walt grunted. "When the group came inside, they gave me a wide berth, but they checked me out pretty good."

"Probably thought you had COVID," Grant snickered.

"You're an asshole. They might remember me. We gotta ditch this vehicle." He glanced over the seat, his eyes devoid of any emotion. "Did you check if she has anything else on her?"

"Like what?" Grant asked.

Walt slapped the steering wheel. "How stupid are you? She might wear a tracker or have a second phone or some shit."

Rissa wished she had a tracker. She memorized all their names: Grant, Walt, and, Mrs. Iglesias' son, Terrance. If she got out of this, she could tell the police.

Terrance nudged her with his boot again. "Nod if you have anything else on you. If you lie to me, your kid will die first."

She whipped her head from side to side. He pressed his heel into her foot again, and pain blurred her vision.

"You should make sure," Grant said.

Terrance bared his teeth. "Don't fucking tell me what I should do. If I check her now, it will stir up the kid. We'll check her at the house."

•   •   •

He wasn't telling Grant, but Terrance couldn't have searched the girl if his life depended on it. His side burned like a fiery brand, and he didn't know how much more he could tolerate. A hospital was out of the question, since a gunshot would be reported, but perhaps it'd been long enough that he could claim something else had happened.

Finally, they reached the house.

Walt punched in the gate code and circled to the garage. "I'll take this inside," he said, holding the food bag. "Grant, help bring the passengers."

Marissa watched him with wary green eyes.

Terrance tucked her wallet and cash in his pocket, ignoring the shoes. "Marissa, are we doing this the easy way or the hard way?"

She stared at him with wide eyes.

Grant yanked the door open behind her, and the girl nearly fell backward out of the vehicle.

"Wait," Terrance said. "Pull the tape off her mouth first."

Grant clamped onto a fistful of her hair and tilted back her head to rip off the duct tape.

"Ow." She pressed her lips into her shoulder, and Grant grunted in pleasure. "Tell me what you want me to say."

"It's simple." Terrance pressed a hand to his side as he slid toward the opposite door. "You can walk inside with your child, or Grant can knock you out, and I'll carry her." He hoped she chose correctly, because he didn't want to carry the kid.

"Walk. Please let me walk," Marissa said firmly, her eyes fixed on him.

Terrance puffed his cheeks, pleased to see his daughter showing some backbone. "The house is secluded. If you scream, no one will hear you, so don't waste your breath. Help her out, Grant."

Gripping under her arms, Grant dragged her backward out of the vehicle. Shelby let out a terrified wail and kept crying.

"Stand," he ordered.

Marissa managed to get her feet under her while shushing the kid.

Terrance slid out his side, and pain radiated through his entire belly. He had to lean against the door frame to maintain the new position.

"Where do you want to put her? In your bed?" Grant asked.

"No." He swallowed hard, pushing down the pain and forcing himself to stand upright. "Put them in the walk-in closet off the bedroom next to mine." It didn't lock, but they wouldn't be here long, and it was downstairs.

"Got it." Grant hauled her across the garage.

"Wait." Terrance circled the front of the vehicle. "Don't fight me, and I'll let the child remain with you. Stay where you are put until I call for you, or there will be consequences. Understood?" When she didn't immediately answer, he clamped his fingers on her jaw and squeezed until she gave a little gasp.

Her eyes filled with tears, but her voice was strong when she answered. "I understand."

He liked her spirit. It might work to his advantage.

•   •   •

A short while later, Terrance sat alone at the dining table under the pale light of the brass and pewter chandelier, twirling his fork in a Styrofoam dish of spaghetti. The room's walls were painted a soothing cream color, which he liked much better than the gold in his bedroom. His body ached, and fatigue dragged at his eyes. He needed sleep, but he needed to take care of business first.

If he didn't return to Austin soon, he would need to reschedule his meeting on Friday with the new buyer, and he was running low on pain pills. Cash was also becoming a problem, but as soon as he obtained a few signatures from Marissa, his access to Amelia's accounts would be restored.

And then there was the kid. Perhaps it would be easier to control Marissa if he separated them, but then he'd have to deal with the kid. He could turn the baby over to Ravago for safekeeping, yet that might give his associate a chance to use her parentage against him. Terrance needed another solution to keep her under control.

He pushed the food aside and dialed Juan Ravago's number. No doubt the two goons had updated him, but courtesy required him to check in. Besides, he needed help getting his daughter back to Austin. Or, at the very least, he needed to stay in this house until Rick arranged their extraction.

Juan answered on the first ring. "*Buenos noches, amigo*. I was expecting your call. I understand you found what you were looking for."

"Yes. Your men helped me track down the right thing."

"Excellent. Since you are done shopping, have you changed your departure date?"

Terrance pressed his fingers into his temple. "I haven't decided. I might extend my vacation, take in some sights."

Ravago cleared his throat. "*Ciertamente*. My men are locals. Have them show you around. I'll send a new car over today."

"I'm in your debt," Terrance said, choking on the admission.

Ravago cackled. "Oh, yes, I'm aware."

"I'll wire you cash for your assistance."

"*Bien, eso está bien*. Perhaps I'll want to visit your fair city one day, and you can take me to hear some of the music."

Terrance hated live shows. They were far too loud for his taste. "I look forward to it."

"Tomorrow then. Call and tell me how you like San Diego."

Terrance took that as a request rather than an order, because he didn't take orders from anyone. "Tomorrow."

He clicked off the call and texted Rick.

Need help to get souvenirs home. Join me for a cross-country drive.

Now he needed to deal with his daughter. It would be better to forgo an audience for their first conversation, but Ravago's men lingered nearby. Whether it was the painkillers muddying his thoughts or sheer exhaustion, he couldn't for the life of him remember their names at that moment. The driver, a lean man with a thick mustache and beady brown eyes, sat on the couch. The refrigerator-sized guy had his elbows propped on the back of a chair. Both watched him like hungry wolves, waiting for him to do something. Damn.

"You both did what I asked today," he said, reaching for his laptop. The quick movement had him clenching his teeth. He breathed through the pain, then continued. "Give me your information, and I'll wire the money."

Mustache joined him at the table and pulled a card from his wallet. The back of the card had a string of numbers. "Put it in this account."

Terrance clicked a few keys and transferred the cash from his emergency slush fund. He considered the driver. Egor? That didn't sound right. Egan? "I'm going to need supplies. Food and whatever a kid that size needs. Also, some more bourbon and whatever we need here."

The big man spoke. "Walt and I have someone on the outside."

"Good." Outside of his boss's business? Interesting. "Money isn't an issue. I want it handled now." *Walt—where the fuck had he gotten Egan?*

"I'll check with my contact."

"One other thing," Terrance said, his eyes roving from Walt to ... Grant. The name came to him. "When I speak to Marissa Parker, I need you to contain her." He hated admitting vulnerability, but he had no alternative. "I'm recovering from an injury and need to avoid a physical altercation." That was an understatement.

Grant made a weird sucking sound with his teeth. "You want me to bring her out now?"

"Let's not set the kid off again. We'll deal with her after we have supplies." Terrance pushed himself to his feet. "I need a drink. We wait for the delivery before bringing her out."

CHAPTER 32

Grant surprised her when he cut the ties off her wrists before shutting them in the closet. Terrance was keeping her alive, but why? And for how long? Rissa struggled to remain calm as terror licked at her heart. She had no idea how much time had passed, but Shelby was finally asleep in her arms, and she didn't want to put her down. Every minute might be the last one she spent with her daughter.

Terrance had told her to stay where she was put, but she had to try to escape. The doorknob turned easily, but when she pushed, it didn't budge. Something must be blocking it on the other side. She pressed her ear to the seam but heard nothing. Grant was probably waiting for her to open the door.

Ironic that she was back in a closet. But there was no escape room this time, and Shelby was with her. Overwhelmed by despair, she sank onto the soft carpet. They would all be safe in Liesel's apartment right now if she had listened to Burn. She was an idiot for breaking her promise and going outside. But she'd had to get her wallet, hadn't she?

A knot of remorse twisted in her chest. Terrance was going to murder them, and Burn would never know what happened. He would never know how sorry she was. None of this was fair to Shelby. Rissa rubbed her cheek against her daughter's tangled curls. Her baby had her whole life in front of her.

Could Terrance be reasoned with? Her daughter was too young to remember what had happened, so she might be able to persuade him to release Shelby. Fear slithered through her, then solidified into anger. She was not going down without a fight.

She gently lay Shelby on the carpet before surging to her feet to pace their small prison. It was eight feet deep, four feet wide, with plush carpet and four empty metal bars for hangers. She attempted to dislodge the bars, but they were screwed in tight. At least the light was on. She didn't think she could stand being in the pitch-black.

Hopefully, Shelby would sleep a few hours, because there weren't any words of reassurance to offer. She had no idea what would happen to them. Or, more correctly, when it would happen. Gulping a sob, she settled on the carpet beside her daughter and pulled Burn's sweatshirt over her knees, praying for a miracle.

Sometime later, the door burst open, and Grant, the man who'd snatched her off the sidewalk, stepped into the closet. His massive frame sucked the air right out of the room.

"Get up," he barked, his beady eyes raking over her body.

"What—what's happening?"

He leered at her, and she caught a whiff of sweat and alcohol. "Mr. Simmons wants a word with you. Be smart or not. I'd like it better if you fight me."

Apparently, things could get worse. Rissa scooped up her daughter and pressed against the wall to support her trembling legs.

Shelby lifted her head in confusion. "Mommy?"

"It's okay, baby," Rissa murmured, half-turning to block her daughter's view of Grant.

Shelby saw him anyway and hid her face against Rissa's sweatshirt. "Home, Mommy," she whispered.

"Let's go." Grant's breath stank of garlic and onions when he clamped his thick fingers on Rissa's upper arm to hustle her out of the closet ahead of him. They'd gone a few feet across the bedroom when he shoved her in the back, knocking her to her knees.

Shelby whimpered, and fury burned through Rissa. She twisted and bared her teeth at him. "You're a real asshole."

"Been told that. Move."

Doing her best to reassure Shelby, Rissa stumbled forward to get some distance between them. As she walked, she tried to memorize the layout of the house: two doors on this wall, then a short hall opening into the living room. There was a long couch and two chairs. Large windows lined the wall to the left of the front door, and a staircase ascended to a second floor. Beyond the stairs was the dining room. She knew that because they'd walked through a kitchen and dining room when they came in from the garage.

Someone coughed. Rissa swung her focus to the room's occupants. When she saw Mrs. Iglesias' son standing on the far side of the living room, bile crept up the back of her throat, and her breath came in ragged gasps. Shelby sensed her mounting distress and began to cry.

"Come in," Terrance said, waving a hand at the couch. "Have a seat."

Shelby. Shelby was all that mattered. "Do what you want with me, but I'm begging you. Please don't hurt my daughter." Surprisingly, Rissa found herself not crying but burning with anger—at herself, at this jerk, at Grant, and even at Burn.

"Have a seat on the couch, Marissa. I want you to be comfortable," Terrance said.

Comfortable? Rissa whispered reassurance to her daughter, quietly begging her to close her eyes. Shelby buried her face in Rissa's neck, still crying softly.

"Sit," Terrance said again, this time more forcefully.

Keenly aware of his gaze, Rissa crossed the short distance and perched on the edge of the center cushion of the long couch. At least she had a wall behind her. She stiffened her spine, awaiting whatever came next.

"I have a story to tell you," he said, dragging a straight-back chair from the dining table and settling it between the cushioned chairs facing the couch.

Her gut soured. Whatever he was about to say, she didn't want to hear it, but she forced herself to play along and keep him talking. Anything to buy them more time. She was sure Burn would be searching for them. "A story?"

He snapped his fingers at Grant. "Bring Marissa a glass of water and juice for the child."

Rissa was ready to beg for her daughter's life. "If you let Shelby—"

"No. Stop talking," Terrance barked.

Shelby whimpered again, hiccupping little sobs as she burrowed into Rissa's hoodie.

Grant returned with a bottle of water and an apple juice container with a rubber car on top. When Rissa hesitated to take them, he slammed them on the coffee table. Then he dropped onto a cushioned chair. The other man, Walt, leaned against what must be the front door—no doubt blocking her escape. Heavy drapes covered the large windows. That exit wasn't an option. Not with Shelby and not before one of them stopped her.

A small hand patted her cheek. "Mommy?" Shelby's eyes were wide and dripping tears.

"We're okay, sweetie. Grown-ups are talking. Do you want some juice?" Rissa kissed Shelby's fingers and not waiting for an answer, she snatched up the car-topped container. She was relieved to see the plastic seal still intact.

"I'm talking to you," Terrance grumbled impatiently.

Rissa ignored him long enough to finish unwrapping the bottle and offer it to Shelby. Then she fastened her gaze on Terrance. "What do you want from me? You said you had a story?"

"Yes. It's something you'll find interesting."

She shook her head. "I promise not to tell anyone if you let us go."

His lips curved, exposing his perfect white teeth. "What would you have to tell?"

This had to be a trick. Keeping her mouth shut seemed like the best idea. "Nothing. I don't know anything."

He inclined his head and lifted his brows dramatically. "Both you and your child have green eyes. Eyes a shade that is somewhat unusual, don't you think?"

Rissa licked dry lips. How crazy was this man? "Yes, we have green eyes."

He scoffed in amusement. "And whose eyes do you have, Marissa Parker?"

Desperate to keep him calm, she played along. "I'm not sure I understand what you're asking."

He waved his fingers in front of his face and drew her name out in a hiss. "Marissa ... whose eyes do you have?"

Shelby shrank against her chest. Rissa wished she could get farther from Terrance, but there was nowhere to go but the wall behind the couch. "You want to know where I inherited them? I don't know for sure. My parents have brown eyes, so probably a distant relative."

"You idiot. What color are my eyes?"

Her lips quivered. "Why are you asking me that?"

"Answer the question," he demanded, his voice rising.

"Green." She stuttered, "Y-your eyes are green."

Then Terrance did something utterly bizarre. He arched his brows and his face split into an alligator grin. All Rissa could think was—psychopath. Too afraid to speak, she kept her eyes locked on him, waiting for his next move, while Shelby sucked on the apple juice container, the sound filling the heavy silence in the room.

"I suppose it was too much to hope you'd be more intelligent than your mother."

Her stomach twisted into tight coils. What did her mother have to do with this? "My mother?"

He ignored her question and checked the display on his phone. "This is more tedious than I imagined," he said, lurching to his feet with a grimace. "We leave tomorrow for my ranch. You and your daughter have decided to live with me."

Live with him? He was crazy, and it was stupid to ask him anything, but she couldn't stop herself. "What? Why would we go anywhere with you?"

He slowly stepped behind his chair and rested his hands on the back. "Why? Because I'm your father, Marissa. Haven't you figured that out yet?"

She shook her head, and blood roared in her ears. "That's not possible. My father is Frank Parker."

"You stupid girl," Terrance snorted derisively. "I suppose I need to spell it out for you. Your mother and I fucked and made a baby. Is that clear enough?"

Her head buzzed as she struggled to form a response. A terrible suspicion bloomed in her gut. This made sense in an awful way. All her life, her parents barely tolerated her. She'd thought they didn't want to have a kid. But it was worse, worse if this monster had fathered her. Had her mother loved him?

"Nothing to say?" Terrance tapped his palms on the chair. "We're done here."

"Wait." Past events, things she'd never considered, tumbled around in Rissa's head. "Are you going to kill us?"

His lips pressed in a thin line before he spoke. "Try to use your tiny brain. Did you ever question why Amelia chose you? Was getting scholarships for school maybe a little too easy? Then, out of all the candidates, even more qualified ones, she picked you as her nurse."

Rissa felt as if she were plummeting into an endless abyss. She shook her head fervently in denial.

"But, dear, it's true. As compensation for raising you, your mother extorted money from Amelia until you turned eighteen. Unfortunately, or perhaps not, my stepmother kept your existence a secret."

Her mind reeled. "No. I don't believe you're my father," she managed, although deep down the undeniable truth lingered. All three of them shared those strangely bright green eyes. For years, people had asked her where she got her unusual eye color.

"What you believe changes nothing." He disappeared into the dining room. Moments later, he returned with a tumbler full of amber liquid.

Grant watched her like a hungry wolf, and Walt studied his phone. If she could only get her hands on that phone.

Terrance belched loudly. "Here are the ground rules," he said, slurring slightly as he eased back onto the straight-back chair. "Are you listening?"

Rissa jerked her head affirmatively. A second later, Shelby's little head moved up and down against her chest as she also nodded in agreement. Her poor baby.

He drained his glass. "There's a bedroom attached to the closet you were in. If you behave, you'll be allowed to use it along with the bathroom. You're my daughter, and I don't want you sleeping on the floor in a closet. But if you try anything stupid, that's exactly what will happen. If I have to restrain you again, my granddaughter will have separate accommodations."

Rissa's heart clambered into her throat at the thought of being separated from Shelby. "I won't be stupid." Not stupid, yet every fiber of her being screamed that the moment she had a chance, she must escape, because staying here meant certain death.

Grant leaned forward with an avaricious stare. "There's an alarm on the doors and windows. Try to escape, and you'll spend some time with me."

"That's right." Terrance inclined his head. "If you open or otherwise compromise a window, Grant or Walt will stop you, and they won't be gentle."

"I understand," she whispered.

"Good." Terrance's mouth stretched in a grin, and his cheeks dimpled.

He may as well have punched her in the stomach. She had the same dimples, same eyes, and hair color. *He's telling the truth. She had the blood of a psychotic killer in her veins.*

Burn would never want her now, but would he still want Shelby?

•   •   •

"You gotta admit, we had fun today," Kama said over the noise of the helicopter returning them to base.

Burn gave a rueful shrug. The last eight hours over choppy surf, coaching newbies, had been exhilarating. No injuries and lots of good skill training, so a successful mission on all counts. "Yeah. A good day on the water."

It was around nine, and Burn still planned to swing by his base apartment for clean clothes. Afterward, he was headed back to Rissa. They needed to talk things through and figure out where they stood. Besides, he didn't like leaving her safety up to anyone else.

"Wanna hit Cicadas for a drink after this? All these tadpoles need to pay homage to their trainers and buy us beer."

Burn snorted. "Sounds fun, but I have somewhere to be." Somewhere he really wanted to be, with Rissa and Shelby—a kid who might be his daughter.

Upon landing, Burn and Kama grabbed their gear, and Burn immediately spotted Pan and Butter standing at the edge of the tarmac.

Kama bumped his shoulder. "What do you think they want?"

"A welcome committee at this time of night is never good." Burn's mind had been focused on how much he was looking forward to seeing Rissa, and now he was on full alert. He hurried over to his teammates.

"What's happening?" Burn demanded.

"What's going on?" Kama echoed by his side.

Pan spun toward the building and motioned for them to follow. "Walk and talk."

Burn ran through possibilities in his head, none of them good. "We're listening, so talk," he growled.

"It's Rissa Parker," Pan said as he yanked open one side of the double doors.

Burn paused, and his gaze bounced from Pan to Butter. "Styles is watching over her. What's happened?"

"Let's move," Butter said, leading them into the building. "Someone called in a suspicious character report on Styles."

"What the—?" Burn rushed behind him, and within a minute, they were inside the team's locker room. "Talk while I offload gear," he said, unlocking his cage and peeling off his swim gear.

Butter's gray eyes were clouded. "The cops arrested Styles. They didn't hold him long, but by the time he was released, Parker and her kid had vanished."

A red haze fell over his vision, and Burn released a primal growl. He whipped around to face his men even as he pulled out his cell. "From the apartment?"

"No. They were outside," Butter said softly.

"Dammit!" Burn kicked the locker and plugged in Rissa's number, his thumb hovering over the send button. "Did you speak to the night watchman at the desk? Rafferty?"

Butter nodded. "I did. Rafferty wasn't there when they left. An older guy named Dean was on duty."

He barely resisted kicking the locker again. "What did Dean say?"

"That Rissa left the building to take her kid for ice cream around six-forty, right before he went home for the day. Rafferty didn't get there till after seven."

Burn called Rissa, but it went directly to voicemail. He hit call again, and the voicemail replied again. He pocketed his cell and stooped to lace up his boots. "What time did Styles get arrested?"

"Around the same time," Pan said.

An invisible hand sucker-punched Burn's chest. He'd left, and Rissa was gone. The question was, had she been taken or had she run? He hated that he didn't know for sure. They'd disagreed, but it hadn't been serious, had it?

"What are you thinking?" Butter asked.

"We had a disagreement this morning before I left. But I don't think ... She doesn't have the resources simply to disappear. This wasn't her leaving on her own."

Kama slammed his cage shut. "We'll find her. Someone had to have seen where she went."

Pan shrugged. "So far, no one's come forward. Styles called us when he discovered Rissa wasn't in her apartment. We tracked down the security guy and confirmed the time she left on the camera."

"And the cops?" Burn had to get over there. See for himself what was happening.

Pan inclined his head. "Styles raised a ruckus after they arrested him until they called Officer Dalton, the detective working the break-in. Dalton got Styles released, but it was already too late. Rissa was gone, and no one saw anything."

"Cam, Styles, and Coal are there now, canvassing the area," Butter said. "Nothing so far. Wait, I got a text." He fished out his cell. "It's Styles. Jimbo's Creamery is closed, but Styles found a bag with two cartons of ice cream on the curb halfway down the block from the apartment."

"Shit," Burn muttered, his pulse hammering as he grabbed hold of the situation.

Butter rubbed his chin while studying his phone. "We can't confirm those cartons were hers. He's trying to track down the owner of the ice cream shop."

"Un-fucking-believable." Someone scooped her up. Burn was sure of it. Rissa had left the apartment and been snatched. He never should have trusted that she'd be safe on her own. He loved her, and even if it was one-sided, he was determined to protect her and get her back. "I need to get over there. Someone must have seen something."

"Let's roll," Kama said.

The four of them jogged toward the parking lot.

His team had his back. Pan, Kama, and Butter right beside him with Cam, Styles, and Coal already on site. Scoot was still out recovering from a head injury, and Mac was recuperating in Germany.

"I'll ride with you," Butter said as he climbed into the passenger seat of the truck.

Burn dialed his brother before dropping the phone on the console. The ringing tone came through the speakers and only rang once before Paul answered.

"Hey, brother. It was great to spend time with you on Sunday. I was going to call you today because I learned something interesting about your girlfriend—"

"Paul," Burn cut him off. "I've got trouble."

"Listening."

"We believe someone grabbed Rissa Parker and her daughter on the street near the apartment. I'm on the way there now to search for witnesses and see if any cameras caught a tag. Can you help?"

"Roger that. I'll reach out to my FBI contact and meet you there. Text me the address and any details you have," said Paul in his give-no-quarter police voice. "We'll find them."

Burn's throat felt thick with gratitude. "Thanks," he said, punching the gas on his truck. His job was to protect Rissa and Shelby, and he'd failed miserably. Now he was going to get them back and annihilate whoever had touched them. It was his fault for leaving them alone. Regardless of what Rissa had said to him, he shouldn't have listened.

CHAPTER 33

Terrance awoke refreshed on Wednesday morning. He'd taken two antibiotics before lying down and had a good night's rest. Or perhaps he'd slept well because he now had the girl in his possession. Not just any girl, but his daughter. The thought gave him an odd sensation, and he wasn't altogether certain it was pleasant. He checked his cell and found a text Rick had sent during the night.

Be there in twenty-four hours with a truck.

Good news. He could send his guests back in the truck with Rick and fly home. Put this mess behind him and sleep in his own bed tomorrow night. In the meantime, he needed to manage Marissa Parker. He'd already decided to leave the child with her, but did he have other options? Perhaps he could use the boyfriend to his advantage.

After showering and dressing his wound, he put on slacks and a white dress shirt, forgoing his usual tie and jacket. He slid on his boots and strolled into the living room, expecting to find Walt and Grant waiting for him.

Only Walt sat on the couch with the news blaring on the television.

"Where's Grant?" Terrance asked. He could use the muscle man to guard his reluctant daughter when he brought her out again.

"He's taking a shower," Walt said. "You hungry? Our guy dropped off takeout, and I brewed a fresh pot of coffee."

The pair had made decisions independently. His men back home would never dare without consulting him. But what the fuck did he care? He'd be leaving town in another day. "Fine," he snapped.

Walt gave him a sly glance. "I paid the driver in cash."

Anger tingled down Terrance's spine. He'd like to drop the man in his tracks, but he was too exposed in this city. He'd have to tolerate him a little longer. He rolled his head in a slow circle, making the joints crackle. "How about I send the money to you to disburse?"

"Sure," Walt said, an odd glint in his brown eyes. "The girl is your daughter. We had no idea."

"Which is none of your concern." Terrance lowered himself onto a chair at the table and opened his laptop. "The money is transferred. I'm going to get coffee. While I do that, bring out Marissa and secure her in one of these chairs. I don't want to deal with any histrionics."

"You got it." Walt unfurled from the couch, stretching every fat vertebra in his back, before sauntering toward the bedroom.

After he disappeared down the hall, Terrance pushed quickly to his feet. Too quickly, because something popped in his side, and pain radiated through his abdomen. He clenched his teeth to smother a moan and fought the black edges creeping into his vision. With a white-knuckled grip on the table's edge, he waited for the agony to pass before slumping back on the chair. He drew air in and out of his nose as he worked up the energy to try again.

It seemed only a minute passed before Walt returned with Marissa and her child.

"Sit there," Walt ordered, yanking a chair away from the table.

Marissa leveled a glare at him but didn't argue. The child had her thumb stuffed in her mouth—her eyes wide, round orbs of green.

Terrance sighed. He had another headache. "Be easy with them, Walt. I'd rather the smallest guest not begin crying too early."

Walt secured one of Marissa's ankles with a zip tie and arched a brow at Terrance. "Good enough?"

"Yeah, it's fine. Push in her chair and then get me coffee. Also, whatever they need." Terrance's chair was across the table from Marissa. He folded his laptop and pushed it aside. "Have you processed the information I gave you yesterday?"

She stiffened and nodded. "I did."

"And?"

"I believe you," she said, her gaze darting around the room. "I don't like it, but I believe you."

He smirked at her bravado. "You must embrace your new circumstances. You belong to me now. Even so, I'm curious." He surprised himself by chuckling. "Let's discuss other genetic traits."

"What do you mean?" she said.

He watched her expression when he said, "My granddaughter. Tell me about her father."

"I ..." Her mouth flattened to a straight line. "I don't know who he is."

Terrance reared his head back in surprise. "Your SEAL doesn't know he's the father?"

Rissa's shoulders rolled forward, and she wouldn't meet his gaze. "He's not."

"Here," Walt interrupted, plopping down a box of cereal and a pair of bowls. "I'll get your coffee now."

"Crunch?" Shelby reached for the box.

"Okay, baby." Marissa pulled a bowl closer to shake out some dry cereal.

Drumming his fingers, Terrance waited. When she met his gaze, her expression told the entire story. Cruz was the father, but she didn't want to admit it. "You're a liar. I wonder why."

She pinned her shoulders back to glare at him. "I swear he's not her—"

Terrance interrupted with a bark of laughter. "Shut up. All you're telling me is that he doesn't know. That's good, since we're leaving tomorrow. A clean break is best."

Walt returned with a cup of coffee and placed it before him. "Need anything in it?"

He almost said no but shrugged. The liquor would take the edge off. "Bring the bourbon."

Rissa spoke as Walt spun back toward the bar. "Can I have coffee also?" she asked, her eyes glinting green sparks.

Walt raised his bushy brows at Terrance.

He shrugged. "Get it for her but dilute it with milk." There was no point in giving her something hot to toss on him.

Walt set the bourbon on the table and returned to the kitchen. A minute later, he returned with two more cups of coffee, and when it seemed he planned to join them at the table, Terrance shook his head.

"I'll call you when we're done. But stay close while we converse."

Rissa's hand trembled as she picked up her coffee, and it sloshed over her fingers. Terrance liked that she hid her fear otherwise.

He sipped his bourbon-spiked coffee, enjoying the way it blazed down his throat. Then he gave her a sly grin. "Shelby's father is Bernie Cruz."

•   •   •

"Burn?" Shelby asked, her eyes gleaming with hope.

Rissa shushed her, glaring at the man who held their lives in his hands. "She can't eat the cereal like this. She needs milk with it."

"Walt, get it," Terrance ordered.

Rissa watched as Walt rose from a chair by the couch and returned to the kitchen. He wasn't as bad as Grant. He hadn't hurt her when he'd brought her from the bedroom, and the tie around her leg wasn't very tight. She'd lain awake all night thinking about reasons that Terrance hadn't killed them outright. There was no doubt in Rissa's mind that he needed her for some reason, but what? She was glad he did, because she and Shelby would be dead otherwise.

"I'm curious as to why you haven't told him, but it does seem to be a pattern. Is someone in his family offering money for your silence?" Terrance snickered.

Panic surged through Rissa, and her heart skipped. If he knew for sure that Burn was Shelby's father, it would give him one more thing to use against her. So, she doubled down on her lie. "You're wrong. Burn isn't her father."

Terrance scoffed and tipped the bottle of bourbon over his coffee mug a second time. "Just when I think you aren't too stupid, you try my patience. How about this? My business associate has offered to send a sharpshooter to take care of Burn for you. That way, you won't have to share custody of my granddaughter."

"No," she blurted, louder than she intended.

Walt returned to place a tall glass of milk on the table. Shelby reached for it, and Rissa barely prevented it from tipping over.

Terrance reclined in his chair, watching her over the rim of his mug. "Hmm. Your fire is more interesting than pathetic whimpering. It's nice my daughter has a backbone."

"Please, leave Burn alone. He doesn't know. I never told him, so he won't be a problem," Rissa pleaded desperately. She hoped that if Burn weren't seen as a threat to whatever Terrance wanted, he wouldn't hurt him.

"You care for him," he stated, placing his phone on the table. "Let's see if Mr. Ravago, the owner of this house, can help us with this."

Rissa's blood stalled as he dialed a number and put the call on speaker. After four rings, a deep and heavily accented voice answered.

"My morning is rushed. I didn't expect to hear from you today. Is your vacation over?"

"I need a favor," Terrance responded, his gaze never leaving Rissa's face.

"We should meet in person. Phones are not secure," the man suggested. "Let's have an early dinner. Walt knows the place."

"See you then." Terrance clicked off the call and sipped from his mug.

"Milk," Shelby whispered.

Rissa's hand trembled as she poured milk over the cereal. The overwhelming uncertainty and fear of what might happen next threatened to consume her. "What're you going to do?" she asked, her voice cracking with emotion.

"It's simple," Terrance replied calmly. "You'll do everything I tell you, or there will be consequences."

"Consequences?"

"The first is your boyfriend. If you refuse to comply with my requests, attempt to escape, or do anything without my explicit instructions, I will have him killed. Better yet, I'll have someone shoot out his knees and ruin his life. The second consequence is your daughter. That should be self-explanatory." He pointed a finger at Shelby and mimed pulling the trigger of a gun.

Rissa trembled so hard her teeth chattered. "Do whatever you want to me, but please don't hurt Burn or Shelby. If I knew she was safe, I … it would be easier to do whatever you want. You could let Burn take her."

"Now you're asking me to send my granddaughter to live with a stranger, someone who has no real connection to her except for shared genetics. He left you alone to raise your child. Or did you push him away?"

Heat flushed Rissa's face, and she shrank back from his gaze.

He snorted derisively. "I guess you are an idiot."

"I—"

"You made it easy for me. Think about that, Marissa. This is your fault." Laughter charged out of him, and he slapped the table. "When we're back in Austin, perhaps I'll let you call the SEAL and break things off. Tell him you found your real father and are starting your life over." He absently pressed a hand to his side, and a pained expression flashed across his features.

What was wrong with him? Then it dawned on her. "You were shot."

He tilted his head to study her. "I was. Did you see it happen?"

Rissa almost said yes, but decided the less he knew, the better. "No, but I heard the sound, and I can tell you're hurt." She relaxed when he seemed to accept her explanation. Now she needed to think of ways to use his injury to her advantage.

"Where were you hiding in Amelia's house?" Terrance asked.

She licked her lips. "I didn't see anything. I hid when the alarm went off, then a gun went off. The keys to the car were right there, so I took them."

Shelby knocked over her bowl, dumping milk and cereal onto both their laps. "Uh oh," whispered Shelby.

Rissa closed her eyes briefly. When she opened them, Terrance watched her with lifted brows. Ignoring his scrutiny, she reassured her daughter, "It's okay, baby. It was an accident."

Shelby whimpered, "Me wet."

"Kids are a giant pain in the ass," he said. "You are a wet, stupid girl because you made a mess."

Shelby burst into tears and buried her face in Rissa's sweatshirt.

Rissa cuddled her. "It's alright, baby. Mommy's not mad," she reassured her daughter, never taking her eyes off Terrance. "I need something to clean this up with."

"Are we clear on our arrangement?"

She conceded with a nod. No point in arguing. The man was unhinged. "I'll do whatever you want. Please don't hurt Shelby. Or Burn."

This was her fault. She'd pushed Burn away, and now his life was in danger because of her. He didn't even know Shelby was his daughter, so how had Terrance figured it out?

Her freedom might be over, but she'd do everything she could to keep Burn and their beautiful daughter safe. She loved them both so much. Terrance planned to move them tomorrow, so she needed to get Shelby out of here before that happened. Burn would take care of her daughter if something happened to her.

Why did it take a deranged kidnapper for her to realize how much she loved him?

CHAPTER 34

Burn's jaw muscles clenched beneath the stubble that shadowed his cheeks. His SEAL team stood in a line behind him as he faced his brother and the lead FBI agent. The tension between the groups buzzed as sharply as an electric current.

FBI agents tracked down this property through an operative on Juan Ravago's security team. The DEA had been looped in because Ravago was a known drug dealer, and Burn had been with Paul when he got the call. Now, the FBI, DEA, and Whiskey Team had converged outside the fence encircling the property.

Satellite images showed a triple lot with expansive lawns and a high fence surrounding a two-story stucco dwelling. The residence boasted a tile roof, a three-car garage in the back, and an elaborate camera system. Behind it was an in-ground pool and a deluxe cabana enclosed by a separate chain-link fence. The corporation that owned this property had plenty of disposable cash. A corporation, in turn, owned by Juan Ravago.

Paul's DEA people and the FBI agents wanted to gather intel using drones before formulating a plan of action, but there were no drones on-site yet. Burn knew they could never have too much information before breaching a location, but time was running out. Rissa and her baby were in the hands of a psycho, and Burn needed to act.

Paul's expression was unreadable, though his eyes betrayed his concern. "Brother, we have to be patient."

Burn shook his head. "We wouldn't have found this place so quickly without your help, but now we're here, use my team to do what you can't legally, without more concrete evidence. Rissa's tough, but I can't—I won't let her down." He tugged Paul aside for a private exchange. "There's something else."

Paul didn't ask, just waited for Burn to speak.

"It's Shelby." Burn's throat closed, and he had to clear it before finishing. "I'm almost positive she's my daughter."

"Freaking amazing," Paul said, gripping Burn's shoulders, his eyes full of sympathy and love. "We'll have a party when we get them back." His gaze shifted from the fence to Burn. "Right now, I'd want to rush in there and grab my family, but think about it. Shelby needs a father, and it's suicide to go over that fence with no visual. What if this is a false lead?"

"Nothing matters but getting them out of there."

"There's something else you need to know." Paul's hand tightened before he released him. "I'd hoped to tell you this differently."

"What?"

"Yesterday, an attorney contacted the FBI in San Antonio about Marissa's former employer. The woman, Amelia Iglesias, died in a fire a week ago."

"I know all that."

"Did you know that Terrance Simmons, the man we believe is the kidnapper inside this house, is Amelia Iglesias' stepson? According to that attorney, Marissa Parker, is the sole heir of Iglesias' sizable fortune. We're talking hundreds of millions."

Burn sucked in a breath. "She didn't tell me."

"He said she doesn't know, he's trying to find her to tell her. The bottom line is we're pretty sure Simmons needs her to get his mother's money." Paul hesitated. "That's not the clincher. Simmons is Marissa's biological father."

The weight of that revelation nearly knocked Burn off his feet. "What the—?"

"I'm only telling you because maybe you don't want to kill him." Paul's deep brown eyes held compassion. "Let our teams handle this."

"Paul," Burn growled through clenched teeth. "That may all be true, but what if he hurts her or Shelby? I can't wait for the drone. Your men can stand down, but my team is going in."

"That's great," sneered the lead FBI agent.

Burn turned to face him. "What?"

"A SEAL team operating on American soil brings consequences. You need to leave this to us," he said, pointing a finger at their group.

Styles moved forward, shoulder to shoulder with Burn. "I'm just a friend standing with my buddy. No SEAL action is needed here."

Burn's throat thickened with gratitude as he faced his guys. No uniforms, no body armor, and sidearms were their only weapons. His family in all but blood. Butter, Styles, Pan, Coal, Kama, and Cam. But he didn't want to risk his team if there was another way. That would be trading one family for another. He had to keep everyone safe.

"Rushing in blind isn't the answer," Paul pleaded.

A second FBI agent, a man with sharp eyes and a sharper suit, nodded in agreement. "Waiting is the smart move."

"Alright," Burn conceded, the warrior in him bowing to strategy.

•　　•　　•

Shelby slept on the king-sized bed while Rissa paced the oversized bedroom. After the breakfast confrontation, Terrance stuck them back in here, and they'd been alone for hours. At least they had a television. Her daughter had watched cartoons well into the afternoon before falling asleep.

They needed to escape. Rissa figured her odds of getting past Walt and Grant were slim, so they were going out a window. She'd checked all three in the bedroom and decided the best option was the one facing the front of the house. Terrance had told her no one would hear her scream, but he could've been lying. She had no idea how close they were to the other homes.

The property was surrounded by a tall wooden privacy fence, except for the metal gate at the entrance. The vertical poles on the gate curled up eight or ten feet, like giant black candy canes. Rissa imagined climbing over them with Shelby in her arms. She didn't think they could squeeze through because they were too close together. Maybe she could open the gate somehow or flag down a car. It was a risk, but returning to Texas with Terrance would be a death sentence.

Leaving the apartment had been a foolish mistake. An ID could be replaced, but her daughter's safety should've been her main concern. She had allowed herself to be swept along by circumstances for too long, reacting and getting through situations instead of taking control. Her parents had made it clear they thought she was inferior in every way, and at some point, she guessed she started believing them.

Then she met Burn. She had been afraid to search for him. Then, afraid to tell him about his daughter, yet he had stood by them without question. She loved him, and because of her, Terrance threatened to maim or kill him. She pushed Burn away, and now she and Shelby would die if she didn't find a way out of this house.

Rissa hardened her resolve. Things would be different if they survived this. She'd tell Burn that he was a father and make sure he knew she'd share their daughter, regardless of whether the two of them stayed together.

The past was exactly that. She'd made mistakes, but she could make better choices in the future. More determined than ever, Rissa crossed to the window she'd chosen and traced her fingers along the frame. A rectangular sensor protruded from the corner, but there was no light or indication the alarm was active. Maybe it wasn't supposed to have a light, or maybe it was only active if the main alarm was turned on. There was no way to tell.

She would wait. It would be safer to try the window at night, while everyone was asleep.

By midafternoon, the sour stench of stale milk and urine on her clothes was making Rissa nauseous. She used a rag to clean them as well as she could without actually undressing, but it barely helped.

Shelby sat up on the bed and rubbed her eyes.

"Hey, did you have a nice nap?" Rissa put an arm around her.

"Yes," Shelby said. Then she looked at her expectantly. "Me eat?"

"I'm sorry, sweetie," Rissa said, scooping her daughter onto her lap. "We don't have anything right now. Let's watch some TV and maybe later—"

Someone tapped lightly before pushing open the bedroom door. Rissa immediately rose and put herself in front of Shelby, ready to face the new threat.

Walt stepped into the room, an unreadable expression on his face.

Fear was a sharp tang in Rissa's mouth. "What're you doing here? Terrance won't like you coming into our room."

He pressed a finger to his lips before setting a pair of juice containers, a box of cereal, and a package of pull-ups on the floor. He backed most of the way out, then paused to whisper almost too softly for her to hear, "Trust me. Everything will be okay." Then he was gone.

What a strange thing for him to say. Rissa was glad to have the items, especially the pull-ups, but what had Walt meant with his whispered words? Was he going to help them, or did he have some new plan with his boss to take her out of here? She had no idea if the Ravago person would be a better or worse alternative.

Her stomach rumbled. At least he brought something for Shelby to eat. There were no cups or bowls, so she poured a small pile of cereal on the bedspread.

Shelby's mouth was a round O. "Mess?" she asked softly.

"It's okay. We're having a silly picnic," Rissa said, turning up the cartoon's volume on the television. Her daughter giggled and munched on the cereal. Rissa peeled the plastic from both apple juice containers and handed one to Shelby. Then she took a big gulp of the second one. Very sweet, but she'd need the sugar for energy if they were going to run tonight. She grabbed a handful of cereal and peeked out the front window in time to see a black SUV leaving the gate. Probably Terrance, leaving to meet the Ravago fellow. She thought about trying to leave right now, but she had no idea if Walt and Grant were still in the house. It was better to wait for darkness.

The afternoon stretched, and eventually, Shelby fell asleep again. Rissa watched the gate, hoping for a miracle, but only saw the SUV returning a few hours after it left.

The sun set, and finally, the time on the television read 10 PM. She waited almost another hour to make sure the men were sleeping. Then, gathering her courage, she crossed to the bed and gently lifted Shelby.

At that moment, the bedroom door slammed open, banging loudly against the wall. Grant gave her a malevolent glare. "Mr. Simmons wants to talk to you. You can leave the kid here."

"I ..." Rissa would never leave Shelby alone in this house of horrors. "I'll bring her. She'll be scared and cry if I leave her."

Grant folded his arms over his chest and tipped his chin.

She took that as agreement and squared her posture. "Don't shove me. It'll make Shelby cry, and Terrance won't like that. She's his granddaughter." The words were acid on her tongue. She didn't want to claim any relation to the devil, but she'd say anything to protect her child.

Grant shrugged and turned sideways to make room in the opening, but she still had to pass him. Rissa marched regally forward, increasing her pace to put distance between them, and, to her relief, Grant didn't touch her. He trailed behind them down the short hall and into the living room.

Terrance stood on the opposite side of the room with a gun trained on ... Walt? He swung his gaze to her, the weapon in his hand wobbling as he poked the air in Walt's direction. "Marissa," he spoke through clenched teeth. "I found a traitor in my house."

Walt was backed against the wall near the entrance to the dining room. "That's not true. Tell him, Grant. I haven't done anything."

Terrance squinted and waved the gun. "Grant says you've been naughty. What have you done, Walt?"

Fear rippled down Rissa's spine. Terrance appeared to have completely lost his mind. He held a bottle of bourbon in one hand, a gun in the other.

Grant moved closer to Terrance, obviously picking a side.

"Marissa?" Terrance hissed out her name.

Rissa wasn't sure what he wanted, so she remained silent.

"Why?" He licked his lips. "Why do you think I had Grant bring you out to witness this?"

She slowly shook her head. "I don't know."

Shelby was awake and trembling, but kept her face buried in Rissa's sweatshirt.

"Of course, you don't know. We've established that you're stupid. Walt, get on your knees and beg for my forgiveness."

Walt immediately dropped to the floor. "Mr. Simmons, I have no idea what Grant told you. I gave your daughter some diapers and juice, nothing more. It was to keep the baby quiet, nothing more."

"I'm talking about you communicating with someone outside, you asshole." Terrance pressed the gun into Walt's forehead, right between his eyes.

Rissa scanned the room. The front door had a deadbolt. Terrance would shoot her if she ran past him to reach the garage exit. Where could they go? Stairs. It was a big house. There could be a deck or another way out of this house upstairs.

"Did you hear me?" Terrance barked.

She swung her gaze back to find him glowering at her. "Y-yes," she stuttered.

"My daughter even agrees." Terrance took a slug of bourbon and refocused on Walt.

Rissa edged toward the bottom of the staircase. Unfortunately, she'd have to move closer to the three men to reach her goal.

"Mr. Simmons, if you call Ravago, he'll vouch for me."

Terrance stuck out his lip like an overgrown toddler. "I don't trust him."

Sweat trickled down Walt's face. "I understand, but if—"

"No! I don't trust anyone," Terrance roared, waving the gun wildly, briefly pointing at her, then Grant, before fixating back on Walt. "Grant told me you had a second phone hidden in your room. Perhaps I should trust him."

"My extra phone is a burner that Ravago asked me to carry."

"You call him with it?"

"Sometimes," Walt panted, bobbing his head in agreement.

Rissa was more than halfway to the staircase. Shelby lifted her head, and Rissa whispered, "We have to be very quiet."

Shelby jammed her thumb in her mouth and burrowed into Rissa's neck.

"Mr. Simmons," Grant said, "we should call Ravago. If you kill him, there might be problems."

"How much?" Terrance said, enunciating his words slowly.

Grant's brows pinched together. "How much trouble?"

"No, you fool." Terrance spat on the floor. "How much money for you to shut up and take orders from me until I leave this damn city?"

Rissa had reached the bottom step. All she had to do now was swing around the big knob of the banister and run up the stairs.

Then what?

Walt lunged for Terrance and the gun went off. The sound exploded through the house twice in quick succession.

Someone screamed, and Rissa knew it was Walt's last scream.

"Shit, man! Don't shoot me! I'm on your side!" Grant bellowed, his hands in the air.

Rissa didn't hesitate to grab the banister and swing around to run up the stairs, keeping her body tucked low around Shelby. Her heart pounded so hard she could barely breathe, and Shelby clung like a barnacle, whimpering in fear.

CHAPTER 35

The piercing sound of gunfire shattered the quiet darkness, and Burn's mind instantly filled with an image of Rissa's vivacious life draining from her body. He turned to his team. "No one has to go with me."

"I'm with you," Butter declared.

Pan and Coal nodded in agreement.

Kama grunted out, "Hooyah."

"Let's do this," Styles joined in, smacking Cam on the back.

Paul threw up his hands. "If there's no stopping you, at least wait for me to create a distraction at the front gate. It'll give you time to get inside," he said, snatching up a flare gun.

Burn and his team quickly mobilized next to the fence. They were going in without night vision or their usual gear. Luckily, the moon was full, and the ground floor of the house seemed to have all the lights on. Burn suspected there were motion lights outside the house, but they would avoid or disable them quickly.

Pan and Coal cupped their hands to boost him up the ten-foot wooden wall. Farther down, Kama and Butter stood ready to lift Styles.

•   •   •

Rissa's heart pounded in sync with her racing feet as she ran up the staircase. Terrance let out a cruel laugh somewhere behind her, but there were no more gunshots. After reaching the second story, she stayed low. The carpeted catwalk was extra wide, but if he were looking, Terrance could see her through the open rails from the living room downstairs.

There were three closed doors along the wall. She pushed open the first one and stepped into a spacious bedroom. It had an ensuite bathroom and no balcony. She hurried out and tried the second door—another bathroom. Thinking fast, she clicked the thumb lock and shut it. That might buy her a minute or two if Terrance believed she had locked herself inside.

One door left.

She entered and quickly thumbed the lock, scanning the bedroom for anything she could move in front of the door. Nothing. The furniture was too heavy, and she didn't want to waste any more time. This bedroom didn't have a balcony either, but it did have two large windows facing the front of the house.

Shelby popped her thumb out of her mouth long enough to whimper, "Mommy?"

"We still need to be quiet, baby. Mommy is going to get us out of here." She hoped.

Tucking Shelby on her hip, she yanked back the curtains. There was a short section of tiled roof below both the windows. She guessed it was for the porch overhang. If she could climb off that, it wouldn't be such a long drop to the ground.

Rissa could hear Terrance calling her name as he searched for them. Help wasn't coming. There was no choice but to take her baby out of a second-story window.

"Sweetie, I need you to stand right here so I can open this," Rissa said, putting Shelby on her feet so she could attack the latches with both hands.

Suddenly, a bright explosion of yellow light illuminated the darkness above the iron gate.

"Burn," Rissa whispered and for the first time since they'd been taken, hope bloomed in her chest.

•   •   •

When the flare went off, the team propelled Burn and Styles up the fence. They easily slid down the other side, diving in opposite directions to avoid sniper fire. Burn didn't need to check to know his team would follow close behind. He scanned the yard but didn't immediately find a target.

The FBI's inside man hadn't provided a headcount of the bad guys, so they had to be ready for anything. With practiced hand motions, he directed his team to spread out around the house.

•   •   •

Shelby whimpered and clung to Rissa's leg, one thumb securely in her mouth.

"We'll be okay," she said, praying she wasn't lying to her daughter. The latches didn't budge at first, but she finally managed to unlock both sides and push the window open.

The alarm beeped, but it didn't matter. Terrance was about to find them anyway. She snatched up her whimpering daughter, perched on the windowsill, and swung her legs outside. Her bare feet rested on the short section of clay-tiled roof.

She kissed Shelby's head. "Sweetie, I need you to hold tightly to Mommy. Don't let go no matter what, and don't look down."

Shelby clung to her with shuddering sobs, and her little fingers twisted into Rissa's hair.

Gripping the window frame in one hand, Rissa eased forward to gauge the distance to the ground. Fear clogged her throat as she thought about how badly that fall could injure her baby girl.

•   •   •

Burn's heart nearly stopped when he spotted Rissa and Shelby emerging from an upstairs window. The top floor of the house was dark, but she was easy to see in the bright moonlight. Rissa teetered precariously on the narrow ledge over a small section of clay-tiled roof extending over the porch.

"Hang on!" he shouted, sprinting across the yard toward her.

Shots were fired from the house, but Burn didn't stop. Rissa and Shelby were about to fall, and he had to catch them.

"Watch your one o'clock!" Styles' shout reached him an instant before a bullet whizzed past his ear.

Burn crouched and spotted a figure at the front window. Before he could lift his weapon, someone from his team neutralized the threat.

•   •   •

The sound of gunfire below gave her hope they would be saved. Maybe she should go back inside the bedroom and wait for rescue. Indecision froze her in place. Shelby started crying, and Rissa whispered as much to herself as her daughter, "We'll be okay—"

Something hit her from behind, sending her sliding onto the shingles. With a strangled cry, Rissa twisted to grip the bottom of the window frame with one hand, her other clutching Shelby. Her knees scrambled for purchase on the clay tiles, and her feet dangled over the edge.

"Hahahaha!" Terrance's laughter was that of a madman. "I own you. You'll die before I let you go. Give me my granddaughter."

"Rissa!" Burn's urgent voice cut through the din of her adrenaline and fear.

"Burn?" She turned her head but couldn't see him over the roof's edge. Hope and relief had her shaking. "Help us!"

"He can't save you," Terrance singsonged above her.

•   •   •

Burn skidded to a halt beneath them. He holstered his gun and spread his arms to catch them. "Let go, Rissa! I've got you."

A wild-eyed man, probably Terrance Simmons, leaned out the window above her, a gun in his hand. "You are too late!" he cackled.

"No, please!" Something happened and Rissa began sliding over the roof's edge with Shelby in her arms.

The world slowed to a crawl, and when the sharp crack of a gunshot rang out, Burn held firm, even as pain exploded in his shoulder. He stumbled backward, arms outstretched, and knees locked. Rissa and Shelby landed on top of him, and he allowed their momentum to carry them all to the ground. His team would finish the job. Team was family, and family would take out the threats.

The fight drained from his body and the void swallowed him.

•   •   •

The impact when they landed knocked the breath out of Rissa. She recovered quickly and ran her hands over Shelby, checking for injuries, grateful they were both alive and relatively unscathed. She rolled to kneel beside Burn, still holding her daughter.

"Burn, you got here—" she began, and her breath caught at the sight of the huge red stain blooming on his shirt.

"Me Burn?" cried Shelby, struggling to reach him.

Bullets pinged the ground around them, and Rissa threw her body over Burn with Shelby tucked between them.

"Marissa!" shouted Terrance from the second-story window. "Come back right now, or I'm going to shoot you all."

No-no-no! Fury surged through her veins. Terrance had hurt or maybe killed Burn, and now he was threatening to shoot her daughter. Rissa yanked Burn's gun from the holster, aimed it roughly in Terrance's direction, and pulled the trigger. The gun recoiled so much she nearly dropped it.

Then Styles was there, taking the gun and yelling for Kama to check out Burn. Rissa sprang into action, yanking off her sweatshirt and using it to staunch the flow of blood. Kama appeared on Burn's other side.

"Chief. It's not a good time to lay around. Can you hear me?" His words were conversational, but his actions were those of an experienced medic checking him over.

"He's still bleeding," Rissa said.

Kama didn't glance at her as he checked Burn for other wounds. "Bleeding is a good thing, right now. If he's bleeding, the bullet didn't stop his heart from pumping."

Rissa held the sweatshirt in place and Shelby in her other arm.

"Will you let me take the munchkin?" asked Styles.

Her immediate response was no, but then Shelby reached for him, so Rissa allowed it. Burn needed her more right now. "Don't let her out of your sight."

"She's safe with me."

Paul rushed over to join them. "Ambulance is on the way. How bad is he?"

Kama rocked back on his heels. "Keep that pressure and let me know if you get tired. The bullet missed his heart as far as I can tell. I'm fairly certain it got his collarbone. Maybe a rib or two." His brown eyes fixed on her. "Are you injured?"

"I'm fine," Rissa said, but her teeth had begun to chatter. She didn't think she was that cold, it was most likely shock.

"Butter," Kama called. "Anyone got a rescue blanket? I need two."

CHAPTER 36

The EMTs didn't let her ride in the ambulance, but Burn's brother, Paul, had a booster seat in his truck and drove her and Shelby to the hospital. She rode in the back with Shelby.

"You told the EMTs you were fine, but are you certain you two aren't hurt?" Paul asked.

"We're good. Burn saved us," her voice hitched on the last word. He'd saved them and now he was hurt all because of … her father. "Is Terrance dead?"

"Yes."

She had to swallow past the lump in her throat. "Good. He was psycho. And Paul? He has a police officer helping him. He was there in San Antonio when he killed his stepmother."

Paul's mouth flattened, and he glanced over the seat at her. "I'm going to need more information about that."

"I told the officer. Manny Dalton. The one who came when the men broke into the apartment. He didn't believe me, but I told him everything, and he wrote it down. Terrance also said the name Juan Ravago a few times and called him on the phone. He was going to have Ravago …" her voice broke, "hurt Burn."

"Not on my watch," snarled Paul.

By the time they arrived at the hospital, Burn was in surgery. Rissa and Paul were directed to a surgical waiting room, and the whole team—Styles, Kama, Coal, Pan, Butter, and Cam—packed in with them.

Styles charmed Shelby, keeping her entertained while Rissa barely held it together. If Burn died, it would be her fault and if he lived, she would tell him that he shouldn't forgive her. Maybe Shelby would be better off with him anyway.

Paul startled her when he put an arm around her shoulders. "Rissa. There's an officer here who wants to talk to you. Says you know him."

She shook her head, "Please, can it wait?"

"I got this," Paul said and walked over to where Manny Dalton, along with a second police officer, waited. He returned a few minutes later. "They'll come back after Burn is settled in a room."

Rissa nodded and pulled her knees up to her chin. Her sweatshirt had gone in the ambulance with Burn and was no doubt in the garbage now. She was cold and stank of blood, milk and sweat, but she didn't care. She was staying right here until she knew Burn would be all right.

Later, when a nurse came in to check her and Shelby for injuries, Rissa refused to leave the waiting room and Paul ran interference for her again. At some point, the same nurse returned with a pair of slippers for her to wear. She'd forgotten her feet were bare.

"Thank you," Rissa whispered.

They'd been waiting over an hour when Burn's parents arrived. His mother came over and pulled her into a hug and all Rissa could do was cry.

"Honey, my Bernie is tough and he's going to be fine," she said, settling back on the plastic seat and keeping an arm around Rissa. "Call me Latrice. That's my husband Ed over there with Paul. Here, you must be freezing," she said, wrapping a thick cotton sweater around Rissa's shoulders. "Hospitals are always so cold."

Rissa didn't think she would ever be warm again.

Burn's dad stepped outside with Paul, and the waiting room was quiet. Shelby left Styles and crossed to Rissa, her thumb in her mouth.

"Mommy crying?" Shelby's lip trembled. "Me want Burn."

Rissa scooped her into her lap. "I do too. I want you to meet someone," she said, shifting her daughter to face Latrice Cruz. "This is Burn's mommy. Latrice this is ... my daughter. Her name is Shelby Bernice Parker."

"Bernice, huh? Well, isn't that a nice name?"

Shelby popped out her thumb and her gaze bounced from her to Latrice. Then she promptly crawled into Burn's mother's lap like she'd known her all her life.

"Well, aren't you the sweetest thing?" Latrice snuggled Shelby with one arm and used her other hand to pull Rissa's head to her shoulder. "You're both exhausted, why don't you close your eyes and rest a minute?" she said, then began humming a low melody.

Shelby promptly closed her eyes and fell asleep.

Burn's dad came back in the room and sat on Rissa's other side. Not touching her, just a solid wall. A protector like Burn.

Real families did this for each other. Burn's guys, his parents, his brother—everyone together. They all sat quietly until finally, a doctor entered the waiting room to speak with the family. Latrice kept an arm around her while the surgeon explained what they'd done.

The bullet had hit the central third of Burn's collarbone and nicked the subclavian vein, which was why he'd bled so profusely. The doctor told them that if the bullet had gone a centimeter in either direction, it would've hit the jugular vein or an artery, and he wouldn't have made it to the hospital for surgery. For now, he was out of the woods, but he'd be in the hospital at least a week, maybe longer.

After Burn was moved to a private room, his parents took care of Shelby while she talked to the investigators about Terrance Simmons. Rissa had zero remorse that her biological father had been ended that night.

By the time she finished answering all the questions, it was mid-morning. Burn hadn't woken yet, but the doctors assured them it was his body's way of getting the rest it needed, and he was recovering as well as expected.

In the late afternoon, Burn's mother offered to take Shelby to her house for the night and tried to talk Rissa into coming home to rest, but she wouldn't leave him. She could live without sleep, but not without this man who never gave up on her.

Rissa clung to Burn's fingers and rested her cheek on the edge of the cool sheet. She was stiff and achy from sitting in the hard chair beside the hospital bed but unwilling to close her tired eyes. She hadn't really slept since the night before they'd been taken.

Her mind replayed the echo of gunfire, her fall with Shelby from the upstairs window, Burn catching and protecting them even as they hit the ground. That's when the whole world slowed to a heart-stopping crawl. She was glad she'd shot back at Terrance with Burn's gun, although many people were shooting and there was no way to know whose bullet had found its target. The results were the same. Terrance, her father, was dead.

"Please wake up," she whispered, her thumb caressing the rough edges of his knuckles. "I need to tell you I love you." She pressed her lips to his hand. "I'm sorry I didn't trust you. Please give me the chance to tell you that."

At this late hour, the corridors of the hospital were quiet. A police officer sat outside the door, and some of Burn's team lingered nearby in case Ravago's people tried to retaliate. Terrance's accomplice, Rick Brown, had been arrested after Rissa identified him in a photo.

Her phone vibrated against the side table, and a text lit up the screen.

Shelby just fell asleep. Don't worry, we've got her. She's safe and loved. Mom.

Their beautiful daughter was wrapped in the loving arms of Burn's parents. A tear slipped down Rissa's cheek, gratitude and sorrow blending together. His mother had asked Rissa if it was okay for Shelby to call her Nana, and Rissa had cried, telling her that of course it was, because it was true. She hadn't meant to tell them, not yet. It wasn't fair for them to know about Burn's child before him.

"Come back to me, Burn," Rissa said, smoothing a hand over his cheek. "Shelby needs you, and I need to tell you she's your daughter."

If she hadn't been staring at his face, she might've missed the slight motion of his brow. Then his eyelids tightened as if fighting a great weight. It was the barest movement, but to Rissa, thunderous as her pounding heart.

"Burn? Can you hear me?" Her breath hitched. The hand beneath hers tensed, and she could sense him inching his way back to the surface. "Open your eyes. Please come back to me. To me and your daughter," she softly encouraged.

His eyelids twitched. "Rissa?"

That one raspy word was the most beautiful sound she'd ever heard. "Yes, it's me. I'm right here."

He blinked his eyes open, revealing the deep golden pools. "Shelby?"

"She's fine. Great even, thanks to you. She's with your parents, her grandparents."

"Good." His lips curved up, and he weakly squeezed her hand. "About time you told me."

Shock coursed through her. "Told you? You already knew?"

He laughed softly. "I'm a trained tier-one operator. Took me a while, but I figured it out. Is there water?"

She snatched a Styrofoam cup from the bedside table and held the straw for him to take a sip. Tears clogged her throat. "Are you angry I didn't tell you?"

"You weren't ready." He shut his eyes again. "What happened to Simmons?"

"He's dead."

Burn gave a slight nod. "My team?"

"Lots of people were shooting. I even grabbed your gun, but I think he was already gone. And I've never shot a gun before." She rubbed his hand against her cheek.

"Get up here," he murmured.

She didn't hesitate to lower the rail and climb onto the bed next to him. "Shelby and I survived because of you."

"Safe ..." Burn's fingers tightened before he relaxed into a restful sleep.

"I love you," Rissa whispered in the quiet room.

CHAPTER 37

Burn savored the rich coffee on his tongue. His mother had a passion for flavored brews, but thankfully, his dad drank plain dark coffee. He shifted, turning enough to prop his foot in one of the two chairs across the table. This breakfast nook hadn't changed since his high school days, although the bench beneath the bay window had been wider and longer in his memory.

Hearing laughter outside, he turned to watch Shelby and Rissa playing fetch with his mother's cocker spaniel in the backyard. Shelby adored Trixie, and the pair had become inseparable. He'd been in the hospital for several days and longer here at his parents' house. It'd taken all that time to recover from blood loss and surgery. Yesterday his doc had cleared him to drive, which meant next week he'd be on light duty at the base.

He had a one-bedroom apartment on the base, but he hadn't wanted to rush his relationship with Rissa. They'd begun with a one-night stand, and he wanted them to get to know each other, before they went forward. And they would go forward.

Rissa had explained the circumstances that prevented her from searching for him after she discovered her pregnancy, and he mostly understood. At this point, it was water under the bridge. Shelby was his daughter, and that would never change.

The problem was that he couldn't see a way forward between them. Rissa was an heiress in San Antonio, Texas. He'd seen the paperwork. She was now a billionaire with thousands of acres of land, a strip mall, and multiple homes. The money might have tainted origins, but there was plenty of it to make amends and still have some left over. So why would Rissa remain in San Diego when she had so much there for her in Texas? There was no way he was letting her or Shelby out of his life, even if he had to give up his team and his career to be with her.

Shelby burst into the kitchen, chattering about something silly the dog had done outside. He could only make out a few words, but he laughed and helped her climb up on the bench, Trixie right beside her.

"Did you have fun with Trixie and Mommy?"

She giggled. "Yes, Daddy."

His heart tripped. Would he ever get used to hearing that? He and Rissa had told Shelby he was her daddy as soon as he was out of the hospital, and now it seemed "daddy" was her favorite word. He'd better save for whatever sports car she wanted in fourteen years. But then her mother could buy her anything.

"Why the frown?" Rissa asked as she took a seat on the opposite side of the curved bench. Her cheeks were flushed, and her hair was twisted up on her head.

His fingers itched to tug off the scrunchie and delve his fingers into the dark strands. These last days, he'd kept his hands to himself, but that was about to change. Maybe it was time to move them all back to his little apartment. They needed some privacy. He wondered if Rissa would let his mother keep Shelby for a few days so they could spend some time getting to know each other before he went back to work.

"Burn? Are you in pain?"

"No, I'm good. I was thinking about something."

"Thinking," Rissa nodded, keeping her gaze averted when she spoke. "I'm still sleeping in the guest room with Shelby. Would you be more comfortable if we moved back to Liesel's apartment?"

"No. I don't want you to leave."

Rissa turned toward him, and her eyes were cloudy with confusion. "I don't know how to act here. You say you don't want me to leave, but do you really want me to stay?"

The wistful tone in her voice made him realize he was hurting her by not being honest, by not telling her his concerns about their future.

"Stay!" Shelby shouted, clearly listening. She patted Burn's cheek. "Me stay, Daddy?"

"Yes, my princess." He kissed her nose and grinned at Rissa. "The vote is in. You two are staying with me. My base apartment is an option, but it only has one bed. We need to get a bigger place. In the meantime, my folks will let us stay here till we figure things out. If it's okay with you, we'll take it slow."

Rissa gave him a tentative smile. "Slow and steady sounds good to me."

"Steady, Daddy." Shelby giggled and jumped down to roll on the floor with Trixie.

CHAPTER 38

A few months later.

"Happy birthday to you, happy birthday to you, happy birthday ..."

Rissa bumped her glass against Liesel's as they sang along with the well-wishers. Strange to be back in the same place three years later. Only this time, Burn stood at her back with his arm resting on the bar. His solid strength was an anchor in the crowd and in her heart.

Liesel beamed. "It's our birthday, we can—"

"Do what we want to!" Rissa finished, and they burst out laughing.

Burn's lips brushed against her ear. "I like the sound of that. I know what I'd like to do."

She turned her head to look at him. "Someone will hear you."

"What? Hear me say I want to make love to my woman all night?" Burn cupped her cheek, then leaned to cover her mouth with a kiss that left no doubt about what was on his mind.

"Get a room!" a man yelled, and she thought it was Styles.

She loved Burn wholeheartedly, but showing affection in public was difficult for her. She'd grown up in a family that rarely offered any physical touch. Rissa lay her cheek against his chest and breathed in the delicious scent of Rollo's chocolate candy.

Tonight's party at Cicadas was private. Only friends, teammates, and Burn's family were present. His mom and dad had a corner table where they entertained Shelby, the twins, and little Jackson.

She didn't know how to process Shelby having grandparents. Her mother and the man she'd believed to be her father had never treated her with kindness, and now they were dead. Killed by Terrance. Even Mrs. G. had been ... a surrogate aunt, at the least. All her relatives, except her daughter, were dead, murdered by her father.

Her mother had used her to extort money from her step-grandmother, who in turn kept Rissa's existence a secret to use as a bargaining chip. Terrance Simmons had only seen her as another tool in his arsenal of ways to improve his life. Her family tree was awful.

Burn wasn't like anyone she'd ever known. He charged into the situation without caring for his safety because he cared about her. And he forgave her for not telling him about their daughter. He was a straight arrow, smart and loyal to those he loved. How could she be enough for this wonderful man?

"What's got that look on your face?" With his arms around her, he steered her toward an empty corner at the side of the stage.

Her gaze drifted down, and he slid a hand in her hair to tilt up her chin. "Talk to me."

"I ... I don't know how to be this person," she said, unshed tears filling her vision.

"What person?" He dipped his head to trap her with his golden eyes.

She licked her lips. "This person who's good enough for you to love."

He rubbed his thumb over her bottom lip. "Not only me. Everyone here."

"Most of them are your friends."

"Riss, you are family. My family. By extension, everyone here is like ... your cousins. Except my folks. They're much closer kin."

A laugh sprang up her throat. "I love your parents."

"I love you. Have I said that today?"

She slid her arms around his neck and pressed into his hard body. "You might have said it once or twice. I love you too."

"Then it's time for you to prove it."

"What?"

He knelt on the floor at her feet and held out his hand. "Marissa Parker, I love you. I love Shelby, and I'm asking you to be my family. Marry me. I want to grow old with you. Maybe have a few more kids."

She gaped at him. "I ... are you sure?"

He threw his head back and laughed. "Say yes."

"Are you asking me or telling me?"

"There is only one answer I'll accept. If you aren't ready today, I'll keep asking until you are. If you need to move back to Texas, I'm going with you, because I won't be living with my heart in another state. I don't care about that fortune you inherited. I love only you."

Tears streamed down her cheeks. "I love you, too. So, yes, I'll marry you."

He lifted her off her feet and spun her in a circle. "She said yes!" he yelled.

Everyone in the bar cheered.

When he stopped spinning, she clung to him for balance. She never wanted to let go. "Let the lawyers handle everything in Texas. I don't want any of that. My life is here with you."

He growled something unintelligible and slanted his mouth over hers, devouring her in a kiss that made her toes tingle. He kissed her until the room dissolved around them, all sound around them disappeared, and she rode the wave of his embrace. Here was safety, love, her heart, and her future.

She could have stayed in his arms for hours or forever, but the cheering in the room yanked them back to reality.

"About time, little brother!" Paul called out.

Burn's team toasted and slapped each other on the back. She thought she glimpsed money changing hands.

Rissa whispered, "Did they bet on us?"

"Oh, honey. We were a sure thing."

Acknowledgements

This journey has been filled with so many wonderful people who have encouraged me, laughed with me, and demanded I keep writing, even when life felt too big to squeeze out words on the page.

Thank you is not nearly enough, but here it is anyway.

Thank you to my best friend, lover, partner, and husband, Jimmy Miles, for your constant source of love and support. Thank you Jeanne H. Taylor, Sara J. Walker, Val Czerny, Jenny Jones Johnson, Danica Winters, Sally Murphy, Vickey Wollan, Melody Johnson, Charlee Allden, Abigail Sharpe, Vanessa Kilmer, CS Bennett, Glo Ferguson, Kate Aras, Paula Robinson, Felicia Mason, Sherrie Lea Morgan, JP Bastin, and all of my fellow authors in the First Coast Romance Writers. Without the encouragement and feedback of my friends and family, this book would still be an idea in my head.

My heartfelt gratitude also to Reagan Rothe and Black Rose Writing for taking on my debut novel, and Colleen Oefelein (MacGregor and Luedeke Literary), who believed I had what it takes and agreed to be my literary agent for Baby ConSEALed.

About the Author

Leah Miles is currently working on a Contemporary Romantic Suspense series with thrilling action and military elements involving take-charge heroes and women who stand up for themselves and the people they love.

She grew up in Atlanta, Georgia, and planned to have a career as either a television reporter or a successful author. After getting a bachelor's degree in English and Communications, she worked at CNN for more than a dozen years—sadly, she never managed to sit on the anchor desk.

Her second career is managing an insurance agency in rural Georgia, along with six brand new Airbnb-type cabins with her husband. When not writing insurance or cleaning cabins, she cherishes quality time with her hubby and their rambunctious cocker spaniel. They have three adult kids: a doctor, a lawyer, and a journalist.

Please visit her website, leahmilesauthor.com, and sign up for her newsletter to get updates on current work progress and new release information.

OTHER BOOKS BY LEAH MILES

- *Romancing the Holidays, Volume 1*: A Pug Thanksgiving: An adorable pug is the catalyst for love in this Thanksgiving tail.
- *Romancing the Holidays, Volume 2:* Stolen Christmas: A Navy SEAL and a single mom join forces to save a little girl's Christmas.
- *Romancing the Holidays, Volume 3:* Fireworks Again: Fireworks bring them together, but she must face down her past, and he must accept his future before they can find love.
- *Romancing the Tropics:* Love in the Conch Republic: Her future is bright until the long-lost son of her employer returns to steal it from her. Tensions mount along with attraction for the one person neither of them wants to love.
- *An Autumn Embrace:* A Barking Chance: When they are forced to work together at a dog training center, Zane and Beth find more than memories in the office files. Can they forgive their past mistakes to catch a criminal and save their future together?
- *For the Love of Winter 1*: Marry Me by Midnight: Navy SEAL Kendall Nelson can't manage a successful proposal, and single mom Luisa Sanchez has no time for romance. Their journey of love unfolds into a race against time to secure their future together.
- *Romancing the Tropics 2:* Not Another Jack: Her final wedding gig takes an unexpected turn when a hunky Navy SEAL crashes the party, reigniting old flames and stirring new misunderstandings amidst the choppy seas of love.
- *For the Love of Winter 2:* Mistletoe Magic: A holiday romance rekindles when Navy SEAL Michael Rodriguez runs into his old flame, Nora Geller, and invites her to his family holiday gathering. Will they mend old wounds and find love again, or will misunderstandings leave their hearts out in the cold?

- *An Enchanted Encounter at the Matchmaker's Inn:* Will Trish and Brent be able to unravel their misunderstandings and embrace the enchantment that binds them, or will shadows from the past tear them apart?

- *Aura of Destiny:* In Pinevale Valley, Ruth Fairfax hopes her gift for seeing auras will stay buried with her troubled past. But when she falls for ranch owner Hinto Miller, she'll have to choose between protecting her heart and embracing her power to save the man she loves.

- *Cindy Aurela—A Cinderella novella*: A city girl finds her true path and unexpected love—in thrift store hiking boots.

- *The Brewmaster's Kiss*: A Halloween novella released in a shared world of the "Border House Ghosts." Fifty-five years of longing and a love that transcends death.

- *Christmas Wishes:* Tied Up For Christmas: Hostages on Christmas Eve. Tied together. Falling hard.

Note from Leah Miles

Word-of-mouth is crucial for any author to succeed. If you enjoyed *Baby ConSEALed*, please leave a review online—anywhere you are able. Even if it's just a sentence or two. It would make all the difference and would be very much appreciated.

This is just the beginning! *Baby ConSEALed* kicks off the seven-book *SEAL & Shelter series.* Each book stands alone, but you'll get glimpses of your favorite characters as their lives intersect throughout the series.

Next up: *First Note of Danger.*

Thank you
Leah Miles

www.ingramcontent.com/pod-product-compliance
Lightning Source LLC
Chambersburg PA
CBHW032059050726
47590CB00001B/341